ONE
HUNDRED
DAYS
AND ONE
NIGHT

SAM HUNTER

BALBOA
PRESS

A DIVISION OF HAY HOUSE

Balboa Press books may be ordered through booksellers or by contacting:

Balboa Press
A Division of Hay House
1663 Liberty Drive
Bloomington, IN 47403
www.balboapress.com
1 (877) 407-4847

Print information available on the last page.

ISBN: 978-1-9822-2711-1 (sc)
ISBN: 978-1-9822-2710-4 (e)

Balboa Press rev. date: 05/09/2019

CONTENTS

DEDICATION

To those who seek and cannot find, to those in love who lose their mind, to those hopeful that a world of harmony awaits as a cloud of illusions departs. To those who believe in a magic of words.

ACKNOWLEDGMENTS

While writing this book, I was engaged in multiple writing projects and research. Throughout the process of revising and finalizing my academic projects, I found a guidance and feedback of my faculty mentors to be most helpful in my growth as a writer. I am thankful for their honesty and patience. I would also like to thank my editor, Jane VanVooren Rogers for helping me make the final revisions of my book.

FOREWORD

This narrative contains three seemingly disconnected stories told in three obviously dissimilar voices. The first is an account of a silly, short-lived crush that reawakened a painful memory of a longer yet unfortunate encounter of two people whose lives intersected at a point of turbulence and uncertainty for the one, and a point of midlife complacency for the other. Their lives were shaped by different times, different places, different roles, expectations, and experiences. This encounter, in turn, inspired a story within a story—a third narrative whose intensity, poignancy, and plot bordering on fantastic ultimately surpassed the framework, in which it was conceived, of an ordinary life of an introspective woman.

The first two narratives chronologically follow each other — one very short and amusing and the other one long and serious — and represent two different stories of rejection. The first one might appear facetious and silly, while the second one produced a serious disconcertment and heartache. Both combined produce a sort of a revelation that it would be possible to experience one's own life as an entertainment — to oneself and others, even when circumstances would grant a more serious outlook.

Bella, the main character, likes this exact revelation, but simultaneously fears that it's nothing out of the ordinary and ascribed. The old legend of Scheherazade dangerously resembles her state: she narrates to stay alive, or to keep someone in her life. At the time of her struggle, the line between the two do not seem to exist. Although she frames her response to a typical, human concern of one's importance to others in what she sees as an artistic and atypical way, she fears that ultimately, she is not able to use all her potential and that she couldn't step out of the ordinary. At times she also feels that no known experience can help in justifying a strange succession of events. The third narrative, a story within the story, fills in the gaps of what her ordinary experiences can't.

This third story, however, is not part of her storytelling, leading to a Scheherazade revelation. As a result, and unlike Scheherazade, she does not live—in a metaphorical sense. Thus, she ultimately buries an entertainer and the typical, however symbolic that role is to her. The third narrative is a story of deeper human suffering, out of the eyes of anything predictable or entertaining. What makes it so mystical is its timelessness and that it is intentionally 'hidden' from view. In this way, neither Bella nor the person she so passionately tries to captivate with her stories, can trivialize this most poignant story of rejection—a rejection resulting in writing off a human being and human dignity. Through a succession of voices and moods, sharp turns and pauses at unpredictable points, the struggle and failure of one voice might give birth to another, more serious and worth hearing. All three of these voices are captivating, and even though one might seem to hold a greater attention span than the other, they remain interim and interchangeable.

PROLOGUE

L ong time ago, young school children in a far-away land had to read a story called "Aska and the Wolf." In many ways this fable of a witty sheep and a bad wolf resembled the tale of the thousand and one nights that inspired narrators throughout times and across nations. The teachers told the children in school that Aska was not eaten by the wolf because she kept distracting him with her dance. The moral of the story: at times one needs to be clever and outsmart the stronger enemy to survive. An explanation that sometimes one needs to learn ballet or any kind of art to survive escaped conventional analyses it seemed. The narrator, first and only laureate of the Nobel Prize from the exotic and hostile Balkans, surpassed any interpretation in his own account of the power of art over death, stating, "We don't even know how much strength and how much potential are hidden inside every living being. And we cannot guess how much we are capable of. We exist and pass on, without ever realizing all that we could have been and done."[1] The teachers wanted the youngsters to transcend a meaning of plain dance into cunning intelligence, while the most powerful message lay right in front of their eyes. Both Aska, first and foremost epitomizing femininity, and Scheherazade entertain—to stay alive.

Sultan, in the legend of the thousand and one nights, had many women, all virgins, but he killed them all, all but Scheherazade, a woman who volunteered to spend one night with the king. Sex alone did not interest him. Sex before Scheherazade came along had been offered as a sacrifice, a plea for mercy, but it was only good while it lasted. Sex leading to departure and rejection was one of my greatest fears and it is possible that it was founded on a tale of Scheherazade, who told Sultan a story each night, not finishing each story before the morning. Sultan kept sparing her life to hear the end of her stories the next morning, and for 1,001 nights,

---

[1] Ivo Andrić

this pattern continued. At the end, Sultan had fallen in love with her and decided to spare her life.

What I saw in this was a slight advancement, *sold* to us as a slightly better deal, was a deliberate sex, carefully planned and executed, so that a promise of care in return might envelope a shroud of those dreadful submission and servitude. It is here that *plus nous changeons, plus nous restons les mêmes*[2] found its most welcoming home, passing the test of time over and over again. Along with virginity. Anachronistic? Hardly. *"Women should stay virgins because they are not special anymore once they lose their virginity,"* I once heard a young millennial girl say on TV. This "not special" verdict must have been her version of being dead. Raising a "special" stock in hopes to trade it, when the price is right, for bits of respect and a nicely elaborated happily-ever-after tale never ceased to mesmerize me.

I could, however, be mistaken and anachronistic in summoning words that lost their power and potency as such. But, it is not the words only which deceive. We are all masters of renaming things and if the harshness of *servitude* could not withstand the test of time; its denotative sister *service* was there to make an imprint. We are all here to *serve*. In the language of economy and education, "innovation" and "creativity" can only emerge as by-products of service. And the logic of service, in its lowest or highest expression of goodwill, and as a most remarkable trademark of an era, would make or break what might be called "special." This kind of lifeless *special,* filled with fallacies of undeliverable promises, has saturated our reasoning and conscience. It is a fallacy to believe that what we *possess* and must inevitably lose or replace would make us special, rather than that which wouldn't have to be sacrificed but nurtured and cherished. What lies beyond virginity? Only life was special, I concluded as I recounted the tales of Aska and Scheherazade.

Some people say they've had a near-death experience that changed their lives forever. I had a near-insanity experience of my overworked imagination about a backhanded coworker, followed by an arduous process of cleansing my mind of the dregs and refuse and ending in a self-discovery that began giving shape and meaning to a seemingly erratic life course. I turned out

[2] The more we change, the more we stay the same (French adage)

to be a product of my time more than I could wish for—entertainment is a service, though I thought I have discovered something, a sort of a hybrid fueling its growth with a different source of energy. Suddenly, Sultan and Scheherazade, and Aska and the wolf *principle* emerged everywhere, even in a one-man-and-one-woman union, though not granting it the allure of a lasting union. I found it fundamentally wrong to think so. I found these allegories to be only snapshots in time and yet to signify a lasting struggle to justify existence, to occupy space, moreover to create space in the universe for oneself, to stall rejection, and to give and take in the cycle of life. In the process of this struggle, we become more special, the more stunning and more remarkable our tale is. A Sultan would not get to decide about life and death of his Scheherazade, rejection and continuation, but he could stimulate, he could actively nurture the subsistence of her life. Sometimes, he would be even able to emanate a certain linguistic bravura, a great honor for any Scheherazade who then must not mistakenly interpret his gift to her as a redundant yet empty chivalry because, often, if she does so, the turn of events could endanger his existence and purpose too. I happened to be a Scheherazade, *he* happened to be a Sultan, but these roles are not inevitably gendered. Finally, what makes any tale stunning and remarkable is the intent, not content.

I

Never in my 36 years of life had it occurred to me that a human life, a life of a female human in her prime, would have so much in common with the existence of a butterfly. A feeling of "falling apart," as in Bonnie Tyler's "Total Eclipse of the Heart," marks an end of a short- or long-lived season outside the cocoon and entering of a dormant stage anew. I am a butterfly in multiple incarnations, each one of them a mind-blowing, long- or short- lasting, mentally and physically draining mating season—with or without a mate. There is only one feature that butterflies and I, as far as the mating is concerned, do not have in common—when mating or lack thereof is followed by an ultimate death. However, in trying to describe how this statement may not be completely true, to use a cliché, something does die in me each time my virtual butterfly existence is supposed to come to an end—with or without mating—but my overall physical existence somehow always overcomes a near-death experience, pushing me promptly into a new interval of a life cycle.

Have I chosen this path to mark the years of my fertility climax? Self-respect I have left would scream no, but the secret compartment of emotional waste I accumulated is already boiling into a critical mass of self-accusations that no one in her right mind would build such a *history* of crushes on emotionally or otherwise unavailable mates without deliberation, or pull her emotional strings until they break or are close to breaking. My lips still part in bafflement when remembering my friend Sally's confession that, though in the third decade of her life, she only had two men in her life: one of them her ex-husband, and another a man she met six months after her divorce. I was not able to peek into her soul to see if there was any waste there, but the outside manifestations signaled what I suspected, a role she faithfully played as a woman: her job was to please and—as she proudly self-proclaimed to be a hobby or a kind of a liberating endeavor of hers deeply engrained into her personality—to clean. Selfish or egalitarian, and in these matters, it was always a matter of perspective, I resented such a price to pay for something that would not be sufficient to satisfy whatever purpose or needs we might have.

While resenting a predetermined course of life, passed on from generation to generation of docile members of the *weaker* sex, I developed some very peculiar emotional characteristics, a certain emotional charge attracting exactly those men granting me such a course of life. The ensuing consequences regularly appear in a form of a said emotional waste, as a result of futile hoping that perfect love must be achievable at some point in life, love on my own terms, equilibrium of giving and receiving. Now I must dig deep into my waste, pull all the trial and errors so that I can ask myself what was it exactly I was or wasn't looking for, accept or reject the above hypothesis that I am a butterfly in multiple incarnations and come to terms with living not even resembling the one God gave us, or so we were told. Pardon, my intention here is to delve into those replete and burdensome personal dregs and emotional waste that have nothing to do with God, but one might emerge in the process, and I imagine it would be a Goddess. I won't refer to her, however.

In case I don't return to a god of any origin, it would be wise to state right at the beginning that the ultimate goodness is out of mine and everyone else's reach here and now, that ultimate goodness and love some of us would like to claim to know so intimately. And yet, we only weep in the dark for forgiveness, unable to even conceive a good and dignified life for ourselves and others. We use the words of others lightly, as the original message ought to be secondary to our self-aggrandizement or pleasing the audience. One of those feel-good quotes I just recently heard, misheard at first, compelled me to mourn ever more the emptiness of the words used in vain. I imagined I heard someone spouting in a microphone, "Justice anywhere is a threat to a justice everywhere," wondering who could have possibly publicly questioned the brand of "universal" justice that ought to be transposed anywhere and produce more justice. No, I argued with myself for days afterwards, those couldn't have been the slogans for public ears, they would transpire in a classroom full of graduate students or a club for dissidents raging against colonialism, imposed way of living as some kind of "justice" that could kill the life it was imposed on. And every time I researched the said "quote" I would get this result, "Injustice anywhere is a threat to a justice everywhere."[3]

OK, now we were back to mainstream: trivialized, lip service kind of mainstream, but I'd rather deal with that than with the dissidents taking over. My sanity, I then decided, did not hinge on misinterpreted quotes, my sanity and peace of mind hinged on recreating: my life and the whole world! This sounded easy as it first occurred to me as a possibility, but then I realized that my emotional waste and its critical mass tended to threaten my life and dignity in ways unforeseen.

With a naiveté of an inexperienced explorer, I decided to wallow in my mental waste compartment, passionately and thoroughly, hoping to filter out something to live by, something essential in meaning making, something I might have discarded and forgotten about. This attempt at soul cleansing started after a most recent silly and absurd crush on a fellow graduate student and a colleague, an outcome of a dilettante's flirting and wishful thinking. This crush not only blurred traces of rationality I thought I possessed, but also occasioned waves of flashbacks of another, grander and by far more significant crush—the crush of a lifetime. I tended to jettison less unpleasant or even pleasant experiences from my memory, while those most burdensome and mind-blowing continued to sediment into a growing aggregate of refuse. The most recent addition to the waste I mentioned above occasioned the flashbacks of the one before as well, the one I wanted to forget the most. At some point, however, I had to decide whether to allow the unhealthy critical mass of the waste to be recycled or to crumble under its weight. In retrospect, I did recycle the waste, but not before allowing another fantasy to take on a life of its own. It started, or intensified, as a chance encounter at a half-deserted college campus a few weeks before the chaos of the new semester ensued. It was then catalyzed by a series of real and imagined events, ultimately showing me over again the effects of the power of an unlearned lesson.

After a due time of living in a cocoon, another metamorphosis into a butterfly transpired one evening in my office while finishing some paperwork and getting ready to leave. The subject of my crush came in and sat at the desk next to mine and after only a couple of minutes of

---

[3] Dr. Martin Luther King, Jr.

3

busying at his desk hurried through the door. The butterfly flapped its wings in my stomach when he bumped into someone on the way out and in a short conversation said to a passerby that "the girlfriend was gone." We were colleagues for about six months, and I thought it appropriate to say, "Sorry about your girlfriend."

"That's OK," he replied, adding that each loss was an opportunity for a new gain, or so he hoped. "Are you still on vacation?" he then asked and I said I was coming back to work in three weeks and just needed to tie some loose ends and pick up a book I left in the office.

"See you then," he smiled, looking at me for a long moment.

If someone else were telling me this story in these exact words as a prelude to what later developed into a full-blown crush, I would . . . simply not believe it. One equivocal promise "See you then," followed by a longer-than-commonly-acceptable-among-acquaintances gaze does not give enough material for a fantasy built on foundations of a sandcastle, but I pulled the additional material from another split of a second-long episode, or rather a spark elicited by a short exchange a couple of months ago when he told me in an equally equivocal way that I could teach him something I was working on at the moment. The spark he ignited then was short-lived, and if there was a subsequent fantasy, of which I have a vague recollection, it had neither strength nor relevance to occupy my thoughts for long. If I cared to have articulated any thoughts on a subject of the said fantasy, it would have been a defense of my resorting to fantasies as a practical and perfectly normal habit. By interchangeably placing someone into a sexual and asexual state in relation to the provisory needs of my imagination, neither one of us had to risk destroying the ephemeral beauty of the flirt in exchange for the uncertainty and trials of a real relationship, especially if one relationship had to disintegrate in favor of another. Or so I thought . . . But, at the time we both tacitly assented that in our fantasies it was permissible to breach the moral barriers of the taboos involving love, including the one that thinking about sin is a sin. As it turned out, and in my defense, *I* was at a greater liberty than he was to do as I pleased.

Consistent with all I knew about the fragility of a one man-one woman union, my faith in the sacredness of such a union was shaken time and again, especially because some fantasies tended to come out of the closet. And not all of them are created equal. If a pop psychologist encourages fantasies to revive stale relationships, there are rules to follow. After all, diving into the fantasies and living imaginary lives could all be part of an ongoing evolution and navigating everyday life in an increasingly virtual world. The game was on, but I reluctantly participated in it, resisting it for fear of somehow being tricked into staying in the fantasy world. Despite its appeal, the inherent insincerity of letting one's imagination loose created a certain resentment on my end. My colleague had a girlfriend, but when he leered at me at the office door that summer evening, I thought he'd do what I'd do—start anew. Every loss is an opportunity for a new gain as he stated. Thus, those fantasies would and should rightfully transition into a reality. I was wrong there, acting like a monkey I once watched on the Discovery Channel: it got stung by something while trying to pull a nut from a crack in the trunk of a tree, but did not learn the lesson. Every time its hand went in to grab a nut a painful bite forced it back, and this repetitive action went on for longer than I cared to watch. I wondered afterward which one of the parties involved got tired of the repetition first: the cameraman or the monkey.

My colleague played a game, a well-known conventional game that must be more enjoyable if one happened to have a spare partner. I thought I had a successful return to normal before that evening in the office. Our fantasies remained in the fantasy world until he blurted that the girlfriend was gone and then, leering at me, "See you in three weeks." My well controlled —in fact,—almost forgotten past flirts with him replayed in my imagination, as if the summer reruns on TV were not satiating enough. The relativity of time is best evident when we anticipate: minutes are hours, hours are days. I had to return to work in three weeks from our unexpected encounter. The first couple of days of my, now-boring vacation went by as usual—by finishing some books I started reading long time ago, downloading songs on my iPod, but then it struck me one morning while driving to a grocery store how beautiful the perfect love was in the song "Amazed". I immediately identified with Lonestar's lady, grabbing my colleague who broke up with his girlfriend into yet another fantasy. This time it was unforgettable! "Smell of your skin, taste of your kiss, the way you whisper in the dark …" I was simply melting while lying on my late-summer-sun-bathed deck, while listening and fantasizing about a perfect love. If I ever contested a one man-one woman union as untenable, a return of a strayed sheep felt ever sweeter and the idea of this union captivated my thoughts anew.

I admit that, on the one hand, a crush of this proportion required perhaps something more than a gaze. On the other hand, as I remembered, a couple of kisses of my greatest teenage love fed my infatuation with him for no less than four years, long after he gave up courting a sixteen-year-old virgin. Now it was one look and a casual, "See you in three weeks"! Later, even after recollecting all the memories about this encounter in the office, I found nothing but one flirtatious ogle and a small talk to have set my imagination loose. I went step further this time and confided in another colleague, Anne, an act that made the fantasy almost real and public. "He's handsome," she commented. "We'll see what happens."

Nothing happened . . . after three weeks. Upon entering the office, he lilted his usual good morning and then we had our usual small talk, in which others participated as well. Not expecting such a sluggish transition of our *just colleagues* into something more intimate, I felt slightly disappointed. Nothing happened . . . until, one afternoon I thought he timed his leaving the office at the same time I did. He returned as if he forgot something on his desk, while I was still getting ready to leave. We headed down the stairs together. This must have been a sign of something . . . anything, I thought while descending the stairs right in front of him. It was about time I chanted silently; his silent trailing must have been a sign of a developing affection unleashed by his newly developed emotional availability. We spent too many days sitting quietly next to each other, each one of us keeping their own secrets.

Now it was my turn to demonstrate that I understood his hint, to encourage him, but haven't done anything of any significance the day he walked behind me. A week or so passed . . . On a quiet Friday afternoon, I simply asked him out for a drink or a coffee. It caught him off guard, as if he was trying to grasp that I, in actual reality, dared to disturb his perfectly ordered worlds! He did not like a wakeup call from a girl next desk, obviously mixing up the unmixable: the safety of a routine, breakups and makeups, and little field trips of the imagination. He stood behind me for a long moment, motionless and expressionless, and when he finally managed to say something, a lame, "Now?" came out.

"Now, later, whenever," I replied, playing nonchalance before he finally agreed to it, "after running some errands."

Those errands took awfully long, and while I was waiting, Anne came by. Her advice to me was to put some lipstick on, and if I didn't have, it she was going to lend me hers. "Eww, why would you do that?" I protested, but she wouldn't back off.

"Here," she reached for a tissue and wiped off the tip of her lipstick. "Go to the bathroom and put it on."

"Why does it matter whether I have the lipstick on or not?" I kept protesting.

"Trust me, it does," and she sounded as if she, not me, knew what was important in that moment. I finally gave in. With due respect to her old-school feminine mannerism, a part of me still protested as I was smearing her lipstick on my lips. On the other hand, my presentability was at stake . . . I applied Anne's lipstick with eyes half-closed and a frown on my face. He definitely was taking his time with those errands, and I extended my end of a common courtesy and kept waiting for almost a full hour.

By the time I stood up and headed for the door, some of my vital functions dangerously approached unhealthy levels. I could almost feel my blood pumping through my temples, while the restlessness that set in largely interfered with my ability to concentrate on driving. Soap operas taught me something that I remembered while squeezing the wheel; if a potential love of your life stands you up, do not cry and drive! And, yes, in soap operas there were many occasions for crying and driving for reasons like mine, but not all of them had to end up with a car hitting the tree. No, I wasn't going to hit the tree, my drama was a glamourless instance of self-pity, by far removed from a grandeur of pain and suffering as seen in the movies. I was bound to suffer quietly after leaving the office that Friday in my Honda, in serious pain and utterly humiliated. Heavens, my lips were burning . . . I blamed Anne and her lipstick. The tears subsided quickly since I realized, now embarrassed more than hurt, that my case was very low on a pain scale. Hitting the tree that briefly crossed my mind as a token of my love martyrdom was completely irrational in light of a ten-thousand-dollar remaining balance on a car loan. With the road construction extending miles ahead I was compelled to exclude any kind of affliction, especially the one placing me at risk of hitting "men at work."

Some powerful, yet non-addictive drug would do, but where could I find such a drug? I quit smoking more than ten years ago, but in occasional rewinding a history of various emotional crises throughout the past ten years I realized in dismay that a pack of cigarettes would always be a part of the remedy. Filthy, stinky and unhealthy cigarettes! Soon enough I was sitting on my deck, sucking up one of them as if my life depended on it. Sanity certainly did . . . . ..

The first bubble of smoke carved its way down my throat like a probe, surprising my lungs the way any uninvited guest would, but after the initial shock every consecutive one went in smoother and smoother, replicating the inevitable nature of every known and unknown addiction; pointless in the beginning, a taken-for-granted necessity in the middle and finally a torture in the end. I wasn't exactly analyzing my smoking cycle that afternoon, while lighting the next cigarette off the butt of a previous one. Some kind of numbness overcame me, throwing me back into my lawn chair for some time after each attempt to get up and go through the motions of some of my late-afternoon chores.

A phone buzz gradually overcame the buzz in my head and Anne was reminding me that we still needed to go to a high school football game later in the evening.

"Did he call or email you? Maybe something came up?"

"No, he did not. How could he call me? We don't have each other's phone numbers. My asking him was just a spur of the moment, but he should've known better than just simply not show up. I can't tell you how pissed I am!"

"There must be some explanation …"

"Oh, just forget it. What time are we going to the game? Not that I am looking forward to that now . . ."

The evening was not a total disaster after all; I endured the first forty-five minutes of the game, cheered Anne's nephew parading in the marching band, and then we went for a drink. Like the city itself at night, only on a smaller scale, the bar was a light dot in the middle of the cornfield. *Children of the corn, I am one of yours!* I thought. If I never saw the scenery of a small-town bar, all the movies that ever depicted such a sight were accurate down to an old, unshaved, skinny guy sitting at the counter and drinking solo.

Anne and I, "Thelma and Louise", sat on the barstools and ordered our margaritas. The old-timer was rewinding who knows which memories, infusing his confidence with the booze that to him might have had a magical power of turning him into a Mr. Charming. He must have not noticed his overgrown hair underneath the visor, a week or so old beard that needed some grooming, and a tremendous age difference when he started his buzzed-up courtship from the other end of the bar. Later, as a karaoke singer, he drew my attention while singing some country song in a rarely heard, amplified falsetto, which made me ache for a microphone to show the crowd how the real singing was done.

Somehow, I gave my desire to sing away and our "cavalier" handed me a huge, laminated index of all songs available. "Would you like to sing?" he asked before I was able to voice my desire to go to the podium. Anne was glancing at me suspiciously, then at our companion beaming in his new role of an impresario, while I first imagined myself as Whitney Houston from "The Bodyguard" soundtrack, then as Madonna, then Beyoncé, but one look around at the crowd who must have all been hearing individuals, and despite a slightly distorted perception, discouraged my ambition. The discouragement, however, dissipated after a few more sips of another margarita and blurry recollections of all passionate singing in the shower. While looking at the names and the song titles, trying to remember if the tune of any of them made me turn up the volume on my car radio, the good old "Total Eclipse of the Heart" caught my eye, a perfect song for a mood of a total loser, as I persistently thought of myself since the late afternoon.

It took another margarita, courtesy of another courtier who paid for it without asking and who then went on to woo Anne. Realizing that I was serious about singing and leaving her alone, Anne gave me a don't-you dare-leaving-me-here-with-him look, but the lady at the karaoke podium was already calling my name. Simultaneously, Anne grabbed my hand and, discreetly motioning to a margarita buyer, said, "Why don't the two of you talk to each other?"

"Why would I talk to him?" I retorted.

"Because I am married," she hissed at me.

"Oh, I see, but if you'll excuse me, I am the next in line to sing." During our muffled quibble, we didn't notice when a margarita buyer left for the patio. It was a pleasant late-summer night and a large group of guests were sitting outside. "Look, Anne, your chevalier found another object of his affection! I think you and your marriage are safe. Look through the patio door," I exclaimed while hurrying toward the podium.

Some advanced courtship was taking place outside, where a sturdy woman bounced up and down, then made circular motions in the lap of our self-proclaimed chevalier. Anne's face looked as if she was about to break in hives, and her rolling eyes followed me to the podium. I promised to be right back, as soon as I finish the song. The lady at the karaoke set was calling my name again and I rushed to her . . .

"Turn around, every now and then I get a little bit lonely and you never come around, turn around, every now and then I get a little bit tired of listening to the sound of my tears . . . every now and then I fall apart . . ." Good, people are smiling, I don't sound like a total idiot . . . With the microphone in my hands and my eyes half-closed, I felt energized, powerful, as if a small performance at a bar in the middle of the corn field were the highest accomplishment of my life. The oldie with the visor thought I did especially well, and my burst of energy somehow had the same effect on him. He was then next in line to sing more of his country songs and then in line at the bar for some more greenish *fuel*. His next question and Anne's intermittent nagging at me to stop looking through the karaoke songs book forced some sobriety into my mind.

"I left my cat in the car at the parking lot. Would you like me to show you my cat?" he asked.

What? Where did the cat come from?

"No," I snapped out of my introspective and *careful* evaluation of the song titles in front of me, trying to decipher what specifically in my appearance and conduct encouraged him to use the cat as a bait for one-on-one time with me. One of us must have been delusional and I cautiously and half-consciously, despite the various sources of intoxication that night, arrived at the conclusion that it must have been him.

"Are you ready to go?" Anne persisted, feeling abandoned and perhaps even remorseful, thinking of her husband waiting for her back home. "I felt never more married than right now," I heard her saying through the chord of another karaoke number.

"No worries," I said, "Can't you see that the one on the patio had his hands . . . . . . pardon, his lap full and the other one with the visor went off to check on his cat?" But, I promised her to leave that bar after trying Madonna's "Like a Prayer." Her expression said *not again*, as I indulged in another song. The acute sense of hurt pride set in again as the night out and a moment of my emotional numbness passed by.

Back home, I looked around an empty place with Alexandra, my daughter, mysteriously absent. The day had more excitement than I could handle. Her friend Brittany told me over the phone that she was not with her.

"After the football game," I stuttered, "where did she go?" My living room appeared spinning around me. "She said she was going to walk back with Sarah." *Life is so unfair!* I lamented to myself in panic. No, I couldn't have articulated what I felt since anything articulated would be an understatement. *My first night out in so long, and after everything . . .* I quietly chanted an incoherent mixture of prayer and cursing, I lamented over everything I could and should have done after properly alarming two other families and the police. Alexandra walked into the house after about forty-five minutes, escorted by Brittany's mother in pajamas. Cruising around the town, Brittany's mom had spotted Alexandra passing by a local supermarket, accompanied by a boy from school. I wanted to close that night, preceded by the day in the office, the same way a dark, heavy curtain in a theater closes in the intermissions and in the way the change of coulisses between the acts brings the transition and the expectation of what follows, without thinking back. I wanted this moment of darkness to pass, just as in the theater, as a necessary and short moment in time before the lights go on again.

That was what I hoped for after closing the door between my family of two and the world, as there wasn't even enough energy left for me to rage over Alexandra's foolishness. Cowering on one end of the living room sofa I just muttered a lame question, "Do you know that what you did was wrong?" and my mind sank into a dark pit, perhaps defending itself from an invasion of self-pity pressing from all fronts of my womanhood: female with her momentous insatiable emotional needs and motherly love, both betrayed. The night finally quieted down, and I remained huddled on the sofa for a couple more hours, motionless. Where was the reward for being a good mother, for sacrifices, for playing a role model the best I could? Reward? If such a reward existed and was granted, how would I receive it? All I wanted was a dose of emotional numbness at a safe place. I longed for the oblivion of sleep.

What do I tell Alexandra? That no one with a real or conceited sense of his own manhood should have the power to distract, deceive or to persuade her into actions leading to her lessened sense of self-worth and low self-respect for a single moment? I took such a vow a long time ago, but was I able to keep it? While lying on the sofa, motionless, this word manhood sneaked in to intimidate and frighten me over again—this time because of her, Alexandra. Would a change of perspective somehow help? The same way Jay-Z's declaration on TV that the word *"nigga"* would always be present in his rap because right there in those chants the word was dissected and stripped of its power—and intimidation. *Manhood, manhood, manhood*, I started chanting to myself . . .

Right when I thought that my lost battles did not matter anymore, Alexandra grew up. Will she have to fight the same battles? A growing conviction that I didn't have any wisdom to pass onto her frightened me. Yes, I could give her speeches about self-esteem; that's what I was going to do the next morning as I frantically thought in my fetal position on the sofa, but where did that come from? The idea of self-esteem, as fabricated today, did not include distancing oneself from sexuality during a sexually immature age, but an exaggerated, yet 'confident' Lolita imagery either to tame or to submit to the opposite sex, or both simultaneously. The "Playboy Club" unblushingly opened the front door to the gaping spectators. What was I going to tell Alexandra about self-esteem and how it's closely tied to how she will interact with men? In a fetal position on the sofa, my emotional waste reached a critical mass again. *You need to be in control of your life,* I thought I heard myself whispering. That would be a good start without a doubt, but if she saw me on the sofa in the same position as two hours prior . . . . . How would my life appear to her? And I wanted to pass on to her exactly what Jay-Z said . . . . . . at which point my thoughts became a ramble, and I fell into a restless sleep.

A long weekend followed. Lonestar's "Amazed" began to sound as a song of a mockingbird, *"The smell of your skin, taste of your kiss. . ."*. One could fantasize like that all the while holding an inflatable dummy! And the way those *in love* parade in front of others, so self-indulgent and selfish, yes selfish, as if the pain and suffering of human kind doesn't bother them since they embarked on their little union-island! How easily they break the promise "'til death do us part" afterward, as if they pinky-swore and had not declared in front of a serious, credulous crowd. A couple of long days passed until I saw my reluctant *mate* and confronted him. He wouldn't say a word of explanation until I suggested that he could have said "no" for a coffee deal instead of just not showing up. A lame "I'm sorry" did not suffice to calm down my boiling rage, but instead of bursting into an undue argument, I just said, "You're good," and, "We're cool," before our already fragile "connection" broke and our next-desk neighborly relationships cooled off for good.

Now, how can one call an end something that never had a beginning? Oh yes, it's called rejection, and the very sound of it felt like a stab into not-fully-healed scar tissue. My current incarnation was coming to a crescendo, without a real climax, and unlike a dying butterfly, I was about to reenter another dormant stage of a cocoon. Why have I even told this story? Well, an end before a beginning is called rejection, even if a so-called beginning lasts no longer than a few days, few hours or a few moments. Rejection makes us to try to reinvent ourselves. The most painful realization dawned on me over the years in a form of self-accusation that I was incapable of a one man-one woman union but, sometimes, certain events catalyze an inevitable epiphany in everyone's life. My shortly lived yet intense crush on a mistakenly-taken-for-available, backhanded coworker, more intensively than anything else before, spurred memories of all the distant and recent past roles, then revealing under the shroud of failed conformity, the most prominent and the most obvious one: a role of an entertainer. If I was incapable to live in a man and woman union, I was most definitely capable of entertaining! I was ashamed at first, but the snapshots of my past kept reassuring me that, to come to terms with my life, I had to accept my role, regardless of how good or bad of an entertainer I was. Then I wondered if an entertainer could change the world if he or she were serious, Buster Keaton kind of serious, but after much introspection and analysis could not affirm this claim. And I always wanted to change the world! As I was trying to recover, not from an unrequited love, but from what I thought to be a self-destructive discovery, a legendary tale of Scheherazade, remembered in the process, aided the rescue of my self-respect.

II

The narratives of the past and present, histories, stories, and fairytales conglomerated into one revelation I then meticulously crafted to convince myself that in each act of foolishness, or insanity, lie undiscovered potential for great wisdom and discoveries about our nature. Stories, as it was continuously passed on to me, appear to be equally important as food or shelter, they are a connection between our past and present, a connection among humans in a worldwide association, only told in different languages. I then began to think that a Cartesian maxim of *cogito ergo sum*, would only make sense if restated into *I narrate, therefore I am*. The narrators, and I cautiously numbered myself as one of them, are a special kind of entertainers—sometimes serious, Buster Keaton serious, and sometimes amusing. My delicate and earnest soul searching in the aftermath of this silly crush revealed to me that I was an entertainer as well. And I began to take my role very seriously. The events of the past few weeks terrified me so much that I decided to venture into recreating my entire past, as something saner, more palatable. In the process, I decided that I was a special kind of an entertainer, a mundane yet no less appealing recreation of Scheherazade.

Days, weeks perhaps, between this revelation and the first serious reflection on the nature of my relationship with a man I named *Sultan,* resembled the delirium of a detoxification patient. The catharsis came in a realization that all the pieces of my story fit together. My most recent silly crush was nothing but a faint resonance of a by far more momentous chronicle about *Sultan.* This new story was therefore bound to be another tale of rejection, chronicled in a course of one hundred days and one night. I set out to recount a tale of my life as a Scheherazade with the passion nothing would measure up to.

For a long time, I wondered if *Sultan* was ever consumed by a remorse, the way I was consumed by pain, but this was an unfair expectation. He received what I offered him, and he thought that I was offering it unconditionally. The other Sultan murdered his boring mistresses, but such an ancient act of rejection does not suit *him*, my *Sultan*. He was my lifeline in a different way. As he tried to cut it, I ultimately tried to cut his as well. And I am incapable of remorse and will not admit that I have sinned since I am incapable of defining the sin committed with him. Besides, how could I articulate my sins if I am becoming increasingly incapable to define sins of others? Does anyone sin against millions of poor, or do they exist because they are simply less fortunate? We are oblivious to good and evil. In the heat of our conversations, I sometimes asked *Sultan,* "What about the human trade? Who was responsible?", and he'd respond that what I would think of as a human trade, would appear to be a natural flow of supply and demand to someone else.

Sultan was not the only one giving me those occasional reminders that I was not to change the man-made laws on a grand scheme. However, *Sultan* reminded me of it all too often, telling me to not hold my breath if I said to him that something was going to change. He and others liked to advise me to learn how to play the game, a deranging input as it turned out most times since I demanded some sort of fair play, somewhat on my own terms at least, which only led to further detriments. Promising to make the world a better place to live in was not bad, *Sultan* would say, but any *action* to change it was. "Remember," he said once, "if you give charity you are a good guy, as long as you don't ask why there are so many poor." Then, after a short pause, he nodded as if in agreement with himself.

I was having lunch with Sally at a café-restaurant, contemplating how to share with her that I met *Sultan. I am having these wonderful conversations with a guy that I met just recently, and we were not on a date or anything, and he has a girlfriend . . . No, no, knowing Sally, she won't miss to find a red flag as soon as I mention his girlfriend . . . Anyway, what is wrong with having conversations with someone?* I was pretending to be very interested in the menu when she interrupted me, "Guess what? I just learned that Emily, a girl I work with, had sex with twenty-seven men in the past few months!"

Sally, a pharmacist in her former life (her former *incarnation!*) was working as a certified nursing assistant at a senior citizens facility. The first day I met her she told me she was not going back to school. "I am not going to pretend that I can live a normal life again," she explained.

"She counted?" I asked, my jaw dropping.

"Yes, she kept tally," Sally sighed, "And I am here stuck on a two-man island . . ." *Or triumphant,* I thought, since her sex life was still richer than mine, possibly even richer than the twenty-seven-men girl's sex-life. She played her role as a woman, she never mistook sex for *Wuthering Heights* of love, she patiently waited for years until her first orgasm with her now ex-husband, and who was the first man in her life, by the way. She would still play her role if he didn't find a "cougar" and moved to Florida. Whatever respect she was hoping to get in return, her saga bespoke otherwise, even to those less inclined to seize any opportunity to grab a faulty man by the collar.

As much as I tried, I couldn't put myself in her shoes since an old virginity-for-respect trade never appealed to me; besides, I missed a window of opportunity and traded it for my own version of marbles. Some Freudian shrink would now perhaps shout *"Eureka!"* upon my subconscious admission that virginity I once had was a jewel indeed, a diamond I did not appreciate enough, preferring deception about some kind of liberation over it. Ultimately, I wouldn't let anyone think that my first had an honor of deflowering, and one of them obviously did—it just turned out that the occasion and the surrounding were not calling for fanfare and his indebtedness to me.

After years of contemplation, I have concluded that we would continue to be dealt a short shrift as long as Sallies of this world kept attempting to trade their virginity for bits of respect and as long as we continue to keep expecting to get transformed from Cinderella into a princess—by a prick. I forced a sad smile on my face, while thinking of all known clichéd representations of love, as if they had any power over much stronger human preference for hypocrisy. Fornication has found its place even among God-fearing individuals, or else there wouldn't be much to expiate. Even a hunt for a one-night stand is appropriate, if brought about in pursuit of happiness, or at least the wrong idea about happiness, and even if only followed by guilt and remorse. Tickets to heaven are never sold out and most are left to believe that a price to pay is a bargain: some lying to oneself and the others. Well, this was not right for me, I declared in my latest rant against this . . . . .. morbid scheme, but how much more or less anything "morbid" was, compared to my existence of a butterfly?

III

I was in my perennial, emotionally-available state when we met in front of his department chair's office. I needed some volunteer hours tutoring his English learning students from Central America, and he accepted my offer with arms wide open. Back in his office, he presented himself as a linguistic virtuoso, quite impressed with my polyglot's intellect as well. He was the first man ever who acknowledged, and was pleased by what he saw as my intellectual gift. The ones before him, even if impressed by said flairs, shunned them as a hindrance to a normal course of life and a sort of an anomaly, as if wondering how a person without a real and redoubtable power could think she had it all figured out. In plain language that I am now trying to avoid and am afraid to use in this reminiscing, such an individual could not possibly be taken seriously. I, on my end, never thought anything, except that my thought process was developing into something abnormal over time. Gradually, my intellect appeared to me as a malignant gene mutation, standing in the way of my happiness. I was in a permanent state of unhappiness, but trying to change, trying to adapt.

With *Sultan*, chair of a musty department at a community college, I felt as if I had something to trade for bits of respect. I was trading years of learned eloquence and linguistic virtuosity since with them I was a newborn virgin over and over again—with every subsequent incarnation of a butterfly! Plain servitude transformed into a desire to appease, to please and entertain with the words. *Sultan* was bald, a part of his egghead naturally so from male aging, and another part shaved to give the natural process a youthful appearance. It did and, along with his over six feet of height, cowboy boots, a turtleneck, and the glasses the size of slightly enlarged eyes, his guise appeared to me bigger than life. He enjoyed talking to me, and after only a couple of minutes, I felt released from the expected strains of carrying on a conversation with a stranger—and on his turf, for that matter. His whole demeanor screamed freedom from conventional bounds, though a well-behaved freedom of a department chair, tamed and confined within ten-by-ten feet space stuffed with boxes of recently ordered textbooks and windowless walls of an office almost covered with shelves. After all, true freedom was overrated, *"another word for nothing left to lose"*—who could've ever said it better than Janis Joplin? *Nice comparison,* I almost patted myself on the back; then it occurred to me that Janis Joplin must have been on the list of personalities to whom he would make a similar reference considering, well, he must have grown up listening to her songs. It also occurred to me that I was multitasking in analyzing his appearance and taste as our conversation progressed, but notably without sentiment or sarcasm.

"Nice talking to you," he said, "We should do it again sometime." He closed our initial meeting with a courteous invitation to do it again. We both understood the sacredness of our words (that much was clear to me I thought), we didn't use them to play with their meaning, but we both also knew how to use them in creating a story between the lines, an open-ended communication that could go in either direction. The department chair at a community college invited me to talk to him again. Anyone else's invitation in similar circumstances, anyone else's but this benevolent teddy bear in the turtleneck's invitation would be dismissed as a latent lure into sex and lies under the cover of an old bard's charm and chivalry. I was very pleased to meet this department chair, later I was happy to see him in the hallway on my way to the tutoring sessions, and happy to continue our seemingly never-ending conversation. Days of my voluntary engagement at the community college quickly turned into weeks, and my fortuitous encounters with the department chair into deliberate parleys of idea exchanges and uninhibited chitchat. And then I realized that what I heard on occasion in quirky movies and bland installments of TV wisdom was true—the most important sexual organ in a human is the brain. If all the right thoughts were coming from our brain, body would be just an executor of the mind's wishes. Mind controls the body; mind of another person is what pleases us, what turns us on. I started living in a haze of a newly and rapidly developing desire to share with *Sultan* what I never shared with anyone else, to seduce him with the words I was cultivating and multiplying in my mind all my life and not just the words of one language, but a multitude of them, all mixed up in a conglomeration of discourses, important philosophical thoughts and other intellectual hodgepodge.

The body, as an executor of what mind wanted, needed to materialize and exemplify those wishes. In my line of thinking, only a perfect mind could have a perfect body, and I made sure that in my future appearances in front of the department chair, all my brilliance shone through a perfect appearance. For our meeting to discuss the syllabus, I appeared in front of him wearing a pencil skirt and a matching "feather-light," as Victoria's Secret advertises, V-neck woolen sweater. That day I brought *Sultan* a draft of a syllabus because he stated in one of our conversations that I could teach "for him" not only tutor. On a said day, as if having forgotten the nature of my visit, he asked politely and with eyebrows raised, "Can I help you?"

Hmm, he was expecting me, did he forget that he asked me to modify a syllabus for an eight-week class he invited me to teach? I wondered. Carefully erasing even a slightest hint of irritation, I blinked and replied politely that I had a draft of the syllabus ready for his view.

This attitude did not completely fit a teddy bear *Sultan* I came to know, the one who was open, who embraced me, the one who enjoyed my company and, most importantly, the one who adored my intellect. His compliments were diamond earrings lingering in my ears for hours and days at a time, nurturing my ego like no other words ever before. I was speaking to an equal, the one who belonged to the same trade and spoke the same lingo as I did. I said yes to his unofficial offer to teach a class, and almost screamed into a phone receiver one early afternoon in October, when he finally called to make an official offer. *Have I overdone it?* I secretly scolded myself thinking of the effect my carefully-selected outfit might have had on him.

Struck by a lighting metaphor fit the state of mind my new circumstances elicited, releasing whichever hormone responsible for a certain mood, when the lips are stretched in a constant smile and libido threatens to implode the body. However, my body appeared timid in an outfit I chose for the meeting. It was the energy bursting inside my body that sealed his eyes on me while showing me around the building. It appeared that I was making an . . . . . . impact on him? As I was never overly confident in my body, I never saw the body per se as a potential. If I ever believed in the power of seduction, this was my first attempt. What I lacked in confidence was overcompensated by my body's electrical charge, disguised underneath non-conductive attire and sparking occasionally through the eyes and the tips of my fingers. The tips of my and his fingers dangerously gravitated toward each other when I was ready to say good bye. Meant as a nonchalant wave, my hand slipped into his when he suggested that we should do a "handshake," taking an immeasurable moment for him to finish our encounter by caressing the palm of my hand with the tip of his index finger. He glued his eyes onto mine while repositioning in his chair in a series of gawky motions. His words at that moment, though eloquent, seemed like a belated reaction to something he contemplated a moment ago and his accompanying physical actions appeared to be reflecting diffused stimuli, causing a slightly noticeable inability to control the inner turmoil by filtered and cultivated outer responses. Thus, it was difficult to tell whether a Neanderthal or an evolved human inside him prevailed when our skin touched and he exercised the urge to stroll his finger up and down my hand. On my end I wasn't sure whether he just violated me or began a courtship, which was going to depend on the events to follow. The answer was not in sight when we met the following Monday. *Sultan* cleared up his throat murmuring "Good morning" in passing and popped the inevitable question if I needed anything.

Later that day he introduced me to various program coordinators and went over the final draft of the syllabus with me in his office. "I am confused," I blurted once we were back in his office. He looked at me as if I exposed him to a sudden danger and asked if I would like to close the door. "I am confused," I reiterated, "because I don't know what you meant by your gesture . . . . . last Friday."

"Oh, that," he smiled and added quickly, "That was a mistake, it won't happen again." *Just like that?*

"Well, I wasn't quite immune to your touching me like that . . ."

"Are you . . . are you trying to say that you are attracted to me?"

"I . . . . . . might be. But what about you?" He sighed, then looked at me, then made a face as if laboring in sorting out his primordial from his male-in-a-twenty-first-century-corporate-world's hormones. Finally, perfectly composed, though slightly "behindhand", he announced that he had a girlfriend. He might have had mentioned her before, but I wasn't sure which one, among the ones he mentioned, the most recent one was. There was an ex-wife (it could not have been her), a German girlfriend (whom I knew of it occurred to me later—small world after all), then the one he used to ride his motorcycle with ... It must've been this one, but I spent too much time fighting for my breath to think about it.

"I . . .. . . don't know what to say . . .. . . you . . . . . . didn't appear to me like a person in a committed relationship. You looked at me as if you had feelings for me too. I don't understand..." Then he stood up while his six foot, three-inch body filled up much of the space of the windowless office and he pulled me into a bear-hug. I felt comforted and safe until he started shaking and telling me that I was a "woman." Though slightly distressed, but aware that it was apparent to everyone that I was a woman, I made a mental note to ask him about my rediscovered "womanhood" some other time. In a slow-motion, he turned me around and moved to a nearby guest-chair. He sat down, putting me in his lap, not easing up on his grip. Soon he became giddy, and "You are a woman" reappeared in his speech several more times.

Such a turn of events was new and amusing to me: an electrified and passionate encounter turned into a coming-of-age, summer camp chit chat. "So, I am a woman?"

"Yes," he said, simultaneously kissing my neck, my cheeks, my lips, "it means you are not some silly girl, silly." By the time I felt his tongue in my mouth, I almost wanted to stop. It felt musky and dry, not minty and succulent as we like to fantasize. He was a master of seductive words and compliments to my soft femininity as he called it, but when the words turned into action, my brain stopped its activity for a moment and then turned into a centrifugal force to preserve the original feeling and the original desire, along with complementary bodily fluids. My brain would do anything to induce the water into its mill, to induce me deeper into *Sultan's* allure because my brain first and foremost knew that I asked for it; a physical expression of my desire had to be of a secondary importance.

Sultan had an assemblage of more-or-less-desirable effects underpinning his carnal acts and an insignificant fact that I stimulated my arousal by all mental, not necessarily physical, means drowned in a new influx of emotions his words brought about. He was rubbing my back, peeked into my cleavage, and caressed it with the same finger he stroked the palm of my hand, while whispering something like, "How often do you see this?" He sent a new stimulus to the most important sexual organ of mine, an organ which, unlike its plain genital representation, possessed logical reasoning and power of inference, in this instance an inference that his middle-aged (as I suspected) girlfriend's breasts could not compete with mine. *She cannot compete with me,* I triumphantly concluded, melting in *Sultan's* arms and letting him process every part of my body through his lexical grinder. Another equally strong, primal force to defeat a rival female emerged right after his lagged announcement about her existence.

An episode of remorse on *Sultan's* end followed our moment of passion, resulting in his declaring that he could feel connection to two women at the same time. Not expecting this, as I saw it, nebulous turn of events, I insisted instead that such a connection was not possible and "against human nature." This part I admitted was a slight exaggeration of what I truly thought about human nature, knowing perfectly well that men could certainly feel "connected" to more than one woman, but that kind of connection had more to do with the blood flow in a certain direction, ironically opposite from the direction where *my* most important sexual organ was located. I insisted to know how old his girlfriend was and he told me she was about his age. *So, fifties, score two for me.* Score one was the breasts, and I remembered his astonished whisper only moments ago. Then I wanted to know what kind of body she had, and *Sultan* told me it was not all about perfection; she was much slimmer when they first met, and then became rounder as the time passed. *Have I just scored again?* This was in the grey area of advantages and disadvantages since the body negligence was a characteristic of a great majority of fellow females—and greatly accepted. The *girlfriend,* with the curves in certain places, would still be competitive I reasoned, but certain . . . . . other gravitational forces might be to my advantage.

Body neglect is a sort of a trademark of long-term relationships, convenient to a point at which an out-of-shape partner would beg to stay in the relationship since the idea of having to bring themselves in shape and having to attract someone else were more unbearable than an indefinite humiliation of pleading to not be abandoned. My office coworker confided in me once that she performed a regular *ritual* with her boyfriend, a timorous pleading to not abandon her at times of his reoccurring intentions to leave. She couldn't say why she wanted him to stay, but the idea of getting back in shape for someone else seemed unbearable. An overwhelming number of long-term partners seem to live in a tacit agreement that physical appearance loses its importance over time. Was *Sultan* in such a relationship? As I was listening to him sprawled on his chair, an allegory of the cat in a cage came to mind; as a teen I had an insatiable appetite for, at the time, heavy existentialist applet, but years after swallowing Jean Paul Sartre without much understanding, I became familiar with the writing of his companion, Simone de Beauvoir. Her cat was an allegory of a woman: small, tender and sweet in the beginning, kept in a large cage with bars far apart. She is free to go in and out of the cage, but her generous helpings of food are served inside it. The time comes when her body is too large and too fat to leave the cage by sliding between the bars, in fact she doesn't even see the purpose of doing so since plentiful meals are still coming whenever she is hungry. The cat is fed, happy, and trapped, but she doesn't see it until the moment her master doesn't like her anymore. And she'll beg, yes, she'll beg for all the comfort and security she once had, but she won't change . . . . . she can't change.

"What do you like on me?" *Sultan* asked me the next time we were sitting in his office. "Your forehead," I immediately replied as if expecting such a question. "It personifies your intellect, your charisma."

"Hmm, I never thought of that," he responded, slightly puzzled, but then went on talking about connection with two women, a repeated confession I attentively listened to and even occasionally nodded. Slowly pushing his office chair behind me, I stood up and gracefully stroked one of his boyish cheeks. His lament about a *connection* was my invitation to a foreplay. Every subsequent time, I would stand in front of him in a carefully selected outfit, confident that my hand on his chest was enough to dissipate his disconcertment. This was a ritual. He'd start by stroking my back through one of my best cashmere sweaters with the one, and turning the lights in his office off with the other hand. The gesture of turning the switch off would sometimes be followed by a heavy sigh—to legitimize his sorrow, or to delve into love martyrdom in succumbing to the desires of a "woman," or both. My desires in those first days were nothing more than to be in his presence. The allure of our secret trysts was their innocence, a desire above all else to simply admire each other.

Sultan's linguistic esotery soon concretized into very real, erotic, and bold demonstration on the guest chair in his office. He generated another one of my erotic fantasies while having an intense sexual experience with all our clothes on and with me sitting on his lap. I wrapped the legs around the chair (and partially his waist) and cupped his knee with one hand, pressing gently the back of his neck with the other. I was amused by his body's motions simulating a real intercourse and his laborious breathing undoubtedly leading to a culmination. He only intercepted his act to voice a hoarse, salacious appeal for me to "get it out," an appeal intended to reassure my slowly melting body that the ultimate end of this act was supposed to be a real climax, not a fantasy. Ironically, a benevolent plea to get it out, a verbal aid we were both well acquainted with and we both preferred to a physical act, had the opposite effect on me. I realized shortly after that it was going to stay in for the day—namely my orgasm. Our encounter left me somewhat restless. Later, I could not stop visualizing our bodies in one of the most exquisite sexual poses, the one we simulated so passionately earlier that day, which made me desire him even more. His hands seemed to have been multiplying all over my back, my hairline, my waist . . . . . He was taking me with him for a moment, but then we came to different places. He actually came, and I was grounded on a sexual starvation-land.

IV

Everything about me was pleasing to *Sultan*: my eyes through which he saw an entire universe of my intellect, my softness as he called it, my figure, my taste in dressing, my smell, my voice. He rejected nothing in my appearance and our interaction at first, yet occasionally, an expression of anguish would appear on his face and I knew that this "connection" business of his was going through its ups and downs. *Sultan's* ups and downs were mine too since I never knew what our next meeting would bring: more connection or more rejection. His dual nature granted me, generously and interchangeably, both. He amended rejection with demands for a friendship, perhaps even friends with benefits as he said. "There is too much stupidity in this world," he shook his elliptic head and the deep crease deepened and almost divided his forehead on a right and left hemisphere at the mention of this dreaded word. "I need you around, I need you . . . . . . people like you . . ." I on the other hand had my own claims and needs, I needed him to justify and reconstruct all the linguistic fancies he manufactured about me, I needed his words to take our encounters to the next level and spin my brain round and round on the waves of climax. I would do anything in return: give him my stories, restore his youth, boost his ego, please and appease.

Tectonic movements of my cocoon bursting open added somewhat to the intensity of the emotional waves he had ridden on. They were hitting me straight into face the moment I'd think that he could become mine, my slow-moving Cyrano de Bergerac. Around the time of our greatest trials we started our correspondence, our "never-ending conversation." October turned into November and the flamboyant days of a relatively warm Indian summer into gloomy mornings, colorless afternoons and much cooler nights. Was I his fair game and his friendship parlance only an easy way out of an emotional mess we created? He didn't have my body, not completely, but it seemed as if he had my soul. I suspected that to him, unexpectedly, I came package and some of it he didn't need—not for a price he'd need to pay. I said no to friends with benefits and that meant only one: he'd need to break up with his girlfriend. Traces of my old self would protest, trying to disentangle out of his grip, but all I did resembled a helpless flapping of a fish when taken out of the water. In one of his moments of doubt, he said he didn't want . . . . . . the physical part of our relationship, a statement that left me betrayed and as if losing a much-needed life support.

Assembling all my strength and determined to stop the vicious cycle of our mental Jekyll and Hyde, I wrote to him one of those gloomy late fall mornings:

> *While you are still in your glacial movement mode (he said once that his intellect and his reactions were as slow as a glacier, but that "there was passion"), I can't help but notice that my thinking is like electrical impulses or lightning. We'll have to put our friendship on hold, but that doesn't mean we won't be able to have a good professional relationship. It says a lot if someone writes you a story and you reply in two sentences, calling it a 'Hemingway moment'. You found amusing my silly, unconventional blabber without much interest to sense the true flavor of what you knew was there. It stunned me how abruptly and coldly you backed off. If you wanted my friendship you would have worked harder on it. I am not sure whether we should meet for a lunch on Monday, but will leave that decision up to you. I will respect either one of your choices and will find strength to think of what we had as something wonderful and worth remembering. And how could you separate the friendship from everything else we shared? Would you perhaps like the best of both worlds and do you know what that would do to me? For my own sanity I can't allow that, even if any other alternative to it would kill me.*

A response came as a blessing; no, he didn't write back, it would slow the communication down—he called the following morning and told me that severing all the ties we established would be impossible for him. "We are connected and it is strong, let's see where this is going. I'll see you Monday," he said. Right in the middle of our conversation, he threw in something about having only one date in high school. I didn't quite know how to connect this piece of information to our main topic, but was grateful that he opened up to share something that must've had a great impact on him. Otherwise why would it matter in a phone conversation more than thirty years later?! The day became brighter suddenly, if a cliché could depict the true excitement I felt, and for the rest of the weekend I was free to let my imagination loose.

We sat on the sunny side of a restaurant bar. The sun enhanced the surrounding landscape of a harvested cornfield. Nostalgic for the summer, I let the sun bathe my cheeks and kept the sunglasses on. This would make our eye contact easier I thought, which was never one of my strengths. We talked about our past, movies and music, as if on a first date. I told him about my most recent fascination with the movie, *Saigon, The Year of the Tiger*.

"There was this guy, madly in love with the main character, who was also the narrator, and she said something about his departure back to England after she rejected him . . . But first, after she rejected him, he made a scene at the bank in Saigon where they worked. He looked pathetic, no doubt, to the audience, to those spectators at the bank, but . . . . . . let me see if I can remember this correctly, the woman said that his leaving Saigon after that incident was dignified compared to how the rest of them left months later . . . . . . I remember once, years ago, I was leaving a city in an overloaded bus driving on the recently plowed dirt roads in circumlocution around the *enemy lines* and thought how humiliating and wrong was it to be transported like that, but then . . ." I stopped, meeting at the same time his curious gaze and just said, "Never mind, we learn sooner or later that there is always *less dignified*."

"True," he asserted, "When thinking about my leaving my ex-wife. Let's say . . . . . I left the house in a "less dignified" way when she found out that I was having an affair. The affair, um, in all likelihood, just catalyzed the process of dissolution of our marriage, but I didn't have the courage to leave . . . I spent quite some time in therapy afterwards, trying to figure out what was wrong with me."

"Why would anything be wrong with you? People divorce all the time, or have affairs for that matter." I almost put the hand over my mouth and bit my tongue for this uncalled-for remark.

"I know, but I just felt as if somebody was acting on my behalf, some 'master of puppets that was pulling my strings'" . . . " He changed the subject, "Have you ever heard about speed-dating? I've done that. That's how I met . . . . ." then he stopped again.

In our reminiscing, we mutually decided that one topic was a taboo, I on my end hoping that his relationship would disintegrate and wither away if not made a central topic of each of our rendezvous—while simply (and conveniently) dismissing a gamut of other known and unknown possibilities in the jumble of unpredictable human actions.

Nevertheless, I felt radiant and as a winner, humbled by recent pain and suffering over *Sultan's* indecisiveness yet enriched by his ultimate grace. He kissed my forehead right by the hairline and embraced me in another one of his bear-hugs when we parted. Little did I know about the turmoil of sexual encroaching! Next time we briefly met in his office, he was in yet another dual state, contemplating his predicament amid half-full cardboard boxes, sprawling in a yoga position between the desks, shelves and a couple of chairs. He pulled me gently into his lap and began his soliloquy, "You are beautiful. You smile with your eyes. I know I shouldn't be touching you, and part of me doesn't want to, but at the same time I want you so badly. I wanna fuck you . . ."

We were sitting on the chair in our quasi-sexual embrace, and he pulled me fast with both hands onto his chest as soon as he uttered the word "fuck". This one stroke sent waves of pleasure into my stomach, a sensation not roused by the proximity of our sexual organs, but a combination of unsatisfied desire, and his skill to tastefully wrap and deliver the trite and distasteful word *fuck*, a simulation of a short and intense intercourse and a moral dilemma whether he should do it or not.

"Could you do it only once," he then asked, a question that depleted those waves of pleasure and energy in a split of a second. Sliding over his knees, I dropped into another nearby chair.

"I couldn't. It would hurt me more than you can imagine. And I don't know why you are suggesting something like that!?"

"Could you . . . . . . share?"

Oh, an upgrade! "Maybe . . . . . . in the beginning…"

"And maybe not," he concluded. The passion he was stirring up with every move of his body, with every stroke of his hand, made me forget this verbal contract we've been drafting simultaneously and what words couldn't accomplish (after all words were not omnipotent). I thought that a lascivious non-verbal promise of my giving myself to him and a gentle unsaid entreaty to not hurt me could. *Sultan* was shaping my desire like a clay, preparing me to become the other woman and, above all, torturing my sexually starved body by hitting the right spot here and there, laying his hand between my legs in an urgent and passionate grasp, then pulling it back and meandering around my stomach in an upward motion to one of my breasts.

This hint of something I yearned for, a promise passed on with every touch that there is more to come and this other more cue of some future other mores was simultaneously exhilarating and exhausting. My late afternoon joggings turned into an unpleasant obligation now that the nearby park, my only connection with the nature, was losing its picturesque outlook as the winter was approaching. However, they gave me some temporary relief from a constant and mind-blowing sexual tension, fueled by *Sultan's* imminent swaying into the certainty and comfort of his *mediocre relationship*. *"He found himself a mommy,"* I sometimes thought of Sally's remark in aggravation; *"she'll take care of him."*

In the following days, he seemed extraordinary passionate about me, and I thought his Hamlet-like dilemmas were beginning to resolve. He was rediscovering me and the potential no one before him even began to understand. Dare I say that these were subjective observations of a corrupted mind? And body? My meetings with Sally turned into counseling sessions, as she eagerly tried to put things in a perspective. Above all, she was adamant about my insisting on clearing up the air vies-a-vie the girlfriend, "You don't know what he is thinking, but keeping quiet could only signal him that you are OK with the status quo."

"No, he knows I am not OK . . . . . I just want her to depart—with honors. And quietly, without much fuss. In fact, I don't even want to be the reason for their breakup."

"And how exactly do you think that would be possible? I am telling you, if you don't say anything now and it doesn't matter what you said before, he won't do anything. Why don't you introduce me to him? Why don't I throw a little party, and you invite him!"

"I don't know . . . . . . wouldn't it be somewhat premature? I mean, he's all consumed by his personal dramas . . ."

"And why do you feel sorry for him? I don't get it, you are painting me a picture of an infantile, whiny sissy and now I just wanna smack him. I hate men like that!" Sally started pacing around her living room.

I started acting all hurt. "Look, you and I see him through totally different lenses. I can't explain…"

"There is not much to explain," she interrupted, "it all seems black and white to me."

"If only!"

After this conversation, and indisposed to credit Sally for her insights, I wondered when everyone became Dr. Phil, in this case by oversimplifying the complexity of romantic triangles. Besides, she called me a sissy too. Back in the solitude of my home, I continued my never-ending discourse with *Sultan,* releasing myself (and him) from all the trivia of everyday life.

> *Where do I begin? I wrote. I love when you say something to me in my mother tongue: my identity is tied to it. You probably sense the importance of acknowledging it and it is cute, although 'cute' might be just a euphemism for how I really feel about it. The identity is truly a "thorny issue" (in your words) but one needs to be in my situation to completely understand. There are a mixture of anger and a sense of betrayal when I think about my identity and the same reasons, with the addition of a naïve wish to be a citizen of the world were contributing for me to embrace languages and what I could do with them. But the resentment I once felt is not so strong anymore, and all the identity shifts I had*

and still am having (as we assume identity is rather fluid not a static entity) almost give me an advantage in comparison to those who take their sense of belonging to a certain group for granted.

I've heard enough for another lifetime about "linguistic oppression and imperialism" in some of my graduate classes. I posed a question once in class about a choice to be a conformist when it suits you, debating with myself whether I was one of those conformists. "You are not a conformist," said the professor, but he doesn't know me. I can boost anyone's ego and am doing it in most situations. I like to call it empowering people, but on some occasions, it boils down to good old sucking up. Sometimes I think that life itself is all about sucking up to the right people. Then when you don't receive a proper level of politeness from those who are supposed to serve you (in our consumerist world) you just snap. There is such an obsessive need for many, whose job is to listen to others, to speak up without thinking. I like to think that it's not symptomatic of something more serious than someone's not being suitable for a job. When you said you didn't feel French, even though you are learning a language, it's normal, I think. You are not a fabric of the French culture because you don't live there. Living on the fringes as a long-term visitor (like you in Japan) is yet another issue. By the way, have you seen Lost in Translation *and* Fear and Trembling? *Let me tell you, I would not like to become "Japanese" the way that poor Belgian girl did… Oh, and I would like to see you right now. You said once it was primal. I think so too.*

He asked me the day before what language I felt most comfortable using "these days" and, "If we had many languages available to us, which would you choose?" The "identity matter" interested him and he began his response to me by restating his previous claim that the issue of identity was a thorny one:

Language is but one aspect. Although I enjoy French, it is not so much a part of me, not an identity, other than that of "speaker." I did develop somewhat of an identity, or at least a role, when I lived in Japan. I can "be" Japanese to a certain extent and it's easier to do when I'm speaking Japanese. But again, I was not fluent enough to really enter society and interact. I was out there on the fringe, as you said. Self-identity and self-identification are very interesting to me. That which is "me" is a combination of what I've done, what I've seen, what I've hold dear, what abilities I believe I have and how I think others see me. And that's probably the short list.

I like to say that we're all "puppies in the pack." I also believe (and I think this is documentable) that we are designed to be tribal, not national. When a group gets large enough so that the direct relationships between any two individuals are weak to non-existent, then the tribe itself weakens. I'll leave it there for now. What say you?

I said that the notion of being tribal, not national puts us back in time—at least by standards purported by a modern part of humanity, one fighting against tribal quibbles, vengeance, and division (which usually ends up in inducing them, as our human nature never stops exhibiting unlimited talent for manipulation and destruction). The modern part of humankind is also exuberant in support of those individuals breaking up with questionable traditions and ideologies, leaving one to wonder why declaring a support to one or another ideology would matter in matters of personal liberation and even survival. How is then being national better than being tribal, I wondered afterward.

I, perhaps no less of a nomad than Ayaan Hirsi Ali, a Somali woman who escaped bonds of arranged marriage and ongoing oppression, as she stated, of Muslim women in a world where clan is holier than a nation and a female slightly above property, would not be inclined to understand Hirsi's affinities. On the other hand, I did not walk in her shoes, at least for the part of absolute submitting to what her tribe saw as "God's will" and female genital mutilation. She loathes *tribal* and celebrates modernity started with Enlightenment, which I on my end started to loathe for my own reasons, identical to reasons of an army of feminists, among others, possibly not tortured by traditions light years apart from the Enlightenment. "Hirsi's strength astonishes, yet her unconditional support of modernism confuses me," I said. In *Nomad*, she wrote a letter to her grandma, and I shared it with *Sultan*:

> *The secret of a Dutchmen's success is his ability to adapt, to invent. The Dutchman's approach to solving problems encourages him to bend nature to his wish rather than the other way around. In our value system, Grandma, like the thorn trees, like the baobabs, like dawn and dusk, we are all set firmly as who or what we are. We bow to a God who says we must not change a thing; it is he who has chosen it. When our people wondered through the desert from oasis to oasis, we did not create permanent wet spaces, we didn't bend rivers and lakes to our will or dig deep into the earth for wells.*

Yes, modern man did all that, I wrote to him, but where does his arrogance put the whole civilization? We take from nature what we need, we take from other humans what we need, thinking that the whole universe would submit to a law of the more powerful. Just because nature didn't have the weapons of mass destruction didn't mean that a man could "bend" her and adjust her to his own needs for as long as he needed. The nature is taking the turn in a ferocious response to a civilized man's exploitation. And what about people civilized man thought submissive, primitive, and powerless? An individual's power of being human is dangerous to underestimate, including a power to procreate, power to communicate, and power to persuade. But Hirsi is not ignorant, I wrote to *Sultan,* for she also said the following to her grandmother:

> *But even if you had done nothing and stayed in your hut made of thorns, even if you lived all your life dismantling the hut, loading it on the back of patient camels, traveling in a caravan to the next green pasture with your husband and children, and their children, and the wives and children of*

35

> *your husband's kith and kin—even so, modern life would*
> *have come to you. In the shape of bullets and bricks, decrees,*
> *men in uniform—it reaches into every part of the world.*

It is not the primitivism that disturbs a civilized man, I said, it is the space that "uncivilized" ones occupy and every speck of that space, virtual or real, is now needed to fulfill the new world order visionaries' envisions. Would there be so much displacement, tragedy and destruction if the tribes never got a hold of arms of mass destruction produced in *civilization* and generously supplied to them? *"Modern life would have come to you. In shape of bullets and bricks, decrees, men in uniform . . ."* Sultan's reply disturbed me a little:

> *I always identify myself as a 'homeboy,' even though I've spent*
> *significant parts of my life either outside the state or outside*
> *the country. But, while I claim my roots, I do not ever want*
> *to go back to the city where I was born; I don't like the way*
> *that I saw myself then and I don't care to build something*
> *new there now. I am also American; that I cannot and need*
> *not deny. As you've noticed though, I am in a minority of*
> *Americans in that I love languages and can learn them. I try*
> *them on like suits. :-) And I get to play different roles. There*
> *was a silly movie in 1986 called Soul Man, in which a rich*
> *white student needs money to go to Harvard because his father*
> *decides (for his own silly reasons) to pull the plug on the kid's*
> *support. So, the kid uses his friend's tanning formula to make*
> *himself look black, which lets him apply for a black student*
> *scholarship. The rest of the movie deals with stereotypes. OK,*
> *after all that buildup, here is the kicker: when he's found out,*
> *James Earl Jones, who plays a professor, says that he knows*
> *what it's like to be black, the student answers, "No, I don't. I*
> *can change to white whenever I want," to which Jones replies,*
> *"You really have learned something."*
> *   If I simply gain some facility in a language, then I am*
> *just taking on a face. But if I actually join the culture, nay,*
> *even more importantly join a small group of real individuals,*

*then I have become a member and I have changed. And that
begs the question of whether one really can be a member of
two cultures at once or one creates in oneself a new culture.*

I did see Lost in Translation. *I've been to some of the
places shown in the movie, and I definitely have lived it. I
could talk for hours on that alone, maybe will sometime. I've
not seen the other film.*

*The Japanese are a mixed bag. I've often said that the
Japanese get far less credit for creativity than they deserve, and
Americans get far more than they deserve.*

I have to get to class. More later . . .

I was on the spur to give him a piece of my mind for this and didn't
care that it was already past midnight. He may even read it tonight . . .
considering . . . it must be awkward between the two of them. His reading
my letters would mean that I get the attention. Instead of old(er) couple's
sitting in front of the TV, the only show she was capable of performing, I
give him fireworks in our, sometimes dialectic, dialogue. Why didn't he
marry her after five years? In whose house they are living? Nah, those were
the issues I didn't consider worth thinking about, once their relationship
ran its course. This was something Sally would dig into, but her life and her
interests involved concrete things; nothing exotic about mixing chemicals
for a new medication, or now, in what she was doing now. Maybe she
missed that kind of control and responsibility. Why wouldn't she go back
to school? And here, I was the more practical one. No, I won't ask about
the house, or the dog slash cat, or progressing of the break up, my course
of action was to tap into the core of our interaction—our appreciation for
others, for diversity. *Sultan* once said, when he first officially acknowledged
her existence, he liked the domestic aspect of his girlfriend's personality,
making me infer that I was somehow "imported." Then he spent some
time explaining that what he meant was in no way implication what he
thought about me. Now this identity and race *pen-pal* crisis needed to be
resolved. Maybe we got lost in translation.

His intellect may have been bigger than life from my subjective, heavily
corrupted perspective, but I wasn't going to tolerate even the delicate

indication of his white male privilege to govern his thoughts and belittle my female, though white (but that didn't matter, it was "imported" white) non-privileged position, as I immediately classified it after reading his letter. Member of two cultures, connected with two women—why was he obsessing about this split in two all the time? I remembered reading a Robert S. Chang's article where he says, "What have I lost in my struggle to become American? What is it that I hope to recover?"

The issue of identity in *Sultan's* view may have been identical to another Chang's question, "So whom do I root for, and how does the question of whom I root for connect up with where I feel rooted. And perhaps more importantly, how does this affect the possibility of critique?" My claiming a *stake* in America came as natural to me as to any American-born person, but the clash of opinions might challenge that stake I am claiming and I am claiming it to, in Chang's words, "legitimate [my] criticism . . ." How could I just be considered a guest? Where else could I go?

In my graduate class I heard opinions from some ex-military individual that borders should be closed and that United States is not a "kennel." I wanted to say to him that borders should get closed only when the last American soldier comes home, but until then they need to be open for the displaced, some of whom losing their livelihoods for the very involvement of the United States in world-wide conflicts. I wrote back to *Sultan*:

> So, you can change back to white whenever you want. Is that the point? Trying on languages like suits and then simply taking them off if they become uncomfortable? What about those who are stuck in their suit, forced in their suit and don't have an option to change? Anyway, I think you should know that a problem in communicating with the people coming from a background different than yours is that you always should be aware of their potential vulnerability.
>
> TV promotes some black and white friendships and the way mass media do it is kind of like the 'soft news' I was telling you about. There is no digging through the shameful past, just fun. You are bringing up some interesting points. But then why would you hold onto something you wouldn't go back to? I, for example, like to think of the funny side of

my past (or I make it funny), so when I remember something remarkable and pull it out of a sea of other silliness life is full of, it gives some strength to who I am, or to the idea of who I am—like a counterpoint. One does not have to constantly place oneself in one context of who they are. That one larger picture of who I am does not always have to linger above my identity and tag along everywhere I go, unless I choose to carry it along at all times. Sometimes it is hard to carry your identity around and it's especially difficult at the place where you were born and lived for a while. I have to find the quote from the New Testament when the believers were told to "be the salt of the earth." You see, the necessity of progress by challenging the old ideas about the world was well known more than a thousand years ago. Other religions explore the notion of identity too: Muslim prophet Mohammad had to leave the place where he was born for "one cannot be a prophet in his village."

I am not sure whether I know a comprehensive enough definition of a culture. I am a member of my culture when I see my people and talk to them. Meanwhile, I am a member of (an)other culture(s), not knowing what either of them should represent (keeping in mind that I don't represent anything typical either). But being an American to me has a different flavor. In Robert S. Chang's words, "If the price of the ticket to become an American is to forget who we are and where we come from, then the price is too great." He warns that, "If we accept the admission on those terms, we will have joined the center without reforming it in any way, as John Brown Childs warns us against." Childs says, and I found it elsewhere, that social thoughts of non-mainstream, primarily the indigenous social thought aids us "in our own resistance to mega-business domination." Going back to Chang, he reminds that (even though it is not always 'fun') we must remember our past, "Otherwise, we are doomed to continue rooting for empire, because we will have forgotten our roots."

You are talking about the interaction with individuals from a different culture bringing some potential change, but didn't specify what kind of change that would be. Would you really stand for everything you said to me before, or was that just a part of the rhetoric? When you say you are an American, can you even begin to explain what it means? In Childs' words, some most wonderful concepts such as 'justice' and 'equality' or, in his words again, the "particularistic ones such as 'I love my community and my people'," have been used "as justification for violence and oppression." I can't go into it right now . . . As much as I criticize 'soft news' I'd like to see myself as 'soft' and 'elegant' in writing and in person . . . It's that vulnerability thing. I'd love to say that you don't have to spare me of what you really think, but there is a certain part of me that is not completely intellectual.

People could empower each other if they wanted to . . . We all live through the intervals of dark ages and we don't ever know when it interchanges with enlightenment. I meni je drago sto te poznajem.

The following morning *Sultan* was waiting for me in front of his office. He almost grabbed me trying to usher me through the door, telling me that we needed to talk:

"Hey, I am sorry that I didn't say more than I did. You are right: I do not know you much yet, and I am only now appreciating how much this communication means to you. Please have patience with me while I learn. And please have patience while you learn about me."

That's it. It's official now. I let him continue almost not believing with my own ears:

"I want to delve into you intellectually and emotionally, not strictly separate in my mind, or in some recent studies of autistics." He grinned, pulling me closer to him, "And this identity issue is not a black-and-white issue, not at all. But you really already know that; it's a matter of definition out there in the *larger world*. You know that, *moja* Bella." This word *my* and the intimate sound of my mother tongue sent goosebumps to my skin. We were standing there, firmly embraced in the middle of his untidy office, promising commitment in words and deeds to our small union, with the ties becoming stronger than any conventional, speed- or slow-dating engagement.

"Where would you like to go?" he whispered.

"I don't know. What makes sense?"

"Mmm, does this make sense to you?" he kissed my neck, moving slowly toward the chin, then the lips. I muffled a moan, parting my lips for his tongue, which wouldn't create sensations described in books or shown on TV. Prescriptions how the kissing a right man should look like are a part of a teenage Cinderella syndrome and fireworks do not happen when kissing on a lunch break in the third decade of life. *Sultan* was of a different opinion:

"I want you. I want all of you," he mumbled between the kisses, "I want you now."

"Now? Are you sure? It's hardly midday."

"It doesn't matter . . . We are leaving for a lunch break. . ."

At my place for the first time. I fantasized about his ripping my clothes off, right there on my sofa, but now wasn't sure whether I wanted sex or not. We continued our office-style petting, but this time more daring and with a sense of direction, at least on *Sultan's* end.

"I am not sure," I said.

"OK," he complied laboriously and continued his quest within the next moment, "You are so . . . succulent," he was grumbling while combating the last barrier between our skin-against-skin touch. His hand was sliding against my inner thigh until it gently touched the bottom of my panties.

I was holding my panties, not even realizing how firmly until *Sultan* tried to pull them down.

"What's the matter?" his horny voice was whispering straight into my ear.

"I am not sure, that's all."

He gently threw his shirt onto my lap, taking me into his arms like a baby. In a way, I felt like one too. Before we left his office, he said he needed to make a phone call. There was this semi-anguished expression on his face, which I began to think of as his new trademark. Now, lying in his lap, I was beginning to see his nakedness and, undoubtedly, he was beginning to see mine—later, after I let him pull his shirt away and take my panties off. It looked as if we were examining ourselves and each other in this mother-and-child or should I say father-and-child position, but the resemblance with Pieta was too obvious to give it a paternal swing.

My head leaning against an armrest and his slightly bent and ogling my figure suddenly gave our actions a digressive twist. I'd never seen him from this angle, an angle revealing an unstoppable process of aging. A bow of lose skin was stretching from the bottom of his chin to a neckline and a dimmed day light coming from the opposite glass door played its shadowy game on his face, deepening the lines around his eyes and widening the pores on his full, baby-like cheeks. I felt an urge to kiss the stretch of loose skin, never noticed before underneath *Sultan's* chin and prompted myself on the elbows. The nipple of my right breast, while combing through the hairy patches of his chest, sent a tickling sensation through my entire body, and I pulled my head backward to relish the moment. When I finally kissed the loose tissue underneath his chin, he looked at me as if asking whether I seriously thought this piece of skin could be an erogenous zone. It was a sad look. I on the other hand wanted to acknowledge his nakedness, to tell in my own way that we all have our source of vulnerability, our Achilles' heel we should not disguise in front of people we care about. My lips touching the jiggly skin gave me a sense of control, so that I could display my nakedness without discomfort or shame.

His right hand was resting on his shirt, still covering my intimacy, and then began to float above my pubis.

"Do you want my tongue there?" he continued in the same seductive tone, descending one of his fingers underneath the shirt to the hot, damp spot on my panties.

"No," I replied, remembering that the last time I took shower was this morning.

But he made a semi-loud approval of "freshness" after he swiftly, for that size man, moved downward, parted my legs while putting one of them around his shoulders, took a bite of my panties, removed them from the slick and soaked area of the labia and quickly pasted his lips onto a bare, pink silk of my most intimate self. At that moment we both attacked the panties, our fingers intertwined at moments while pulling them down and after we finished his lips came back to my center with a magnetic force. The activity his tongue and lips produced, weak yet enjoyable contractions, was certainly a step up in our physical contact and almost sufficient for me until the next rendezvous. What *Sultan* had in mind was real sex, and now I was the indecisive one. He sat on the sofa and pulled me back to him into our usual position on one of his office chairs, but this time there was nothing between us. His corpulent body swallowed a disproportionately small penis and, upon noticing, *Sultan* lowered himself down exposing his masculinity in a fully erected state.

I may have repeated that I wasn't ready, but his desire on the other hand was almost uncontrollable.

"You're soaked," he almost shouted, stopping his motion and pressing me firmly against his chest. This time my imagination didn't have time to manufacture various stimuli and transmit them to the most important sexual organ of mine—namely the brain—actual sexual act was short and straightforward and *Sultan's* ultimate action didn't need any help of my mental faculties to want him more. This ultimate action was about him, not me, though I thought I heard a muffled "I love you," dismissing it as a figment of my imagination. I decided to give my imagination a break since this last audio sensation was putting it on a slippery slope of irrationality. I could've asked him if he said something, but *"What did you say?"* is the un-sexiest question of lovemaking. *Sultan* and I did not have a breathtaking, mind-blowing sex that afternoon, but we did have our never-ending conversation, our *connection*. That way I knew he was with me. Of course, we had a penis conversation too, though this one was a cliché that "size didn't matter."

Later in the evening I received an email from him and, as if nothing happened, he continued a flow of thought on the topic where we most recently left off. His knowledge of the Bible was greater than mine, and he found a perfect quote to continue a string of thought after my bringing up the prophets and how they are not honored in their *village*. *Sultan* wrote:

In the King James Bible, John 4:44 says "a prophet has no honor in his own country." And I think, not in his own time. Prophets do not predict future. Prophets do not tell people what they want to know. Prophets tell large truths, often unpopular ones. And so, they are called the naysayers, the foretellers of doom. They are usually considered to be nutcases. It looks as though they are the ones who are trying to break a society apart, while it's often the case they are pointing out the cracks that need to be repaired to hold it together.

Have you seen the movie Copying Beethoven? *In it, Beethoven is written to say "I just write what I hear in my head." How can one be considered anything but a lunatic? And how can anyone do anything else? And how can one be "happy" if one does not listen to what goes on between one's ears?*

I don' think it's crazy to talk to oneself. Dialogue creates movement. Question and answer (actually, response is a term I prefer) leads one places one might never go.

I do not want to end up, though, as a vapid critic, some chain-smoking cynic, the one I described as wearing a beret, grumbling about the world. But sometimes I wonder, is there always a point in going someplace you know? (One response from me is yes. . .maybe more on that another day). What is the difference (nor a rhetorical question) between rambling and heading off in a direction just to see what's there? OK, I think I can describe that difference, too, but I'm trying to practice what I'm saying right now. Free writing, surfing the linguistic waves without regard to the possibility of crashing on the metaphorical beach. I've dropped into word play, fun in itself, but kind of like a snack break during a long trek.

What are your reactions?

V

ultan's "surfing the linguistic waves" reminded me again of his "trying on linguistic suits." And this connection was beginning to feel esoteric. Yes, we had sex, and "discussed" the Bible and other religious texts, but *Sultan* was still separating physical and intellectual in his writing; autistic, as in certain studies he brought up in one of his letters.

Sally came over and I told her . . . I indicated certain details to her, and she listened attentively to my confession. However, her pragmatic nature wouldn't stop inquiring about a home front.

"I don't know," I said, "and now I don't know how to ask."

"Sure, you don't, because you didn't ask at the right time."

"I did!" I protested, "but what time is the right time? I told him I couldn't accept his *friendship,* especially not that "friends with benefits" deal. I told him that would hurt me the most . . . he's not a monster."

"How was the sex?"

"Shut up. Or, how did your reconciliation with Brian go? The second and only man in your life? Instead of interrogating me, maybe you could share some hot news of your own."

"Nah, Brian and I know each other so long, it's like a routine with us."

"What is: housewife in the kitchen, whore in the bed? Every guy's dream! Well, I still think you have seniority over me when it comes to sex life. You want sex, you get it—you don't even have to look for a mate; that is my favorite word now . . . . . don't laugh! And your guy breaks up with his girlfriend overnight. Sally, I think you have a perfect life—pardon, — poster-woman perfect life."

"Don't forget that I cleaned up Brian's house after we had our make-up sex, no, no, I stand corrected, I still don't know where this is going . . ."

"But you cleaned up his house?"

"Yes, and left a dollar on his night stand . . . for his . . . *services*. You should give a dollar to your *Sultan* too."

"Sally, with you, this society can still preserve its foundations; you are this new prototype of a woman, unlike a modern alimony-happy, blood-sucking exploiter of men, dressing the mankind in grey suits and sending them into a brave new world to work for *her*."

"You were saying?"

"For God's sake, what kind of satisfaction does it give you to clean his burrow after you moved out and didn't take *half of what he had*?"

"I don't know, it's an issue of control. At least that's what my therapist thought: if you are not in charge of anything, then some sense of control must be coming from keeping an order in the house."

"But it's not even your house. Sally, you're a traitor of feminism."

"I wonder what does feminism make you, . . . let's see, um. . . we have choices ranging from sissy to . . . oh, that's it."

"I forbid you calling me 'sissy'!"

"And how would you prefer to be called, Bella?"

"Maybe a . . . . . .Scheherazade."

"I don't see the point."

"She is the one that tells stories to stay alive in *1,001 Nights.*"

"Ah, and the beau is *Sultan,* for that matter?! I think you would feel better if you cleaned his house. Oh, I am sorry, we don't know if he has one."

"You are brutal, Sally. Just the other day he said something about *his* fireplace . . . being a real fireplace or so."

"You are so easy to take care of . . . . . .here is the pacifier." She threw her Chihuahua's plastic bone at me.

"It's not funny. I think we share something beyond your materialistic aspirations."

"If you say so."

Back home, I turned off the lights in the living room and stared through the glass door into the darkness of a paved cul-de-sac in front of the building. The clustered complex of buildings gave the neighborhood a sense of cozy protectiveness, and a proximity of living units purported human closeness. There was only a week left before Thanksgiving, which meant new trials. The holidays were a nasty, conformist business, but then I remembered *Sultan's* cynic with a beret, "grumbling about the world," which posed an inevitable question whether he stopped trying to change the world, even if he ever tried to change it and whether his current "riding on linguistic waves" was nothing but a supernova of a dead star. In his last letter, he remained in an intellectual bubble, as if a flap of a butterfly's wings caused nothing but a lukewarm breeze in his, all the while swiping my world away as a full-blown tornado. I've had it—the butterfly effect. The whole point of our discourse was to show how we were changing each other's world, not to passively browse through our linguistic archives. That alone makes a cynic in a beret, not the bravery of letting yourself to be shaped by the world and shape the same world in return. Where was *Sultan's* effect? Did he know that Descartes' *age of reason* and the beginning of the twentieth century's *l'art pour l'art* were over? At least in my mind. One can never miscarry intellectually as long as they give a piece of themselves to the world, or one can never . . . get old . . . *Sultan* was receiving a piece of me in every subsequent *story*, only to suck it up in his bubble, his *black hole,* and I did not know what I was receiving in return. Did there have to be reciprocity, I wondered.

I decided to move on from biblical times, telling him that I didn't study Bible much but wished I did. It seemed that there was a lot of *borrowing* going on: the *prophets* could not keep reinventing the wheel, but the mass media pastors firmly hold onto their claim that the New Testament and gospel of Jesus are God's love child. None of the other religions were about love and redemption. They have me there; but isn't *Savior* a *Slayer* in the old scriptures, according to some recent interpretations? As we now know, interpretations are not immune to which side is one on. *"Self-criticism is a sign of loyalty to one's core values and a sign of greatness,"* I wrote to *Sultan.* In a fluid Age of Aquarius, the shape of things depends on a dish in which the water is poured. Which religion does not say that God is great, but that must be one narcissistic, selfish God, *old* God. We praise *him* by all linguistic virtuosity, keeping the world ideologically static and letting it physically rot, in that sense being the agents of change indeed:

But I will reread the Bible, I will read everything there is. The beauty of reading is transaction—a new trendy expression for eliciting a certain, mental chain reaction when you can connect the text with your cultural schema and hence connect the dots. Doesn't even have to be about connecting the dots; transaction in reading is almost like you knew the message all along and someone only needed to spell it out for you.

Our writing is part of a larger picture if you want. Its fragments wouldn't have a significance without awareness of something unifying. That is the frame, sothat anything you say wouldn't sound like cynical rambling, but perfectly fit into acertain time and setting. 'Fit'; don't you like the word; didn't you say it to me once? I fit you. Think of some of the reasons why we do it, or why we write, period. Could it be a way of life, an intra-dialogue given shape and form, so that we don't go nuts listening to the voices in our heads? What is the emotion in our letters? Would a hypothetical reader know that we have sex? Anything you are able to articulate is intended to be heard . . . And aren't we getting to know each other in this way? Not only, getting to know you doesn't explain it. You are always present in a way that gives you a voice other setting wouldn't.

Happy Birthday. I couldn't bring it up today, but think that any symbolic present wouldn't do it. A little tacky at this point. At the same time feeling this way irritates me. Can you read between the lines?

To my dismay, *Sultan* wrote in return that there was no need to read between the lines. His words that "we are not conventional" felt like a stab in the heart; I wasn't talking about his birthday and presents as being intertwined with conventions. He was reminding me what he said the previous day about

one continuing conversation that starts when two people meet and does not ever really end (until one dies . . . . . . and even then, the one who continues may hear reverberations of that conversation)? Yes, our writing to each other is a part of a larger picture, one that may extend even beyond horizons that we may perceive.

On one hand, we are not conventional. On the other hand, some of the conventions are quite nice and well-founded. Acknowledging highlights in another's life makes a connection. The act of giving a present is an acknowledgment of the highlight. Words alone can be bandied about lightly. But in the context of our relationship they carry great meaning. I thank you—hvala mnogo. We have our words. You and I; we prize them and cherish them, in and of themselves and as the vehicles of sharing that they are. Trust that the sharing has been carried to me.

We've been using our words differently, which did not alarm me; we've been using them as vehicles of fundamentally different kinds of sharing. However, they were revealing; they were taking our clothes off even if not intended to. I found myself *caressing Sultan's* dead tissue underneath his chin while reading his last letter, remembering how he tried to reposition himself, and now, metaphorically speaking, he was gradually changing his grandiloquent vocabulary into a more plausible chat as one of the precaution measures in case I expected his linguistic waves to be higher than his intention of possibly not living up to my expectations.

Sultan's car wouldn't start the afternoon he was supposed to come over, so I picked him up. He was wearing a black leather trench coat; it was a rather heavy piece of apparel, I realized after putting it on the hanger. For the entire time, Sally was prodding me somewhere in my subconscious to bring up a topic I was dying to open—even if it were Pandora's Box or a can of worms. In only one afternoon, I was *Sultan's* personal driver, sex mate, and hostess, which in retrospect almost equaled a house cleaning. Some oldies were playing on the radio, and it felt awfully good that I didn't receive a long, judgmental look while trying to sing to "T-Rex's" "Get It On"; to the contrary, *Sultan* could sing this one and several other ones from the seventies—in the manner of Frank Sinatra. The fire was dancing in my fake fireplace, *Sultan* was singing and our coats, his black trench coat and my parka, were waiting for us to put them on and go to the place that sells car batteries. I had one more errand to run for *Sultan* that day.

"Hey, what's the status of your *other* relationship," I shot (and wanted to add additional question *"In which stage of the breakup are you?"*) but was cut off by the look on his face. It didn't even appear to be the face anymore, it was the head of a very large cat with a hair loss problem.

"What?" he asked, as if not believing that I would bring it up.

"Your relationship," I repeated. "For the entire time you gave an impression that I wasn't just the "other woman" and that you were willing to make sacrifices after that phone call. Otherwise, believe me, none of this would ever happen!" I just felt like my head was going to explode. I wished I knew the courtesans' art of fainting, almost certain that there must had been some benefit from their legendary sighs, followed by elegant falls, oblivious to the world and forgetting it existed for a moment. I needed some memory deletion, so that I could never trace the steps of my actions for the past month, leading me up to this. My mouth felt instantly dry and I had trouble swallowing, while simultaneously having an urge to swallow all the time.

"Do you expect me to tell her? And then I am an asshole?"

"What do you think your behavior is making you now?" I wanted to slap those fat cheeks over and over again, but no, he had his glasses on again, and he was technically a pedestrian . . . I contemplated an option of leaving him in front of the entrance door, but then remembered that it was a chilly day, only days before Thanksgiving. He looked at me again, etching this face of a hairless cat into my memory forever.

"You'll get over it, I know, I've been through this before."

"You did it before? Oh, yeah, you cheated on your wife before . . . . . . probably the same way you cheated on this girlfriend of yours. And why do you think your "relationship" could go on, why do you think it could be based on lies and why do you think she'd forgive you? Maybe if she's crazy or desperate . . . So, this entire time you were in control, you were waiting to see what was going to happen, like a spectator!"

It was close to three in the afternoon, and the "magic" of our trysts had to be over by that time; I had to pick up Alexandra and he had to "finish his work." Though everything in me screamed to do something, to dramatize, I quietly pulled his heavy black leather trench coat from the hanger and handed it to him, signaling that we were headed to the garage.

"You need to tell that person," I said while waiting for him to get out of the car and adding sternly to spare me his thank yous for dropping him off. This time his behindhand reaction had slightly more pathos than all the previous ones, defending his "right to thank me" in a yet unseen grandiose way and followed by equally grandiose gestures. I was still fighting some physiological difficulties manifested as dry mouth, trouble swallowing, and a blurred vision to be able to even grin at the scene at hand, but like his large hairless cat face, *Sultan* etched this peculiar gesturing into my memory as well. Of all possible responses in a situation such as this one, I chose a tacky, loser's good bye, by saying, "I just wanted to be with you . . . . . . and I still do . . ."

> *I told her. And her answer was that her life was still much better with me than without me. Forgiveness and forgetting may be another matter. But she wants me there. And I want to be there.*
>
> *It does something horrible to me too. And that's why there is no easy way to stop. It's either on or off. I was either stupid enough or arrogant enough to think that part would do. Part doesn't; not for me, not for you. And if there were no worth there, it wouldn't hurt. If there were no connection there, it wouldn't hurt. And yes, it hurts. I cannot control my urge. I can only control my behavior.*
>
> *Maybe this is too bloody dramatic, but I rage at the Fates for putting us together now. Why not another time? Why now? And had we met five years ago, would we have connected in the same way? Or if we were to have met in five years?*
>
> *You said in an email that we already know each other that our communication fills in the gaps. We do know each other. And that will always be true. But while we understand each other, there are contradictions in me that I cannot explain. I can want two at the same time. And that would*

> *disintegrate me as well as both relationships. I knew that. I ignored that. A case of hubris, possibly.*
>
> *I cannot ask you to just talk with me; we both know how much would not be in the talking . . . I will always be glad and sad to see you.*

This was *Sultan's* response to my rant that the world is on the man's side and that it is cool to score. He could have suppressed caressing my hand, and all he did was suppressing a grunt while sliding his finger up and down the palm of my hand; all other basic instincts were there.

"Could it have started any other way, but the one we experienced? Why do you say then it happened so fast, using that despicable male excuse . . ."? I was crying to him, feeling haunted by the words of a good friend of mine from years past, who said that I could only have all or nothing from a man.

"And that's what you would give in return," he said. I decided to tell *Sultan* another one of my stories, a very long one and an honest one:

> *You felt tempted to do something that a person who is in love with someone would not do. Nothing tells me now that you wouldn't do it again—perhaps with another woman. If you look into your life and into your feelings the way I would, there must be something missing underneath all the cozy layers of what one tends tocall a comfortably tempered and secured life, although we are not nomads that simply pick up their belongings when leaving their overnight spot. Our life doesn't work that way and I know that much. And regardless how much nicer our life style may seem in comparison, in a way it is an entrapment that gradually strips us of everything, leaving those necessary biological mechanics and routines only. We start thinking of ourselves the way others see us and what they expect from us.*
>
> *In all fairness though, certain point in life may contribute to that and I don't mean it sarcastically. A couple of years ago I wrote in my journal that I wouldn't be forgiven for not then and perhaps not ever approaching a point in life when one gradually starts to grow old. I could very well relate*

to your "I once almost lost everything" and we never really completely heal from such an experience, although it may appear differently. I think I already know your girlfriend; she gets some of your instincts, but she is not an intellectual. In fact, I think she is desperate. And not sensual. No offense to her, but many people are better off being that way. So, for a moment you jumped out of your own skin just to see how it really felt to be 'out there' again and I encouraged you. You cannot imagine how much this hurts, but I would be lying to say that there isn't any resilience building up. I suppose you know the pattern: bashing a person in your thoughts, listing all the cons . . . But at this point it really looks as if this suffering is going to last forever.

The way I seemed to be having set my priorities used to put me on occasion in a situation of not being taken seriously and I rationalized that was the price one had to pay in a mediocre world. I used to think that mediocrity was good for survival of the species ('survival of the fittest') but now I am convinced it is exactly the opposite.

Mediocrity is destroying everything, physical and spiritual, and we are on the final countdown. We all suffer from lack of creativity and ironically, we all think we have it. Was that what you wanted from me? Is 'creativity' now a forbidden fruit one steals from another? It kills me to think after all this time that I set myself up for you may have been just my clash with conventions. Though you are static, you play your game so damn well. You made me believe that you were going to leave your musty department, get a doctorate. Did the possibility of your making your job stale ever cross your mind? And now I don't know how to cope...

I started reading one of Saul Bellow's books, but will have to finish it some other time. One motive strikes me in all his books; he seems to be wondering over and over again about why an accomplished man (such as himself) ultimately ends up with a psychopath "under the same quilt." He is baffled by the fact that all the brilliance of his characters *could not help them to foresee a disaster and stop it. Here they are, distinguished scholars, in a role of an oppression instrument by a female without a single human quality (or at least depicted that way). Men with less emotion and less empathy don't fall for women needing a "savior" and then turn out to be the devil themselves. Bellow teaches other men not to do it, not to go for the 'unconventional,' although not explicitly. For the most part I think that men like Bellow teach other men misogyny since what once was a witch has a modern name—psychopath. .*

Anyway, we are borrowing each others' thoughts all the time, even when making our own point. Pop culture is recycling the notion of a 'freak,' which comes down to he same idea of reluctant psychopaths roaming around. Remember when Carrie from "Sex and the City" met nothing-wrong-with guy and panicked, starting to look for evidence of his "freakness" when he was not around. He barged in, seeing her all worked up with a burning cigarette in her mouth, ultimately turned into a freak herself. That is how I feel now.

VI

As in several my previous incarnations of a butterfly, I spent many a night wondering what struck me so strongly and why him of all men. I found *Sultan's* forehead the only attractive feature on his body, but his corpulence and baldness surrounded his persona with an additional charisma that made up for a bulging stomach, very sturdy legs, more woman- than man-like, and a facial expression of a very large and slow cat. Yet I wanted to throw my life right at him, I wanted my stories to never dry up, I wanted his hearing them to heal me. That was why I wanted *Sultan* to hold my hand the following morning when we ran into each other, while unsuccessfully trying to stop the tears and an announcement that I didn't know how to cope. In return, and even if he meant it as a consolation, the effect of his telling me that he started the day by throwing up was minimal. However, a sigh of relief unintentionally slipped through my slightly parted lips, in the next moment dangerously approaching his. A desire to kiss him mixed with a partially conscious wish that he brushed his teeth after vomiting, which I dismissed before it was fully articulated and as soon as his chapped lips, framed by the newly growing beard and mustache resembling a very wide inverted "V" first tickled my face lightly smeared with tears, and then fully landed on my starved lips. The kiss marked another round of our emotional cleansing after yet another failed attempt on *Sultan's* end to sever our ties. I, on my end, performed additional cleansing—a cleansing of my soul as I saw it, for emerging criticism of *Sultan's* physical appearance, whose slight untidiness or a hint of it was epitomized in a yet un-groomed facial hair. This unspoken and embarrassing criticism scared me, prompting me immediately to ban the disturbances of the ephemeral physical world, letting the physical to dwell in its physical realm and dismissing my disdain for Cartesian dualism, as the new circumstances called for it. We were sitting in his office across from each other and the earth and its laws of mechanics slipped into a relativity when he placed his arms around my waist, lifting me gently and placing me slowly into a protective nest of his lap. He showed no effort in doing it, as if I were weightless.

I don't know how long I was nested in his lap, suddenly content like a well-fed infant, but not forgetting to comment on his latest message to me: "What makes her to forgive you, what makes her utter those words that life with you is still better than life without you? Those words . . . they scream despair, defeat. Why would anyone be forced to say them in the moment of total humiliation?"

"I don't know," *Sultan* replied absentmindedly, the tips of his fingers equally absently but gently scratching my back, then moving up to my neck and the scalp. The anguish of the previous night was melting away, and *Sultan* appeared willing to violate the loyalty of his common-law marriage companion by leaning his slightly coarse cheek against mine and inevitably slipping into more and more tangible and visceral motions of first examining my damp face with his dry lips, then sealing them up onto mine. We established our lifeline again, and the break-up episode awkwardly stuck out in the flow of our discourse as an embarrassing though unintentional exercise in mental sadomasochism.

I told him that there were times in my life when I thought I could fly and be all I wanted to be. I told him that I wanted to start doctoral studies right after finishing a master's degree and asked about his plans: "You know, this job you are doing . . . don't you think it's becoming a little stale?"

"It's becoming . . . has become you should say," *Sultan* confided, adding that he was at the point of doing his job half-dreaming, but without bitterness or cynicism—only stating the obvious. Yes, he was thinking about doctoral studies as well, but never had the courage to tackle it, and at this juncture, it would mean more a moral victory than an "investment into the future." And I was generously investing into *Sultan's* alter ego, hoping to place it in a dimension where a plain terrestrial could live the immortality, not only keeping his fantasy alive by a mere strength of faith.

He asked, "Do you really think I am that smart?" and I replied, but not without a significant moment of silence, to raise anticipation and importance of what I was about to say, "Yes, I do." This *I do*, slightly less ceremonial and of a different kind than the one pronounced in front of a priest, brought an equal joy on *Sultan's* face, sped up his speech and restarted the entire structure of his corpulent body.

Sultan's new invigorated self suddenly erased an expression of a slow, sly cat from his face, an image I struggled to erase when it was invading my imagination in the disturbing moments of my fearing his next move. We continued our conversation at a nearby café for a true *conversation starts when two people meet and does not really end until one of them dies.* *Sultan* just looked at me and said nothing for a couple of minutes. The café owner glanced at us occasionally, puzzled by my tears and appearing to be somewhat disapproving of whatever disagreeable traits he found in *Sultan's* persona. How could a café owner explain *Sultan's* long leather trench coat and his sitting at a small table with an open laptop and a backpack full of heavy French textbooks, next to a crying person! Through the haze of my own pain and suffering, I still noticed café owner's judgmental glances. There in the outside world, scrutinized by people of a café owner's caliber as I thought, my determination to give *Sultan* even more than I did, even more than I could give, grew ever stronger.

"I will be on a business trip in a nearby city the day after the Thanksgiving."

"Are you telling me this because you want me to visit you there?"

"That's a possibility," *Sultan* replied, "We'll see how things go." He then remembered that he missed an appointment with a student, and I was instantly flooded by guilt.

"Next time you write to me your stories. You are telling them in a way that does not seem trite . . . even when using those already overused words... I guess it's because we are language people; we don't simply copy or *ventriloquate*."

"I like how you use the word 'ventriloquate.' I've seen it being used quite prolifically in the articles about language acquisition."

"How do you mean?"

"I am warning you: we may end up talking about identity again." A possibility to continue our *lifeline* of never-ending conversation, even under a guard of an apprehensive café owner re-energized my overworked and fatigued mind. Suddenly, I transformed into a cheerful interlocutor, willing to forgive and forget the trials of the previous day.

"Ventriloquism, in some rather daring interpretations, positions language learners first as imitators, or ventriloquists if you wish, of the language of their surroundings until capable of producing *original* or *creative* language of their own. Words in an unfamiliar language do not produce desirable effect until they are reiterated repeatedly and with a variety of people and in a variety of settings. This may sound like a bad analogy, but it's like telling a lie over and over again until the liar himself (or herself) starts to believe it's true. Or take, for example, the swear words or taboo words. By 'taboo', I mean unacceptable in public interactions."

I leaned over to him, whispering, "If I told you to fuck me in a language you don't use, even if you were familiar with the language, it wouldn't turn you on the same way a familiar and intimate *fuck me* would. In that sense reiteration produces a desirable effect, whereas in other situations we look for synonyms, Latin root words and redundancy to get our point across. Why can't other forms of expression be as simple as a simple *fuck me*?"

"Maybe because we attach to them such an extent of insincerity that we are finally compelled to apply a certain linguistic sorcery to keep our forms of expressions appealing and credulous. Take the word 'leadership', for example; everyone claims it, and by now it is so inflated that it makes me frown every time I hear it! Or it makes me put the beret on, light up a cigarette, and go on a rant against the world."

We left the café followed by the owner's gaze at *Sultan*. Did I really look that much younger than him? Home. Home was my haven—and a site of our never-ending conversation. I wanted to tell him another one of my stories, carefully choosing words and with an unsurpassed effect and passion. After rereading it over and over, I realized I called him a 'flatlander' and ordered him to listen to me. Instead of sending it I saved it in my new folder, labeled 'For *Sultan*'. From that moment on, I decided, a folder with his name was going to receive all my told and untold stories, where our conversation would finally become immortal and safe.

VII

Some men are born to be warriors because to them
death is like a new birth, a new quality of life.
Women who tremble and fear for the lives of their
beloved ones only enhance the purpose for which those men
believe they are born, sending off their beloved warriors with
an embrace and a message that the whole universe is united
to pay its respects to them, to show how important they are.
But did you know that beyond all the glory and pathos fallen
warriors are the ones shaping everything living and dead?
They are timeless and homeless, though in their minds home
and homies are all they ever know. I made this up, although
somewhere and perhaps even someone I know lived this
through exactly as I tell you. You say you are proud of who you
are, but that is so shallow and inconsiderate. Now listen and
try to wrap your mind around my story; it is important that
you do so. A flatlander like you—don't look at me like that—
is going to visit the hills of a no man's land far away from
here. In such a land, boys and men—and even old men—
were gathered to go into a war against other boys and men
and old men, gathered on the other side of the no man's land
and sent into the hills, which were once glorious and gorgeous
and victorious when other warriors fought there. It has been
decades thereafter and all the tales were told, all the victories
extolled, when the people of no man's land were told that
their lives had been a great lie and that there was nothing in
the glorious past to be proud about. Dark, heathenish forces
stole those peoples' identities and pushed them into an ambush
of idolatry and denunciation. They were also told that all

of them belonged to different tribes, hating each other and killing each other for centuries. Young boys and girls of no man's land would not know that, but their elders could not wait to take off their masquerading apparel and show their real, warrior faces, which never stopped dreaming about a return to those hills to vanquish and triumph in a true victory this time, rather than succumbing to the heathenish forces and pretending to be celebrating their glory (their lies) all those years.

Peace that was forced upon the warriors of a no man's land for decades only intensified their yearning for a mysterious, adventurous bosom of their beloved hills, yearning to take off their masks and conquer the heathens. For that matter, the girls were told they were warriors too, and they readily took off their waitressing aprons, left classrooms, and abandoned their lives as they knew them. The ones who could not become warriors became mothers. Now imagine a girl who was neither one; her life must had been a disgrace if she chose neither of the roles, or a waiting line for the remote dreams to be fulfilled. She was one of those youngsters who was born long after the old warriors were forced out of the hills and who did not live long enough to establish an independent adult life before a no man's land stumbled into a new, yet unknown turmoil. The painful process during which she started to believe that life had no alternatives but the ones right at hand, which in the beginning seemed to be no alternatives whatsoever, began when her family disintegrated and she was forced to roam in-between meandering border lines of a new land—land her tribe called theirs. This story does not have an end, and there is more death in it than you can imagine, but what makes it great is a ray of light that two warriors saw when sparing each other's life. The girl, roaming her new land, finally married a boy who was soon deployed into the hills hours away from where they lived. He and his companions were soon wished farewell with all the accompanying honors after which groups of sullen women went home.

The girl, now a woman with a warrior's child, visited him once in the hills. A narrow, curvy asphalted road cut through the hills like a scar until a small jeep with the visitors reached what was once a well-built but small vacation house, transformed into an improvised visiting facility of some sort, beyond which was a restricted zone for civilians. Other warriors with their visitors were gathered there too. The hills, covered with tall evergreens, surrounded a small vacation house in what seemed like a snuggling embrace from afar, leaving only a small patch of indigo blue sky to peek into this wild, dangerous yet intimate scenery, violated on its surface by shifts of warriors in full gear and smelling like moth balls and their admiring, timid, and worried visitors. A young warrior and his young wife embraced each other, and she was playing her role so well. An expression of true happiness radiated from her face, so that no one would ever guess that once she was hopeless, angry, and in doubt about the cause the warriors fought for. There were many improvised beds in the attic of a vacation house and there she fulfilled her marital obligation toward her husband-warrior, lying peacefully in his arms afterward, listening to his intimate whisper.

There he told her how big of an adventure this fighting for a cause was, and that he was awfully attracted to the dangers awaiting him. Yes, he even volunteered to sneak behind enemy lines as a member of an elite diversion group. His young wife's blood froze in her veins, and she did not know whether it happened because of what she was hearing or because of her husband's calm, low, and even casual tone of voice telling her the news. His mother, sitting quietly by the window and staring into the distance as if expecting a message, did not exist in his world anymore; his mind transformed all his females into cheerleaders and his warring into a performance of a lifetime. There were cheerleaders in nearby towns and villages too, and his young wife's heart was burning with jealousy.

Then he told her about a night that set a precedent to heroism in her young heart and soon after began to threaten a fragile symbiosis she lived in with her surroundings. Her young warrior was assigned to go on a surveillance mission behind enemy lines, and while sneaking through the evergreen woods in a pitch-dark night, stopping every once in a while by a tree and using it as a shield, he realized that the dry pine cones' rustling and occasional branch cracking off the shoots were following him and could not have been coming from a nocturnal animal. With eyes wide open and stiff as a shotgun uselessly hanging from his shoulder, the young warrior froze and harked rustling that started multiplying while surrounding him at the same time. Thoughts faster than lightning were exchanging in his mind, all at once telling him that he wasn't up against just one enemy soldier, a member of an elite squad like himself and likely better trained than him. There seemed to be at least four or five of them now, getting closer to him by the moment. He wondered if they knew that he simply wanted an adventure, to experience a true flavor of danger, to feel adrenaline rush and invincibility, and then to safely come back to the base to live and tell.

He lived to tell his young mate that hope had left him that night when a face of an enemy soldier appeared in front of him, close enough to see his burning pupils and a finger ready to pull the trigger. A soldier made a motion with his free hand, a motion that gave new birth to the young warrior and set him free. He was directing him to go back to life and the young warrior did.

Following morning *Sultan* was still under impressions of our conversation at the café and power or blandness of words. He wrote me a letter, his *minor rant* against language abuse.

I used this phrase with you: "I value your opinion," and you said, "Please don't say that."

I must agree with you completely, and therein lies the heart of my rant. I really do value your opinion, but that statement has lost its vitality from overuse by idiots.

I want my language back from the people who have, in my heart and mind, co-opted it and taken the heart out of it. What gets to me the most, besides the use of the word 'leadership,' is an equally abusive utilization of the word 'passionate.' I hear it at work in meetings. I hear it on television in commercials. I hear people use it to describe themselves. It has become cliché.

One can love one's job. One can be dedicated to it. But to say, over and over, that So-and-so is 'passionate' about this or that activity demeans and devalues the concept.

A passion, in my mind, is on the level of avocation. A passion is a deep-set dedication to an ideal or way, one that sets the tone for one's life. I suppose that it could be said that one could be passionate about cycling, but damn it all, cycling isn't important enough to engender such a passion. Passion should be reserved for some higher idea.

Now, having just checked the description given for 'passion' in my American Heritage Dictionary, I may be out of bounds. I know that meanings of words exist, not in a vacuum, but rather in a living group. But I'm a member of the group and I want to express depth and breadth and vision. And these people are blunting the tools I want to use.

There. I don't know that I feel better overall because it will never be the case that most people use language, any language, the way we do—but I'm happy that I have expressed my thoughts to you.

A bit of French: je t'embrasse. Yes, the verb 'embrasse' is the cognate of 'embrace,' je=ja (I), and t' is te (you). It means both 'I embrace you' and 'I kiss you' at the same time. As you said of the lovely black dress, it's versatile. Do sutra.

I always thought of language as I thought of fashion, while loving them both. To use a cliché, there are leaders and followers (and ventriloquists) everywhere, including the use of language. I wrote to *Sultan* that I was afraid it was up to us to look for a treasure on the junk yard. I didn't mean it as devaluation of the whole language, but to point out that words were being thrown around without much care, or because they come in handy to fulfill whatever is on the daily agenda of people using them; digest editions of immortal thoughts of equally immortal people are available and in public domain. At least the copy rights laws say that they are. I remember my attempt at newspaper journalism when I was in the second year of college. *Sultan* would love to hear about this; it'd fit into his rant.

> *a friend of mine convinced me to write about something (not important here). She was a journalist and, before switching her majors worked for a newspaper. Her name would be Desiree, if I were to translate it. Anyway, after I wrote the article, she said it was wonderful, but to be accepted as a piece of information for a newspaper, 'artistic' or literary descriptions would have to be peeled off and basically it would have to be served to the readers as a skeleton or 'naked truth' if you wish. What would be left out of this context is demagogy that some others, more fit writers get to do. They also get to spice up their stories, but this is a special kind of journalism one does not learn in school. A good journalist is never a good writer and vice versa. But you heard this before. It is a craft, apprenticeship, not a talent they say. If you are writing to convey information, your digressive gift almost gets in the way. Some say that people's interactions are now what is called cognitive apprenticeship. No wonder we are destined to borrow each other's thoughts. Where does a true talent begin? I feel like an empty shell after reading some of the magazines…*
>
> *Funny that you mentioned a type writer; my aunt had one and my sister and I always played with it. Please don't remark anything about generational differences, but because I never used it for work it will always have its place in my*

memory as one of my favorite toys. Will write some more later… Ljubim te.

Empty email box, empty answering machine (which didn't bother me as much) were haunting me the following days. *"It does not have to be this way, it does not have to be frustrating,"* I wrote to him, but the reply came two days later. He was talking about the "bloody slow connection" at his parents' place, being irritated at their political views and his being "irradiated during gestation" for holding different said views. Nothing comforted me until he called:

"Hey, I am on the road right now, remember a business trip I was telling you about?"

"Can I join you?" I jumped up from my chair, producing a frown on Sally's face who came over for a belated Thanksgiving dinner I invited her to.

"Let's see," *Sultan* was back to his "glacial" mode, "sure, why not. This is the name of the hotel where I am staying . . . you need to take I-80 and I am not quite sure which exit you take . . . I'll call you back in a minute, OK?"

"Sally," now I was whispering to her, avoiding Alexandra's suspicious looks, "this will be our first night together, after so many days of …"

"Of what?" she looked at me, positioning her inquisitive head askew, a well-known gesture of Sally's disapproval.

"On the other hand," she added quickly, "life is too short to waste it wondering what you could have done, beating yourself up over why you didn't…" Unusually supportive attitude and the piece of advice this time didn't smack of latent sarcasm and she even helped me select an outfit, though suspiciously selecting most provocative combinations.

"No, I don't think my high cut, high heel boots would go well with this skirt," I protested. "What kind of dirty fantasies are you living right now?"

"You're right," she agreed, "these flat ones would look better. See, I am totally supportive of you . . . and Alexandra stays with me tonight."

"You think that is necessary? She's fourteen."

"Doesn't matter. She doesn't look too happy with you going…"

"Sure, she doesn't. I am part of the inventory in this house. Always there."

VIII

Time has slipped into relativity again right between my rush preparations and merging onto the freeway. My sense of time was somehow distorted on the freeway and a fifty miles long trip seemed as short as a drive to a nearby grocery store. At the hotel lobby, as at any public place recently I noticed, including the library café, reality kicked in unexpectedly and brutally. "I am waiting for someone," I said to a receptionist, who replied that she wanted to take a look at me and that I should have approached the counter a bit closer . . . *remain in light* I thought. *In case she has to answer someone's questions the following day, in case something happens...* It was all part of a new-age paranoia. How could three minutes at the lobby of a cheap hotel seem longer than two past hours I glided through as if not of this world? *You're cool, it's OK, you're in love . . . you're educated!* I was chanting to myself when everything else failed to boost my confidence. I was never at the reception of a hotel waiting for a man to pick me up, a slow-motion man whom I now wanted to act fast more than ever before.

When *Sultan* appeared in the lobby I immediately forgot the face of a grumpy woman at the reception, beaming at him, letting him take me into his room through a dimly lit, fungi-smelling hallway, which to me appeared as magnificent as a walk on a red carpet. Moreover, the longer I walked hand in hand with *Sultan, this* moldy hallway seemed to have been leading us into the light, or something equally exalted.

"So, how are you?" I was trying to make a small talk once behind the door of his room.

The moment I looked at him and asked this benevolent question, his piercing look conducted through my body a stream of something very similar to high voltage electricity. I could almost see a sharp, broken up line descending to my feet. *Sultan* gave me a smothering kiss, then looked at me again, paused and said, "This is how I am." We could have frozen our positions and locked in our gaze at each other for the entire night, as no sexual act could have matched this passionate moment. I was sitting on the bed on one side of my thigh, knees bent and the hands pushing against the mattress for support. *Sultan* was leaning over me, half kneeling, with one hand buried in my hair and the other one taking my coat off, all the while fixating me with his eyes, piercing me with their steel-blue light. I lost composure, forgot the encounter with the receptionist and what I chanted to myself while waiting for *Sultan* to pick me up and save me from her, lost sense of space in addition to once again lost sense of time, while letting *Sultan* to peel off my carefully selected outfit for our first night together.

Stealing time together during the day never brought forth such a sense of intimacy and companionship. Every mumbling sound he produced, among which I could comprehend that he wanted to devour me, caused an involuntary, uncontrollable moan, substantially different than the carefully calculated ones I played with before. I let him consume me, to suck me in, though I heard him saying through the haze of my mind that it was exactly what I had done to him. That must have been the feeling of the two becoming one and the antiquated marriage oath suddenly became meaningful and true. "Bella . . . Bella . . . Bella," *Sultan* was calling me, his stretching hand suddenly hitting the attached head board, which suddenly brought me back to the reality and the darkness of a chilly hotel room.

The two can never become one without consequences, without a price to pay for oneness is never permanent, never absolute, but I thought that by giving him another piece of me would prolong our fragile union. The face of a hairless cat would reappear in empty darkness occasionally and I would tap through the darkness trying to grab onto a familiar shape of *Sultan's* large body. We talked for a while and I told him a short version of the story I wrote.

"The girl that visited a warrior in the hills, what happened to her?" *Sultan* seemed interested.

"Oh, the girl. They lived in a village, a very rich one, where each house was as large and as sturdy as a mansion, but they knew that in a time of war each one of those houses could become a pile of debris in a matter of seconds. They knew they were living in a little oasis outside of which were ruins and famine, especially in the cities. The cities were these futuristic sights from which all familiar life had disappeared, missile targets as if they were fortresses, not clay and glass constructions with playrooms for children, bedrooms, kitchens… People were reluctantly walking on dangerous streets, shadows of once vivacious bodies.

"The children, where were they?" *Sultan* asked.

"They were still there, but no one would ever imagine that they could live on places like that, where only soldiers and plunderers pretending to be soldiers thrived. The village was relatively safe, but not for the warriors who had to go in the hills to defend it. Sometimes, they would be brought back in the coffins and the village would be in mourning for days. They were men with wives, children, mothers and fathers, but their martyrdom did not seem to have touched the village in the same way it would in a time of peace. Pardon," I scoffed, "there would be no martyrdom, at least not to this extent, in a time of peace. Someone would bring the news to the family of the fallen soldier, and the ensuing wailing (that was a custom) would tell the others in the village that something bad had happened. After many such occasions the apathy set into hearts of the inhabitants of the village. No one knew how to comfort a family struck by a tragedy and the customary visits of the neighboring women were all those wives and mothers could expect. In a way, the villagers became cruel and insensitive, the circumstances whose intensity and duration they could not foresee induced the cruelty that was once dormant and repressed by the leisurely style of life they led.

The girl, or should I say a young wife and mother, did not really fit into any of the village's groups, though many of them were her relatives; after all her mother was born there. She made some impermissible moves while in the village and was always at a distance with everyone even after they accepted her as one of theirs."

"What did she do?"

"She led this infatuated boy in her life the way her relatives did not approve of and for her there was no way back—back to life of an innocent girl, protected by her relatives' hospitality and generosity. And all she wanted was just that: to be an innocent girl shielded from decay and destruction of the war. When this boy came along she was afraid that he, in his boyish ignorance, might violate her once again restored peace of mind, her deliberate return to innocence and withdrawal from the world she did not recognize as hers anymore. *"I was living in a nearby city,"* the boy was telling her, *"I despise these people here, they are so ignorant and primitive . . . rednecks, despite all the property they have, despite who they think they are . . . And look at these girls, I could have every single one of them . . ."* the boy kept telling her. *"Then why me,"* she asked over and over again and the boy would tell her that she was different, sophisticated, they liked the same music and hated the same tunes that the local media was saturating the air with, but it was all needed for warriors' morale and to preserve people's sense of purpose.

She was resisting, careful not to give out a cue to the boy how vulnerable she was and not only once she wanted to plead, to beg him to leave her alone. Instead, she would let him spend time with her at the playground of a local school, *treffpunkt* for the local youth because there was nothing else to do after the winter turned into spring and the days became longer and warmer. She resisted his obsession with her, his persistence and what she perceived as his irrationality. She thought that there was nothing so stunning about her except that she was, what he may have seen, well . . . available. However, he did not want anything from her except her time, he only asked her to let him admire her."

"Did she let him?" *Sultan* whispered.

"She had no choice. When she said to her relatives to tell him she was not home, he would sit on the bench in front of the house and wait for her. The days in which there was nothing to do were alike, and his visits, his obsession with her had some twisted charm. He would let her into his small car (a luxury in those times) and as soon as she would pull the visor down to check her hair a chocolate would fall into her lap. First time it happened she looked at him in amazement, *"So, you were observing my pattern of behavior,"* she told him and he smiled at her. Chocolate would not fall into her lap every time she pulled the visor down and she never anticipated when it would. This little ritual became a trademark of his love, his love signature.

"Does their love have a happy ending," *Sultan* asked.

"No," I replied, pulling the covers closer to my chin.

"Are you cold?"

"Yes, and I don't think the heat is even on."

"Why do you need the heat?" *Sultan* threw in a rhetorical question, pulling me closer to him.

Over the night it became painfully obvious that we were two, not one; *Sultan's* snoring had a sound of a broken automated saw, waking me up every occasionally, prolonging the chilly night *ad infinitum.* The outlook of two-ness was even more apparent in the morning; I had to go back home whereas he had to tend to his business—pose as a field judge in a silly sport event he obsessed about. That was his freedom, his sanctuary, into which no woman could stretch his tentacles. The girlfriend had a good night sleep after convincing herself that her beau went on a business trip into his sacred freedom and would return to her recharged and as new, *Sultan* had a good night's sleep because I did not snore, which left me as the only one feeling as if ran over by a train. These were my thoughts while driving through a grey morning back on the interstate, flat and endless. Later in the day it started to snow—the first snow of a late fall that made me think about *Sultan* and his silly hobby, an old boy's club of sorts, with *Sultan* as a self-proclaimed liberal among those "old conservatives." *"You don't' know those people,"* he would tell me and I would ask in return why he wouldn't associate with more like-minded companions, what kind of gratification he was getting from associating with "old, conservative farts." As he called them. *"Maybe you are just like them and you wouldn't admit it,"* I was teasing him, which he would them passionately deny.

He asked me about my trip back in a short message later in the evening and I threw in my reply something about starting to get ready for one of my finals. One of my classes was exhausting and I could not wait for it to be over. But I borrowed something from it, something useful for my never-ending conversation with Sultan; life is a continuing discourse among individuals and groups and the more we know about a nature of the *discourse,* the better prepared we are to participate. I borrowed a definition from one of the articles I read and responded to one of *Sultan's* statements about discourse sounding "cold." Sitting in front of the computer I went back to our old conversation about self-actualization, existentialists and discourse. It has been days since we wrote to each other in this way. I almost forgot that he wrecked my idea of self-actualization in his letter. We misunderstood each other, even after I showed him a paper I wrote in college years ago. He enjoyed it and it "spurred" him . . . *"nothing kinky,"* he later wrote, and I delved into his letter as if seeing it for the first time:

> *I do not equate "being one's self" with being "selfish" or "self-centered." At the same time, if one is going to be of service to others, one should be centered, in the Zen sense (and now I want to run off for hours on the web to check my understandings, but I'll never express my basic understandings and approach if I don't get down to it.). Just going off on my own here, I don't like the taste of "be all that you can be" while I can embrace it at the same time. It first smacks of acquisitiveness ("schmecks," ja?). And it also can be very fragmenting if one tries to develop all talents one may have, or try to apply one's talents to all possible situations. Opportunity cost comes into play, as it always does, and one becomes a "jack of all trades, master of none." Then again, to claim to be a master of any skill or body of knowledge really is a case of hubris. One does not master anything. One mountaineer was asked how he felt after "conquering a mountain," and he replied, "Well, I don't know about that. It seems to be in a lot better shape than I am right now."*
>
> *The existentialist tenets of "To be is to do" and "To do is to be" come to mind. Is my "self" what I do, or what I can do? Is it my wants? My needs? (and I mean higher level Maslovian needs (na, klar)). All of the above, I guess. What I do, what I think and believe and figure out… It's all in flux.*
>
> *And there it is. I don't see myself as "actualizing" so much as "being" and "changing." To say I'm developing in a certain direction is so damnably linear. The nearest image I can muster right now is either the growth of a fractal or the growth of a crystal, the former being my preference. Iteration*

upon iteration, without necessarily deleting earlier patterns. The problem is that, now taking the different iterations as versions of a program (a choice of patterns of behavior) is that the iterations start to conflict with each other. If I choose that iteration that fits with myparents, i.e. I keep a civil tongue in my mouth, then have I de-actualized? Or have Iactualized in that I recognize that I cannot expect my parents to follow the flow of my ideas? Or that I've recognized that my actualization may conflict with their actualizations and indeed their view of what form my actualization should take?

Then he mentioned something about sitting at a coffee shop and his friend, bike shop owner's coming over and their talk about kids and Europe and languages. And that he had to get going. Abrupt. I told him so, but in a polished-up tone, *"just noticing, not criticizing."* And I told him that I wasn't promoting some kind of 'be all that you can be.'

And we can have this discourse without walking on the egg shells—as we know.

Remember when you said that 'discourse' to you sounded cold? There is a definition in one of the articles I read for a class and is by far the best definition I know, "Discourse, then, is composed of ways of talking, listening (often too, reading and writing), acting, interacting, believing, valuing, and using tools and objects, in particular setting and at specific times, to display and recognize a particular social identity." And it goes on saying that discourse create "social positions" (perspectives) from which people are invited to speak, listen, act, read . . . and value in certain characteristic, historically recognizable ways, combined with their own styles and creativity... Those scholars like to use the term 'social identity,' but I personally think that communication can and should happen without a constant awareness of your 'identity.'

The only existentialist I tried to understand (not at the right time though) was Sartre. Of all philosophies that one seems the most pessimistic to me but again, I would have to refresh my memory on Sartre's writing to go any further. When I think of people reaching a point of self-actualization I imagine them being playful and witty like Mozart: pragmatic side of success and being of service to others is often of secondary importance. Yes, this is clearly Maslovian, but I tend to agree that There is a quote somewhere in my paper saying that self-actualized people don't really draw a line between their work and life, with one being another... When one reaches that point it is no longer important what others think or expect from you. You might think it means freedom, but not really; your ties with the society just got some 'greater cause' justification, but you are equally dependent on its members. Hence none of those I imagine being self-actualized live in an ivory tower and none of them (ideally) care for their (static) social identity. When I came backhome today, Janice Joplin was singing on the radio again her Bobby McGee song and really, when you think about it freedom is "just another word for nothing left to lose. "But what would all this be without someone else's perspective that could either contradict, or build upon what I am saying. I tend to be dismissive of the power of family over one's actions (even if they are opposite from what the family expects) and I also tend to dismiss all those invisible social ties that everyone voluntarily accepts as part of their life sooner or later. Social ties are always in the equation, but I hate to think about it.

I should go to sleep now. There are more . . . personal moments I would like to share, but the two of us do it differently sometimes. Where does all this tact come from? Or perhaps I should only say the usual since iteration is often like a ritual.

How do you feel about my vocalizing everything? And yes, voljela bih da si sada sa mnom...

Sultan needed some more recharging. It was evident from his brief message when he came back from the trip. Otherwise, he said, he's useless to himself and the others. It just happened so that one of his students abruptly left the class after having a conversation with him and he was venting in his ten-by-ten, windowless office, declaring that he didn't "fucking care about her wanting to make up for classes that were not in session" (and that she paid for). *That was passion*, I rejoiced to myself, and did not care how it was brought about. He was clearly pressed with all the work he had to do at the end of semester and I offered my help. He gave me a pile of papers to read and rate at home. He would come by and pick them up the following morning. Later that day we met for a lunch.

Public scenery again. I was driving carefully down the hill, sticky, heavy snow melting on my windshield, minutes later entering another world in another time. *La Trattoria* was one of those ethnic, yet chic, slightly industrial-looking restaurants, staffed with international, exotic staff to complement already exotic setting. *Sultan* was in his glacial mode again and I just decided to wait for him at the bar. An exotic waiter asked me if I wanted something to drink. I replied that I would be ready to order after my party arrived. Five minutes turned into ten, dangerously approaching fifteen, after which waiting, without a phone call and an apology on the other end, would be completely unacceptable. I finally decided to give *Sultan* a phone call. "Sorry, I got held up with these damn papers and I am on my way now." He did not have to excuse himself; I already had an excuse for him and all I needed was to hear his voice telling me that everything was all right.

He finally trotted through a bowed passage dividing the two parts of the restaurant, leaving a noisy crowd of mid-management white collar clerks in one part and embracing the quieter patrons with a silence and muffled whisper of music in the other. *Sultan* theatrically bowed his head while passing through the opening and the exotic waiter ushered us into one of the booths. Timid and not at ease with the café owner a couple of weeks ago, *Sultan's* conduct with the waiter of *La Trattoria* was gaudy and boastful. "Are you an Italian?" I asked the man to show my goodwill and excuse, again, what started to look like *Sultan's* faux pas. "No, I am a Mexican," he said and I bit my lower lip. "Hope you don't mind," I said, "I get these kinds of questions all the time." As we were sitting next to each other, chit-chatting about the menu and what we liked, watching the implacable snow through the small window right next to our booth, *Sultan* leaned closer to me and deeply inhaled the smell of my hair. "I hope it smells good," I attempted a joke, "why are you doing it?"

"I am putting you in my head," he said. *Was I not there already?* He changed the subject and started talking about Sax fashion. A couple of days prior to our rendezvous at *La Trattoria* he emailed me some images of models in evening gowns and then also sent pictures of various trumpery— lingerie with faux fur hemline, faux leather bustier, brassier, with whips and handcuffs as the only missing elements in the collection... His seemingly erratic actions puzzled me at first, but I almost hit myself in the forehead when he casually asked me about my size. *He was buying me a Christmas present!* I immediately softened the harshness of my view of some of the items he sent my way the previous day, trying to remember if I liked any.

"This reminds me of why this place is still my favorite restaurant," *Sultan* said while biting into a sappy tilapia cutlet. The waiter looked at first as if expecting more trouble, but my friendly smile and a "thank you," along with *Sultan's* favorable grin at the food at hand hinted him to go in peace. In between busying myself with food I gave some superficial thought to my companion's "favorite restaurant" remark and our non-hesitant public encounters. *Restaurants are couples' sanctuaries and if this has been his favorite place, then what about that person, his . . . girlfriend?* I bit my lip at this thought, but couldn't stop the avalanche of rationalizing. *It must have been her favorite place as well and she must have been out of picture now. If she is not, then what he said about being adamant about his leisure-time choices since the divorce must be including visiting his favorite restaurants with whoever he wanted to. She was perhaps still a part of his life...*, I sighed, and he glanced at me surreptitiously, quickly fixating his gaze at the plate with tilapia and continuing to chew vigorously, as if not noticing. I plunged the fork into my salad, extracted a small chunk of lettuce and bit into its crisp texture, purporting equal interest in food and lauding its taste as *Sultan* did.

Maybe Sally was right, I continued my internal soliloquy, maybe she is still a part of his life, his "diaper-changing," "infantile" life as she said, but the adult *Sultan* or how he wanted to present himself to the world was right here with me, and the serenity immediately returned to my face. No girlfriend could encroach the sacredness of this territory. In-between my picking on pieces of chicken, heavily bespattered with dressing as most of the lettuce in my Caesar salad, I imagined his girlfriend barging in and the look on her face after seeing *Sultan* with me. *Life with him was still better than life without him*—would she be able to declare it even if she caught him in the act?! Leaves of remaining lettuce in my salad, sodden in dressing, became limp and not so tasteful anymore, or my mood change and thoughts with which I could not stop torturing myself spoiled a simple joy of dining out. *"She has a sick hold onto him,"* Sally said, but for me it was easier to believe that he was disrespecting her by bringing me here and that it was one of the steps of one's relationship disintegration.

"Imagine them in bed," Sally was teasing me and I did, in many a sleepless night, *"Imagine her, a well fed, five feet two, and your Sultan, corpulent, bulging. . . .in certain places,"* she corrected herself, *"a giant."* And as she said the word "giant'," she made a gesture with both of her hands, adding, *"Don't you ever visualize them in bed?"* Then, noticing my expression of disgust, she added, *"Sorry, I didn't mean to deter your own impure thoughts about him."* Repelling the swarming recollections of Sally's unsparing blabber and my own ragged thought process, I gently pushed away the salad bowl and smiled at *Sultan* who appeared oblivious to my, though well camouflaged, inner turmoil. Our exotic waiter brought the dessert menus and the first and only cake I fixated on right away—tiramisu—once again distracted me from all unsettling, non-gastronomic issues. It was a short-lived relief before a reminiscence of another question from a short time ago, *"Why can't you be with me?"* I asked him after our first mentally sadomasochist breakup, unable to think of a reason good enough for not wanting to replace *her,* followed by a few epithets, another courtesy of Sally, with me—his deity at times. *"I did not want this and I told you so before it started…"* I wailed, but *Sultan* appeared to have heard only my *"we were not conventional"* proclamation. In a way I couldn't articulate, the flavor of an Italian dessert elicited some other sentiments, memory recollections of decadent stories, literature I dreaded in my adolescent years as twisted creations of overworked imaginations. Was it necessary

to read *Madame Bovary* as a sixteen-year-old child, I often wondered, as the sentiment of a French romantic Flaubert nested in my conscience recently, devoting much of my curiosity and insights to finding "truths" in his genius rather than resenting his dissecting of human nature. "But disparaging those we love always detaches us from them to some extent. It is better not to touch our idols: the gilt comes off on our hands."[4] The guilt resurfaced again on the way out of *La Trattoria,* when I remembered asking *Sultan* if he were a pervert… *"Tell me this is because I can't see . . . where your "appetite" is coming from . . . because I don't exactly know how to satisfy it?"*

Out in the cold, dreading the snow and slippery roads, we both seemed to have satisfied our appetite for food, if anything. We both have a gourmet taste, as he would say. Apparently, our transient tryst exuded carelessness of a couple not tormented by fugacious nature of our encounters, split loyalties, departures and secrecy, yet those reemerged in the long nocturnal hours as a recurrent nightmare. "Disparaging those we love…" While I was determined to cherish our moments together, flashbacks of our recent temporary breakup continued to torture my hyperactive mind; *Sultan's* slouching shoulders underneath a shapeless navy winter jacket while sitting across from me and listening to my tearful confession of how much it hurt. His cat-like face expanded above drooping shoulders when he seriously declared that she forgave him. I vividly recalled his gestures, his voice, his anguish and his almost crushed body. His failing attempt to depart afforded me hope that the next moment would bring reconciliation. If not the next moment, then at least the next day. It did and we were striding on the eggshells of our reconciliation now as two convicts who escaped the prison.

---

[4] Gustave Flaubert P.243

IX

The art of seduction is an art of taking a hold over a person, making him believe that nothing and no one could satisfy him better than the lover who ostensibly offers to please and appease, but in reality, seeks the kind of control cloaked in her giving herself and asking nothing in return, extending a sense of freedom until she's able to insert her tentacles into his body and make him dependent on her. *It works both ways,* I interrupted my thought process. *This old school mistress of his is going to turn me into a misogynist!* A numerous times brooded dilemma came back in front of the restaurant, dilemma if his *old school mistress* without formal education, not needing a formal education, knew *the art* better than me, this actress playing on a *you are the man* card, possessing enough wisdom to hunt down her game even at the twilight of her life. *Will I ever be like her? Her kind can wait for years and decades for their paralyzing poison to take effect and to start savoring their game the way a necrophiliac does.*

Sultan tended to die on me and in those moments, I cursed my rival to eternal damnation. He would liven up if our *never-ending conversation* took the right turn and I celebrated it, celebrated his (and my) life, but as the days passed I began fearing that he remained dead-like far too often and too long. And here comes a Scheherazade paradox: is it really that only one of them dies? He went to dance competitions and rode motorcycle with his common marriage companion, but the burden of years and weight took its toll on her and the couch (or kitchen table) replaced the adventurous places they once frequented. They settled down, but unlike couples spending their whole life together, raising their children together, their life together had nothing in common with the dynamics of those married veterans. Her grandchildren were not his and their running around the house was not part of the deal. She knew it and she worked around it; she made *Sultan* a permanent guest of honor in her house and everyone else just a visitor. She infused *Sultan* with life and nurturing love making him believe it did not come with a price. She carefully took the same life out of him the moment her erosion began, still making him believe he was honored and free. And her stories must have been better than mine for I heard *Sultan* saying the day of the breakup that he knew what she, his girlfriend, had been through.

Sultan left a large tip to our exotic waiter, becoming greater than life to me all over again. He again asked me for help with rating the essays and I took a stack of his papers home. His classes were a conglomeration of student guests from Latin America; rural and urban areas of Guatemala, Mexico, Dominican Republic, Haiti and aspiring *permanent* immigrants wanting to learn the language. He was going to stop by my place the following morning to pick up the papers. *Good, he needs me beyond the obvious!* Though there were times when I doubted my attributes, thinking that the physical appearance is but one aspect of a person's desirability, never truly contributing to any substantial good in a woman's life, on the way home from *La Trattoria* I was triumphant. I felt initiated into *Sultan's* daily rituals, able to entertain, ease, appease and—resuscitate. Moments of disheartened mental anguish would have to wait. This was the time of my intellectual and feminine peak! I devoured all literature, not only required course readings, and often found myself locked out of the world as is, and creating my own unconstrained and unbounded universe. It was a kind of a spiritual reincarnation, a *moratorium* on a plain routine existence, on the strains and toils of daily life. The daily life was lurking in expected and unexpected place—as if it would be possible to escape it—but I decided to ignore its nagging presence as much as possible.

Some of my actions were taking place in a different realm, and I favored it over a present and future in which to exist meant to compete, to work, to toil, and to bend under the weight of various debts. A life in the realm of my choice, in the meantime, had a great potential for interesting twists and turns. The *moratorium* on the mundane meant sacred freedom from conventional obligations, even if my construct of freedom appeared to be at odds with reason itself. Opportunity cost and risk assessment were domains I dismissed with the same passion I embraced my personal outlook on priorities in life. My union with *Sultan* was my lifeline, but he hung a Damocles' sword over my head in one of his admonishing letters to me:

> *There is a phrase in economics— "opportunity cost." One may have a large number of choices, but one most often does not get to have everything on the menu. And that has something to do with giving up of personal interests. I've been pretty adamant about my personal choices since my divorce. One needs to keep those choices, or at least some of them. How to describe which ones are paramount and which are not is beyond me right now.*

I was brave enough to proclaim that I would not position myself as one of those economically risky human products of recession that was hitting ever harder, human numbers without job security and health insurance, but also scared enough in the moments when I appeared to myself as a gambler whose luck may turn on any given day. I needed *Sultan* to tell me the future was smiling at me and I needed to rehearse, redeem, and to modify the past with him as a listener and companion. I tried to find what we didn't say that day in the rest of his letter. Yes, he could be a "soul of civility," as he called himself after tipping our waiter at *La Trattoria*. His thinking meandered as usual, a mode of expression awfully resembling a message in the bottle, though in places infused with a personal touch, as a much-needed nourishment for my emotionally starving mind. On the other hand, perhaps to achieve a sense of timelessness as one of the ultimate goals in writing, his letters at times appeared to be addressing someone else, generic audience somewhere in the world perhaps.

> *It is difficult to use language and make the message go only in one's intended direction, yes? Please trust me to not be too thin skinned while I follow the lines (or explore the area) of discussion. Kind of like going through an art museum, maybe? One looks at each painting, but then one notes similarities (whether those similarities exist in some objective form or as constructs of the mind: read someday Fire in the Mind:*

Science, Faith, and the Search for Order, by George Johnson. The heart of the book is that very question of how our minds may be imposing the order we think we find in the world.

Does any of us have a complete idea of what something means? An act? A feeling? I'm not just throwing up my hands here. An act has significance in the minds of the actor and for those for whom the act had a consequence. (This is so Western; I don't like having to split all this apart). There are emotional effects of what we say, even possibly actions. And there is significance. This may be a restatement of what I've just said, but what one might consider a minor pleasantry or a bit of advice may contribute to what is a turning point in another's life. The butterfly effect.

I came back to this point after starting to write this morning, so I'm not sure that I'm picking up all threads. You said that one wants another to feel good all the time. Please do not feel that much responsibility. We each are keepers of our own happiness, as much as we contribute to each other's. You indeed contribute much to my happiness, and if there are matters with which I am not currently happy, they may be short-term challenges on the way to a long-term goal. Again, how Western. They are simply the texture of the path that I walk.

Hodamo, ne? Zelim da hodam pored tebe.

His wish to *walk beside me* frequently ended in a sort of an emotional and intellectual dying on me, which inevitably caused me to panic and fear for my own life. *Sultan's* dying away, as it turned out to be a more than one-time occurrence, threatened to invalidate my narratives, my energy and my wit. "Dead" like that he wasn't mine, he belonged to the person I dreaded the most. He was drifting away, I noticed the day after, pulling me into an abyss of meaninglessness along with him. What happened to him? Yesterday he wanted to walk beside me . . . I contributed to his happiness . . . and I recollected something about emotions too. Yes, he appeared dead and his holding an antiquated Bible in German he inherited from some family member contributed to my fear and intensified the symbolism of an act. With the Bible spread on his knees and head bent down in a gesture of awe his entire body appeared translucent and aged. *Sultan* wanted to show me the Gothic script since I stated once that I could read it, but why all the theatricality? That was the *dead* part… Perhaps he was inviting me to be patient, *thick-skinned* as he'd put it, as he was going through another one of his glacial modes. *She* had the patience to wait, as if waiting for a return of a *prodigal son*, her infantile, helpless *son*. Yes, son, and I resentfully remembered Sally's admonition, *"he found a mommy."* Score one for her.

I carefully took the Bible spread on his knees (cautious to not spoil his moment of spirituality) and read a passage from it. Reading the Bible in Gothic reminded me of my first year in college, how tense, focused and scared I was while reading meaningless and decontextualized passages written in this ancient script as if the future of education depended on college freshmen successfully decoding Gothic scripts. Students of *Germanistik*, however, at that time and place appeared to be by far more pragmatic than anxious bookworms only interested in ancient scripts. Children of so-called *Gastarbeiter,* a special kind of immigrants in Western Europe, legal workers filling a surplus of then insatiable economies of the West, tended to return home to study and if they happened to choose *Germanistik,* they also tended to outshine those who did not have their cultural awareness and linguistic skills. Old-school professors acted as gate keepers of linguistic and academic complexity of *Germanistik*, thus creating a program of study involving anything but the proficiency development. Memories of those countless hours of decoding various Gothic texts resurfaced while reading a passage from *Sultan's* Bible. He appeared to be in *honor thy forefathers* mode, proud to be in possession of an old scripture, silent and distant. His demeanor had a quality of a carefully executed performance, while his unnecessary dramatization majorly interfered with my attempt to reestablish a more mundane connection with him, resuscitate him or myself or both.

"Have you read David Goleman's book *Emotional Intelligence?*" I asked to break an increasingly uncomfortable silence.

"I heard about it… Oh, don't tell me he made a huge scientific discovery. It all smacks of those commercial self-help 'recipes' for living."

"Well, others have found a way to commercialize it, I mean managing emotions is a big deal in the corporate world, but that is not what the concept is all about. By the way, popularization is not always the worst that can happen to an intellectual invention. Living by means of emotional intelligence, not Cartesian reason could revolutionize the very way we cohabitate on this planet. Enlightenment brought us out of the darkness of Middle Ages and emotional intelligence could finally bring some equity into our stratified world."

"An act has significance in the minds of the actor and for those for whom the act has a consequence. Action-significance are in a hierarchical relationship. Again, how Western! Is your emotional intelligence an end of Western thought as we know it?" My question seemed to have sparked his interest, which was good, promising, and a wave of excitement rushed through my body.

"If you mean subject-object relationships, then yes. We objectify nature, we objectify animals, and we objectify others by taking from them only what we need. But what happened to I-Thou relationships, understanding others to a point of becoming others?" *Then you wouldn't ask me about my identity, you would've received my identity without fearfully rejecting a part of me by which you feel threatened.*

"Write to me about it," *Sultan* said.

"Tell me about France," I blurted suddenly and unexpectedly, as his expression was telling.

"What do you want to know?" he returned in a flat voice, all previous excitement I sparked vanished in an instant.

"Are you really going . . . by yourself?"

"I am thinking about it . . . but I don't know if I'll be able to . . . be apart from some people that care about me." Touché. *Could he have meant me?* But there wasn't any eye contact, *and how dare he,* I silently protested, bring *other people* into a conversation such as this one without specifying who those people were so that I could know whether any kind of conflict of interest existed. All my thoughts suddenly and simultaneously spiked into a critical mass of frustration and panic.

"I have to go now," *Sultan* said, lending me his Bible in Gothic script so that I could reminisce about his transient appearance and my once upon a time study of *Germanistik*.

"Write to me." *Stay alive.*

X

During finals, I started searching through piles of electronic files accumulated over the years of my perennial schooling. I promised myself that this was going to be the most remarkable and persuasive piece I ever shared with him, the core of who I was and what interested me. I compiled the most powerful quotes I found, trying to recompose a coherent narrative, traces of which I already shared with him. I was living again.

How could a scope of bigotry, racism, sexism and ensuing discrimination even begin to be measured by standards of 'reason', when cold reason and its Western incorporation in private and public sphere alike brought out the most inhumane traits of both an individual and a group. Hence it comes as a no surprise that, according to recent brain research and findings of Damasio and LeDoux, quoted by Mayer et al., "emotional and cognitive systems in the brain are far more integrated than originally believed." When are we going to stop pretending? How clever to proclaim reason to be the sole relevant factor in decision making and interaction and let a bunch of lunatics call themselves reasonable when all they do is spreading hatred. Hopping on a plane to drop bombs at some other 'unreasonables' makes then perfect sense. Proclaiming to be doing that for emotional reasons, however, would call for some serious evaluations of mental health of the parties involved. For too long reason had been a pretext for the most abhorrent acts against humanity, but for some reason we still cherish it. Some ordinary people like ourselves claim that mass destruction is just a form of control of population overgrowth. As long as they and their loved ones alike are not the target... Die or win'.

Emotions, however, can revolutionize the thought and civilization. Of special interest to me here is the role of emotions in the development of an evolving self of oppressed groups, including women. Historically viewed as more "emotional" and less "reasonable" women are now, in my view, utilizing emotions and emotionality to build an entire world view that does not necessarily embrace any of the erstwhile principles on which the epistemologies (on the one hand) and social order (on the other one) relied. In becoming aware of one's oppressed position and developing, first self-awareness then generating a necessary impetus to change the status quo, emotions play an irreplaceable role.

I wrote about a single individual's ability to make an impact on her environment, however small, but impact that did not have to be measured by standards of "success" and "achievement," as expressed in a quote I found in Highlend et al.

By recognizing that one's culture perpetuates this belief of a "need to achieve and to always be better," one "is much more at peace when he [sic] is in touch with his [sic] uniqueness and inherent self-worth" (p. 14). Chuan Peng calls for transcending ideology and nationalism and states that "to open a space for diverse Becomings—as opposed to consumerist assimilationism under global capitalism, my finding a 'new code' begins with a brief review of the limit of hybridity—a major ontological reconceptualization of postcolonial subjects." She says, "Others should be, and have always been, an inseparable part of the self. Refusing the fact that the Others are within is, in effect, othering the outside as the others." In other words, we are back to the same notion of objectifying the world, subject/object, as opposed to I-Thou relationships.

My best story turned out to be a project and I decided to give it a rest until the following day. Besides, I was worried about *Sultan's* attention span since his cat was very sick and probably dying. He said once he was going to write her a eulogy. However, I was onto a big discovery, the one granting my quest a personal significance in a form of an affirmation of *Sultan's* emotional intelligence. I decided to incorporate these new remarks into my narrative.

> *Linking emotional intelligence to an ability to relegate their importance or conceal them under the pretext of 'acting reasonable' is directly opposite from how an emotionally intelligent person acts in my and in view of Mayer et al., "In fact, emotionally intelligent individual must regularly cope with states of mood instability and this requires considerable understanding of moods. Going back to Mayer et al.'s the link between emotions and a zeitgeist, there could certainly emerge a movement (lasting for decades or centuries) putting emotions and emotional intelligence on a pedestal, making the concept a fad, a trend, to which any would like to link their social interactions and 'personal growth'. In that case, emotional intelligence would be reduced, or is already being reduced to but a movement, such as romanticism, in Mayer et al.'s example.*

Was intelligence even worth discussing? Says Roeper, every single person is hurt by the modern concept of intelligence. On my end I was hurt by *Sultan's* not answering the phone, and found it exceptionally challenging to continue working on my tractate. There was nothing in my mailbox either. How would an emotionally intelligent person act? How do I cope now with my states of mood instability? What does emotional management even mean, when all I wanted to do was to open the window and scream?! Some aspects of that mood instability we call PMS, at least when it comes to women, but that would be a rather narrow definition of a construct aspiring to represent a sign of intelligence. Intelligence or not, my mood stability depended on one person's ability to recover from an embrace of, how I started calling her, a necrophilous woman—in her house. Yes, he was living in her house, I finally discovered. I desperately needed him to stay alive since his attention infused me with life. I entered into this symbiotic relationship not realizing that I was a mistletoe and he was a tree, whose roots would be deep in the ground and whose trunk would still be caressed by wind, sun and rain even if not alive anymore. *Sultan* was a tree; strange how trees persist to exist long after the life is sucked out of them, while everything else once living returns to dust so quickly. The *dust* mortified me, I wanted life juices to stream through my body, and I wanted wind, water and fire too.

The notes for my final papers were scattered around the floor next to the computer, but I was deliriously focused on my project for *Sultan*. I was not just creating a project for him—I was showing him what I could do for the humanity.

I shall not separate emotional intelligence and what it could mean for humanity in my view, from emotional intelligence in populist view. In an era of anti-intellectualism, removing an intellectual debate from the body and the movement of a society would be manifold dangerous, leaving the entire debate to dry out in arid, elitist intellectual circles. Popular interest for emotional intelligence and potential benefits for the human kind ensuing from such an interest are a sign that the western civilization is wiggling and escaping, however painfully, from the claws of Cartesian dualism and patriarchal stoicism. Traditional concept of intelligence is coming under ever more frequent scrutiny, in light of findings that its operationalization is highly culturally biased. If our view of traditional intelligence and how it is currently being measured does not change, we fall into the danger of perpetual ethnic and racial division, discrimination and stigmatization. Therefore, there must be something about traditional intelligence that cuts into an existing epistemology privileging some groups and marginalizing others. By saying marginalizing others I envision an entire process of establishing what counts as knowledge (the dominant view) and who has access to it. Denying access to a standardized body of knowledge, yet defining all there is by means reflecting that same knowledge puts all the traditional views and concepts where they belong: on a slippery slope of refutability that calls for a reexamination of their very validity.

Traditional intelligence also falls under the reexamination process and is now bursting at the frail seams torn from the inside out by force of various value shifts, evident in the development of the new self-identities and everything they entail.

Following Monday appeared as a blessing and *Sultan* needed me. He wanted to talk to me after his class, saying that the day was going to be packed for him.

"Along with compiling grades, or at least beginning to, I have to start writing a report for the chancellor. I opened my mouth a while back about bicycle transportation to campus, so someone suggested me as one who would be "ideal" to write a proposal on alternative methods of transport to campus. And there isn't much of a way to get out of it as the chancellor talked to me about it directly on Tuesday. And given that I have to attend the chancellors' advisory committee since I am a member . . . and it starts today at 3:00 pm, I'd better have at least a little something to say."

"What do you want me to do?"

"I would like you to rate the rest of those papers for me. I'll get you the rubric and the scoring sheet."

"OK, but I also have to do some article review for tomorrow's class and I am not looking forward to it. Or should I say it sucks? I'll find some time… Speaking of 'sucks' by the way, do you know the funniest word in German?"

"No, what is it?"

"*Staubsauger. Staub* is dust and *saugen* means 'to suck'. So, when one says, "it sucks" I think of everything unwanted we have to suck in as part of our everyday life."

I picked *bis bald* from my stack of good byes, taking on a task that would prolong my life of a Scheherazade, searching my mental log as one searches a library for ever new stories, ever new fuel to invigorate our life line. Later in the day I wrote to him that I couldn't even describe the way I feel when I was with him and that sometimes everything happens so fast and we don't even have time to talk, or really be together. Then I went back to my file named For *Sultan*.

> *Roeper, (1998) explains that "we should prevent crude science from displacing sophisticated kinds of human intuition when real human beings are involved" (p. 1). In psychology "the term intelligence has been given a much narrower definition: it is a value term which includes some kinds of human behavior and excludes others." In his words, "any effort to look at basic and fundamental aspects of behavior by simplification to known psychological concepts, inevitably chooses some animalistic notions like self-interest to describe emotions, or a simplified version of physical ability to describe muscles" (ibid). Emotional processing, leading to heightened awareness, which further leads to altruistic and more compassionate outlook on others, is directly opposite from the view of emotions and emotionality in terms of self-interest. Now if I reject the populist belief that emotional intelligence can be learned, I am partially rejecting my own claim that emotional intelligence is empowering. To reconcile this contradiction, I will say that emotional intelligence could become a norm for which individuals in a society strive. Its corruption and misconstruction is possible, however, once it starts serving consumerist ideology. Yes, but only if the society remains stratified and consumerist. Value shift, bringing some unimaginable qualities humans are beginning to value, is intertwined with the changes brought about in research (and popularization) of emotional intelligence. However, Roeper writes, "[W]e must prevent ourselves from developing personality cults, and via them, a class system for the mind. This is a legitimate concern because I find it dangerous for a society to settle, as Roeper states, on an image of intelligence or a virtue...*
>
> *Emotions and knowledge have to merge together at some point to create an individual with an integrated sense of self, fueled by never-ending curiosity about other beings and the world in general, curiosity that need not end in adversity and*

destruction of an unknowable enemy, as demonstrated time and again throughout history effected by a "rational man." This curiosity needs to integrate, not disintegrate each other's sense of self and tuning into one's emotional sphere on the way of integration could change the course of our development and the course of history.

What was the point of all this? I asked myself after hours of laboring over something that can't speak to our connection . . . our bond, our symbiosis in any way? He had my heart in the palm of his hand and what if he misinterprets my theorizing as he did self-actualization by calling it "be all that you can be"? He became my intended audience for words said and unsaid and I decided to create more of my linguistic jewels for him and only him, whether he'd see them or not. Our conversation was moving from a realm of mundane into a sphere of eternity.

Later that day *Sultan* wrote:

> *It is a whirlwind at times. I want to talk with you, too, but the touch is very powerful.*
>
> *I think you said either that 'we think the same way' and/ or 'we have the same feelings'. Do I have that right? We do think along the same lines. (Have you noticed how English speakers use linear and spatial terms to talk about thinking? Especially when it's not such a linear act?)*
>
> *I was thinking about going to France last night, to continue our previously started conversation, and the reality of it scares me a bit. I don't like long flights, and I would be estranging myself for an extended period. When I went to Japan, I had no idea of what I was getting myself into. Now I do. And then, I went with someone, as I did on the two European trips I've taken. This time, I'll be flying solo. But I can do this. I cannot back down every time I get scared. I've got a noon lunch meeting (group with dean of the college, not something I can lightly ignore). We'll find some time. Vidimo se uskoro.*

XI

I n between my attempts to prolong a life line with *Sultan* and to finish up final papers due in a couple of weeks Sally met with me for a coffee. She was back with her ex-boyfriend and spending time gambling with him and his buddies—nothing like esotery I was having with *Sultan*. And while *Sultan* was learning the conjugational pattern of Sally's and my mother tongue, Sally's counterpart was enriching his vocabulary with *kučka* (bitch) and *pička materina* (motherfucker). Sally found it amusing.

"You should see us at the grocery store when the cashier asks, 'Did you find everything you were looking for?' and his reply, 'Yes, kučko! It's hilarious."

Sally was a lioness that joined the foreign herd by biting back—and was accepted in return. I remembered one of the Jacque-Cousteau-type TV series of *Survival* when the team of zoologists tried to assimilate a zoo grown young lioness into its natural habitat. They observed carefully from the inconspicuous distance her first steps into the wilderness and her first encounter with the lion herd. Every step of the way the lioness faced rejection, marked by scratches and bites of angry matriarchs. The poor animal would be left alone to lick her wounds or taken back to the camp and treated—until a new release into her "natural" environment. I told Sally about it.

"Every attempt to introduce her to what was supposed to awaken her instinct for survival and gradually develop a *sense* of belonging was a trial and error and she didn't seem to be capable of adjusting to the new circumstances. Moreover, she was fiercely rejected by her kind."

Sally seemed interested.

"What would she do? Would she fight back?"

"No, she was just trying to withdraw from those attacks, while the male population of the herd watched in what seemed like an amazement at times, a mix of indifference and curiosity. Eventually the males started taking sexual interest in her and the team of scientists thought that could mark a new turn in her *initiation* into their world, the lions' kingdom if you wish."

"Yah, sex is always a recourse, but I bet that didn't end up in a happy ending," Sally grinned.

"No, and contrary to everyone's expectations. They were quietly cheering her on when the first male from the herd smelled her behind and soon she was surrounded by them. Lionesses were forced to watch this time as she slowly laid down and submitted. It was really sad, she just curled her back paws underneath her belly, balancing her body with the front legs spread in front of her. The whole act appeared as if her mating partner was violating her, but I guess it's a matter of perspective. I don't remember it exactly, but think that a couple of males took turns and the crew was exhilarated that she finally became a *member.*"

"And the bitches took revenge, ha?"

"Yah, it was disturbing to watch . . . only an hour or so after the mating. The crew didn't interfere this time; they thought it was a temporary reaction before she would be finally accepted. The males didn't do anything to stop the female rage. No one realized how deep the cuts were and could not anticipate that the infection would spread so quickly. Finally, as she went into some kind of a toxic shock, they took her into the shelter and tried to bring the infection under control. She died . . . quietly and without much resistance… Just like the way she lived."

Sally looked at me puzzled.

"Is everything always a matter of life and death?"

"I think so . . . even if the physical death is the only ultimate death."

"If you look at it so . . . intellectually, so dramatically" Sally's pragmatism surfaced again.

"Yes, but what is wrong with looking at it intellectually? Oh, there is a lot wrong with intellectualism here and now, but some of us made it a mission to resuscitate good old thinking!"

"And good old self-righteousness!" Sally exclaimed. "Why is thinking good? Think about it, pardon," and she grinned at her own oxymoron, we thought we had it all figured out and that *rotten capitalism* and consumerism were terminally ill fifty years ago, but what happened to that ideology?!"

"Sally, malignant cancer spreads allover one's body as part of that body, but what happens to the body in the end? Metaphorically speaking? I am no Rosa Luxemburg..."

"A matter of perspective—as you always say. Don't tell me you are into this neo-communism shit because I can't stand the thought of it. We are too imperfect and too sinful for an ideal world like that. Didn't we prove it already? What was once a *Proletarian Dictatorship* are now dominions governed by mafiacracy. Yes, that's the new form of rule if you didn't know. There is oligarchy, democracy, dictatorship and mafiacracy, or all of them interchanging at the same time and within the same political system..." she burst.

"For an anti-intellectual, this sounds damn academic to me. Do you have a secret life, Sally?"

"No, thank God, I'm not a book worm or . . . what you call yourself . . . Scheherazade. It's not always a matter of life and death."

"I'd like to prove myself wrong . . . there is this book I'm reading as a source for one of my papers . . . an anthology actually for which the two individuals, a free academic and an inmate, Dylan Rodriguez and Viet Mike Ngo, wrote an article together. The inmate summed up his narrative as, "Fuck right or wrong. There is no such thing. It's only win or die." *The dead lioness...* They wrote about radical intellectuals who are captives of the state... I'll find the quote . . . but I didn't understand the imprisonment of one of them as only a physical incarceration, I linked his *radical intellectualism* to a virtually imprisoned mind." ("Radical intellectuals who are captives of the state, insofar as they are defined and categorized as civically dead and therefore outside the pale of civil society and the polity, are formally de-individuated upon imprisonment")[5].

"The dead lioness I told you about can convey multiple allegorical meanings..." *Not a story for Sultan* I thought, *the ultimate death was making it is less palatable and contrary to my hopes.*

"Such as?" Sally appeared unusually attentive.

"The sex slavery, including white slavery, trying to fit into a *natural order* of supply and demand in a world of global consumerism. According

---

[5] Dylan Rodriguez and Viet Mike Ngo, "Ethnic Studies in the Age of Prison-Industrial complex" in *Pedagogoes of the global: Knowledge in the human interest,* ed. Arif Dirlik (Taylor and Francis, 2002), 113-132.

to one of my professors, protuberating sex industry only reflects that order. He said that those women realized that they have something to offer, something in high demand on an insatiable market for a fresh, young meat feeding the oldest trade. Now, imagine how that is working out for dehumanized "lionesses" of the eastern hemisphere… You know, I heard someone lamenting over them as the disgraced descendants of belligerent Amazons. And who wins and who dies, if not physically right away, then morally and spiritually?" *A feeling of powerlessness is the most disturbing emotion a human being can sense. . .* "To win is to end powerful and powerless."[6]

"Hold on, a professor said that prostitution only reflects the logic of the market?" Sally gaped.

"Yes, he is one of those people who can only make sense out of the world by understanding each group's function in a market-driven order."

We both paused for a moment. On my end, I contemplated the ethos by which the wrong can be woven into a fabric of the right in ways that do not necessitate revision and leave no doubt of its justifiability.

"What do you do in those graduate classes anyway?" Sally blurted. "How come you talk about hookers?"

"Sex slaves," I corrected. "Well, we discussed social justice and I told him after class I didn't see much social justice even in places conventionally considered to be democracies. He responded that there was only one global drive—money, not ideology. I thought he was wrong because money determines power dynamics and as such is ideology, which means that ideology is at the core of the new world's order."

"So, what do the other students say?"

"Nah, it's not something others would want to discuss I think…"

"But why not? She persisted.

"I don't know, we don't seem to have the same passions. Imagine a class composed of a middle-aged middle school-, a correctional center-, language-, science- and a gym teacher, and a couple of ex-military guys all in one circle… Some interesting dynamics inevitably develop, as some of them don't feel comfortable to speak, and some of them are radicals . . . ha-ha."

---

[6] Ibid.

Her expression was telling me that she would be more interested in a change of subject until I said that, in fact, there was plenty of sex talk, but it was all, well, educational.

"How so?" she raised her eyebrow.

"You know, not so long ago the schools had to teach *abstinence only* as part of health or sex education, legacy of George W. However, that has changed and they teach about sex again."

"And?"

"Part of the "education" is to demonstrate putting a condom on a banana, with the banana representing a penis... I was skeptical about the educational value of such demonstration since, let's face it, how much skill does it really take to put on a condom? Besides, don't you think that a banana is a slight misrepresentation of a penis, but its use *in lieu* of a dildo only confirms that we live in a phallic culture? Anything can be a representation of penis! And some of those representations are pretty sharp! Sally, every time I see a pointed tip of a tower I cringe in pain, as if being impaled. By the way, that was a favorite punishment of adulterous or fornicating women in ancient China, and of *infidels* in Ottoman Empire. Painful as is, an impaled Chinese woman from a story I remember, fastened on a horse which had been walked through the village, was always in wet dreams of a boy who saw the scene."

"There is something barbaric about those sharp, pointed tips... And the representations of a vagina are neither celebratory nor complimentary. Except for Georgia O'Keefe, of course."

"Sally, the intellectual, speaking again!"

"Hey, you don't own the intellectualism."

"True... There is an interesting graphic on the cover of one of Metallica's albums. The drawing of a coffin, framed by lines that are very suggestive of pubic hair."

"As in, *pussy will kill you?*"

"Hmm, makes sense... I mean, the symbolic makes sense. Nicely packaged and delivered misogyny, but a form of creative expression nevertheless."

I found myself stalling a conversation about a single, most interesting, and perhaps most amusing topic with which I willingly and eagerly treated her in the past weeks or even months. As the time of uncertainty continued, I felt less inclined to feed her curiosity. Instead, I found a particular pleasure in continuing our educational sex talk.

"I recently learned that, years ago, there were real dildos in schools for demonstrations. I mean, objects truthfully depicting its shape . . . maybe not the size . . . since the one mentioned was actually "a size and a half" of an "average real thing." This is a serious concern," I continued, "because if the size of an object of demonstration is exaggerated in either direction the effect of the demonstration is either amusing or ridiculing, but not educating. Think of those ten feet tall sculptures of a lipstick or a coca cola bottle... Is their distortion suggestive of respect or the opposite? I think..."

She didn't let me finish what was turning into a monologue, interrupting me instead with a question, "How are things between the two of you?" In a visibly changed mood and tone of voice, I confessed to her that I didn't know.

"Sometimes, at the thought of the two of them, I just want to scream."

"Well, you are not dealing with this other-woman-ness very well... Patience is the name of the game; what do you think his *granny* is doing right now?"

"But, that puts him on a pedestal—wanted by two women, *his majesty*? Sometimes I think that she has a sick hold onto him, as if she cast a spell in a form of this mantra of hers that *life with him was still better than life without him.* All he'd need to do is to come back and vegetate next to her, and that is somehow more desirable than pushing him, pushing the limits of what he can do, forcing him to write to me... That is a lot of work!"

"Wow, 'forcing' shouldn't be part of the vocabulary."

"I meant it as a more metaphorical forcing... Forcing someone to think. Have you heard of Simone de Beauvoir, Sartre's companion?"

"Simone who?"

"Never mind. Anyway, she wrote this allegory of the cat..." And before I finished Sally burst into a laughter at my incorrigible and persistent references to literature.

"If it's not lions, then it's cats. You crack me up."

"At least we are still in the cat family," I retorted, my facial muscles involuntarily stretching into a grin, despite the attempts to keep the expression of self-martyrdom.

"When the cat is young and skinny, and even though she lives behind bars in a cage, she is still free to go back and forth as the space between the bars is wide enough to let her slim body slide through. The food, however, is always served inside the cage and eventually the cat loses the interest about and the curiosity to go into the outside world. As the time passes, she becomes fatter and fatter and the space between the bars too narrow to let her through. So, she's trapped."

"And who is trapped in your case, *granny* or *Sultan?*"

"I guess both. Metaphorically speaking... I think weight is also metaphorical here. People stop leaving the cage for various reasons."

"And who's feeding them if both are trapped in the cage?"

"I'm working on figuring that out. Possibly . . . the society?"

"Then they live in a paradise! You just created a paradise for them!"

"But it's a trap—there is no spark, no action beyond routine."

"Yet life with him is still better..."

"Oh, stop it!"

XII

Outside temperature in the first week of December suddenly approached a freezing level, but I stuck to my routine of early evening jogging while each exhale was layering the scarf wrapped around my chin with a thin smear of frost. The exhausts of hundreds of cars passing by on one of the town's main roads did not seem to be polluting the crisp, chilly air. I could almost feel the oxygen rush through my blood stream with each inhalation. Heavy parka made every motion loud and screechy. I didn't bother with the I-pod, but instead held my cell phone firmly in a gloved hand. Earlier that day I met with a classmate, one of the former military folks, to discuss the group project we were working on. Veronika, another member of our group, was not with us. I was glad to see her in the class at the beginning of the semester—quickly and spontaneously we established a friendship the previous summer that was solidifying as we continued on the same path. Validation we gave each other did not resemble Sally's and my bond, a bond of mutual teasing and, I liked to think, friendly mocking of each other's flaws. The afternoon prior to my frantic evening jog I needed her presence at the campus cafeteria, to avert Sergio's courtship. *"I think you are wonderful,"* he said to me, and *"I like your confidence . . . your strength."* So, he thinks I am strong... My "strength" was a façade, a wall erected between myself and others to encapsulate life I was preserving for *Sultan* only.

Sergio was divorced for decades as he told me and estranged from children scattered around the country. I was posing an interested interlocutor by asking occasional questions, only to learn that his ex-wife was this "weak," "parasitic" woman who finally found someone to "take care of her." It was never going to be him, Sergio, since the fatherhood and the matrimony were sucking life out of him. He now cherished his freedom more than anything and was coming onto me rather strongly. Outside the campus, dim light of a short December day was almost palpably giving way to a cold, crisp evening. Bare trees surrounding the campus building were hovering over the edges of a parking lot and I felt a sudden urge to shelter myself from my companion and the hostile, persistent coldness slowly permeating through my skin. "Oh, here is my car," I told him and swiftly slid into the driver's seat. A nonchalant parting and a corny "see you later" did not bear hope to see him at a bare, plastic table of the cafeteria or to be willing to listen to another round of unnecessary confessions.

Back home I decided to call *Sultan* one more time after my evening jog; stiff thumb dialed the first number on the display and I almost screamed when Sergio lilted his *hello.*

"Um, sorry, I didn't mean to dial your number," I stammered, and he replied:

"Oh, sure . . . it happens. Well, we parted only an hour ago, do you already miss me?"

"No, I mean . . . I dialed your number by mistake . . . it won't happen again."

"OK, so . . . what are you doing?"

"I am trying . . . I am in the middle of fixing a dinner."

"Good to hear! I thought you and the kitchen were not the best friends."

"Maybe we are not, but one needs to eat, don't you think?"

"Of course, and with so many restaurants around, cooking is a waste of time."

"I never said I only eat at the restaurants!" I retorted, slightly irritated.

"But you could... But hey, I'll cook for you . . . and do the laundry. Go out with me!"

"Exactly in that order?" I attempted a joke. "What happened to a one thing at a time?"

My nervous chuckle set the salve of other propositions and among his giddy explosion of words I heard "white woman" (probably a reference to me), "my friend" and "hates Latinas" and then I heard myself asking *why,* then another series of his nebulous, out of context remarks and, finally, I heard myself again trying to say good night. *Great, now I am nothing short of his booty call.*

My premonition was not too far from the truth when I heard the phone ringing through the haze of my rabid thoughts. It was past nine and Sergio's *did I wake you up* resonated in my ears the way Thomas Mann would describe Mephisto's sinister lure. *I wondered if there was ever a practical reason for reading all the German classics. Now, at least, I understand Mephisto's voice.*

"No, but . . . it's kind of late." *And now the booty call!*

"Are you ready to go to sleep?"

"Yes, as the matter of fact I am." The message came through this time.

"OK . . . talk to you later."

The sleep, however, much desired and much needed, did not come for most of the night. Too frazzled to elaborate on these surreal happenings, one thought shot through my mind: *Sergio just demeaned my attachment to one and only man on this earth.* This man, *Sultan*, remained mute for the rest of the night. *Conversation that starts when two people meet and doesn't really end until one of them dies... And even then, there are reverberations of it...* My electronic life line with him extinguished, but even if temporarily it paralyzed my limbs and thoughts as if a real lifeline stopped streaming through a virtual space. Anna Calder-Marshall flashed through my thoughts and her tragic, yet heroic outcry in "Gone with the Wind", *"Tara, I still have Tara!"* and *"Tomorrow is another day,"* after she lost everything and everyone. I had nothing left of him, except my secret—my secret file where my narrating to *Sultan* started developing a life of its own, at its beginning as a first cry of a newborn baby, but now developing a strength and viability that I felt compelled to feed.

The warrior's little war game was over after the enemy gave him his life back.

Lurking behind enemy's lines painted a different picture about the war from the one transpiring in drunken off duty bacchanalia of his superior officers. His young wife listened to his pillow talk about a lieutenant, a local hero, "never short of pussy and booze" in bars he frequented when off duty. The warrior confessed to her as well the glances he stole from girls in a nearby small town. "Do they know that you are married?" his wife was burning from jealousy. "I think so," he'd casually replied. There, in an attic of a cottage turned into a visitor center, with noises and loud, hoarse laughter coming from downstairs, the magic of their love encounter subsided as if wiped out by a stroke of a mop, leaving a dirty residue of betrayed hopes. She wanted to demand, no, to plead with him about the sanctity of their marriage, but was afraid that the word "sanctity" might provoke his ridicule. He'd dismissed her remarks as 'uncool' and invalided her on numerous occasions, an upshot of a realization that he had the power over her. "Let me at least admire you," she remembered occasionally, in moments of never forgot his words, reappearing over and over again in moments of her total defeat and powerlessness.

The locals in the village did not have a penchant for love stories and displays of affection. Her tagging along when he visited local bars became a burden to him. The locals simply couldn't make sense out of such a gesture since she was now 'domesticated'. An old woman was once looking at him tying her shoes before going out one evening and, before he finished, trotted over from across the street simultaneously waving her index finger. "Do not get her used to that, "she scolded. The warrior reluctantly straightened and looked at the women, equally amused as surprised, ultimately leaving a tying job to his girl. Then they'd sit in a smoky, dimly lit café and she'd endure the giggly glances of a couple of local girls. Was it my hair? Was it my outfit? she'd wonder all ruffled and uncomfortable. On one of those evenings she told him 'Let's go home' and then heard someone say "Home? Your home is far away from here," reminding her of everything she wanted to forget: war, displacement, scattered and incarcerated family. "Take me home," she'd whined to him on one of those evenings, and then he dragged her out of the café, shouting in rage on the way back. *"Why? Why are you doing this to me?"* Not finding anything strong enough to assuage his anger, he then slapped her across the face in all force. First time he did it shocked and angered her, but soon after she was compelled to start learning how to cope with her new role.

She came back home alone that night. *"Why can't you be like everyone else there?*

Why can't you be—normal?" he continued his little tirade after coming back. *"You hit me,"* she chanted as if in trance and he retorted, *"Don't provoke me to hit you again!"* The little room in his parents' house was gradually turning into a place of captivity. He did not invite her to go with him anymore. Too humiliated and too embarrassed to sit in the living room with his family and frequent guests, she would spend the evenings in their room, listening to a loud chatter coming from downstairs.

Preceding summer, while still living with her mother's relatives, her absences in the evening bothered her hosts, an aunt and an uncle, asking her to stay home. *"They have no right to do that, you are not a minor,"* the warrior protested, adding, *"And besides, I will hang out with my friends for as long as I want—even if you can't."* His announcement sent shiver down her spine. Was that his 'sacrifice'? She wondered what happened to a timid boy who would come to her aunt's house and sit on the bench patiently waiting for her. Though he seemed slow-moving occasionally with his eyes bloodshot, she was touched by his devotion and persistence to win her over. *"I cannot be with you,"* she'd tell him, afraid for her fragile, only partially restored peace of mind after months of hell in a war zone and home captivity.

After settling at her aunt's home, she went to an editor of a local newspaper, a war pamphlet as it turned out, looking for a job. The boy-turned-warrior told her that one of his friends worked there and that they *"needed smart people."* The editor asked her to write an article about her perception

107

of the war and she did. The job was hers and soon she was outshining the flock of girls who, like herself, attempted their luck at war journalism. In the beginning, she would be running into her admirer on the way to her new job and he would tell her he was waiting for his friend. The look in his eyes was telling her otherwise; he was waiting to see her passing by . . .

Her aunt found his visits charming in the beginning. "He helped you get that job," she'd say. He came from a respected clan and his mother, a nurse, was deemed a local healer. A couple of years prior the national TV filmed a drama based on an epic poem from the time of Ottoman Empire; an aristocrat's wife was kidnapped by an Ottoman soldier and taken to his military camp in the mountains. She resisted his thrusts in hopes that her husband and his knights would save her. The days and weeks passed and there was not a sign of him. In the meantime, the Ottoman soldier sat on the ground close to her with his legs crossed, smoking hookah and asking her the same question over and over again, "Where is your husband?" He was telling her that he wouldn't come since she was "marred by hands of an enemy soldier" and she resisted for as long as her heart nurtured hope for her husband's arrival. The hope and love were guarding her chastity, but the time and incertitude were working against her, until one night she gave in. Eventually, the husband did save her, but the code of honor was demanding that she be punished by grubbing her eyes at her master's hands. It was a cruel yet common punishment for infidelity and the empress herself suffered from it. The husband went to the empress' chambers (it was his mother) where she was held captive and asked if a woman, any woman, could resist another man in those circumstances. The empress, directing her hollow eye sockets to where the voice was coming from, said, "Yes, if the advances, isolation and uncertainty didn't last too long." The young aristocrat then held his broken sword to his wife's eyes, but the moment she opened her half-closed, crying eyes and looked at him he dropped the sword.

"Let me admire you like no one else before," the boy-turned warrior's persistence and subsequent urgency had something in common with the acts of that Ottoman kidnapper, and his girl finally gave in. "I can't stop thinking of death," he told her in a post-coital embrace.

Well past midnight I pushed the chair away from the computer, rubbing my eyes in disbelief that at least one stretch of time went by so fast. A long weekend was ahead of me, a weekend without a life line. A couple of students I was tutoring gathered at my place to fix us a Guatemalan dish and there I was, epitomizing a popular philosophy of diversity: learn and teach about food. While the two Guatemalan girls busied in the kitchen, handled pots, vegetables and condiments, the third one, a Buddhist nun, was meditating in the living room. "Teach us meditation," we were teasing her. Meditation made her feel happy, she shared with me once. *I kind of need that,* I thought, leaving the open books spread on the desk and motioning her to sit on the floor with me. She crossed her legs, putting each foot on top of the inner thigh with an unbelievable ease—the first hurdle of meditation I never passed. She giggled at my grimacing while trying to bring my legs in the desired position and finally giving up. "Meditation should not be all about the body position," I told her. Next move was to intertwine the fingers, the palms facing upwards. Then came breading and concentration, which I also never mastered in those spontaneous attempts with her in the middle of the classroom and finally told her I've given up. *Sultan* advised me again to keep my distance, follow that I couldn't possibly understand the "ways of those people."

XIII

With the immigrant students I encountered through the graduate school I was learning something about the rest of the world and unimaginable ways of suffering. Last semester I taught a group of Togolese students who have taught me in return about realities, even if only anecdotal, far away from objectives of cameras ready to broadcast a spectacle for a bored, indolent and ignorant audience of a *developed* world. They have taught me, or reminded me, that the human spirit and wit never dies, even in times of the worst oppression and distress. The story has it that, after one of the farcical elections, paramilitary hordes were going through different neighborhoods avenging their party's loss by beating the helpless inhabitants for the undesired outcomes, or simply because the masses of nameless and voiceless were even given an opportunity, however fake, to elect their representatives. It would happen, the students told me giggling, that some households would end up being beaten up multiple times, until they finally decided to put a sign on the entrance door that said *already beaten*.

There in my living room I was watching the nun's peaceful face and motionless, erect and serene body sitting on the sofa. The sadness and not yet articulated feeling of guilt overcame me. I did establish a humane and compassionate connection with them, whereas *Sultan's* conduct consisted of creating a distance. He advised me to keep my distance. I didn't keep my distance, but the feeling of guilt came from a realization that I hosted this soiree only to maintain, however weak, connection with him. By connecting with his students, I was indirectly in touch with him—and the bubble of compassion and empathy burst at that thought.

The weekend was almost over. Sally was playing a spectator in my personal theater, amused with what I'd say or what I'd say I'd do. We were having another round of *tête-à-tête* at her place and I decided not to give her an inducement for amusement.

"Your winter break is coming up—how about a little getaway? Would you like to go someplace nice, or at least to Chicago, to one of those *ethnic* places that play our music?" she suggested.

"I'd love to, but my family in Chicago and I are also invited to a wedding next week. I can already see a vanity parade, infused by nostalgic tunes, schnapps and a mail ordered bride."

"Mail ordered? Did they ever meet?"

"They did . . . forget it. It's just so . . . tacky when a person living here goes back to his homeland only to find his future wife. And of course, he is her savior and she is going to cook, pop the kids and never *Americanize*, which we both know is a myth."

"Speaking of Americanization," Sally intercepted, "have you heard about the anecdote when a couple goes back to visit their home country and the first thing he does when they land is to slap her as hard as he can, followed by *"Who said I can't hit you anymore?"* Then she laughed and I wasn't sure if her laugh meant approval or disapproval of a "right" to slap a wife.

"Jokes like that tend to say something about who we are, as if that should never change. Never change your ways, never change who you associate with, who you marry... I hear well-educated, *cosmopolitan* people if you wish, say 'stick to your kind'. How narrow!"

"I don't know... Maybe to preserve that sense of belonging, something you and I are drifting away from."

"Look, Sally, just because we are physically not in the community that speaks the same language and comes from the same place doesn't mean that we don't belong. I belong as long as I remember. Even Hirsi Ali, though fiercely criticizing Islam she once renounced, is still in the grip of her past. Nothing can erase the experiences one had, even if one wanted them to be erased."

"Hirsi Ali..." Sally echoed dreamingly. "You told me about her. Wasn't she from Somalia?"

"Yes, her first book, *Infidel*, was a bestseller and now she published another one, *Nomad*, an autobiography. She seems to be stuck in the Enlightenment and doesn't see anything that's not filtered through its prism. But considering all she's been through, must be quite a liberating outlook on life."

"Why are you criticizing her? Isn't she a feminist? Fighting for liberation of women under Islam?"

"Yeah, her descriptions of life of Muslim women in her immediate family are rather picturesque or should I say disturbing, but the book turned out to be an assimilationist pamphlet. According to her, all those ethnic communities scattered throughout western countries should be untaught their ways and integrate into the mainstream society by means of giving up their customs and religion. Truthfully, while reading the *Nomad* I began to worry that the third world war has already started."

"And who are the good and the bad guys?" Sally looked at me.

"I don't know... Powerful against powerless? It's a quote I found someplace." I paused.

I was thinking of *Sultan* and my secret file.

"You there?"

"Yes, sorry. . . We can only pretend we understand the shades of gray, but ultimately reduce everything, from wars to opinions, into a black and white binary. Is there a place for anything but the two shades of good and bad? That's what bothers me about Hirsi Ali. She is so enraged at what is happening to Muslim women that anyone with an agenda could easily co-opt her for whatever ulterior motives and *causes* they might have." "But it is ultimately a conflict between good and bad. We know it firsthand."

Her words made me cringe: "Even so, it is not a black and white issue. I happen to have come across some research that considers the newest power relations, threat of terrorism, including East versus West or North versus South dichotomy from a more complex point of view. On the one hand, the images of Muslim girls in Somalia or elsewhere, held by fierce force of *guardians of tradition,* with their legs spread while another fierce set of hands is rasping their clitoris between the two stones (as I have read in the *Nomad*), are way too powerful and way too disturbing to disregard, but on the other hand those images, presented in a certain context, can label an entire culture, an entire civilization as "savage" and unfit for a *civilized* world. I mean, *modern* men and women submit to evils equally horrid as one's unquestioning submission to religious mandates." I paused again. I cringed as a mirage of a ghost image from the past vanished as fast as it appeared.

"Take for example my passion for gambling," Sally laughed. "Oh, I won fifty bucks last night... Forgot to tell you."

"Nice!" I replied, slightly envious at her *joie de vivre* while I was wrapped in my existential suffering.

"Hey, I really think we need to have some fun... Let's go to Chicago the week after the wedding you have to attend."

"OK."

"You haven't heard from him, haven't you?"

"No."

"He's in his *granny's* hands, sitting by the fireplace, reading a book."

"Don't make things worse than they already are . . . Please?"

"I was joking. . . No hard feelings?"

"No. It might as well be true." We laughed.

"And then they go to their bedroom to have a round of twisted sex," Sally added.

"What's twisted sex?"

"I don't know—not ordinary."

"I like non-ordinary things."

"Even sex?"

"Depends. Maybe not."

"See. You are an ordinary person. Talk to you later." And she left after giving me a quick fix, as in those self-help books.

Sunday evening. When have magic and wonder disappeared from my life? I could see them in a flower, in a faint smell that would come and go, in leaves rustling under my steps, in a movie that reminded me of the past or insinuated the future—magic was all around me. I didn't have to create it. Now I do; and it only exists if I give it a life... Can't borrow it anymore, can't simply pick and savor it as if it were at the reach of my hand, all around me. My eyes flashed at the message I was about to open. *So, this explains... Sultan's* cat died this morning and he wrote her a eulogy as promised, titled *Queen Kelly.* He must have loved her very much and I avidly swallowed every letter of the text he sent.

The queen passed today at 10:00 am. She was aided in her passing, but she did not leave by herself. We were there to hold her. At this "we" word' I swallowed involuntarily and skimmed through the rest of his eulogy as if in delirium. *Here is 'we' again. . . oh, God, here is her name. How dare he?!*

I am told that Kelly came to J. Greer when he visited the place where she was born, looking for a cat. While her siblings were acting the part of kittens, Kelly sat, poised and regal, on the table, royalty herself, worthy to be the companion of any king. J. picked her up, and she rubbed her hand on his chin. That was that. She was named Queen Cali, from 'calico', but the name changed to Kelly. She spent the next number of years much devoted to J. and would wait on his bed each day awaiting his return, waiting to be picked up to give him a 'hug', her paws around his neck, her head bumping his chin. There came the time when J. moved away to school. Kelly would come out to eat, but for the most part, she stayed on his bed, waiting. The day came when J. came for Kelly to live with him, but Kelly did not do well living with Puma, who was much too boisterous.

And thus, was how Kelly came into my life, the second cat. The first is Mercy, the rowdy princess. We were worried as to how all would fit together. I was gone somewhere for a couple of days. While I was gone and K. was at work, Mercy cornered Kelly on my desk table and would not let her down. That situation was amended when I came back. I have not mentioned yet that Kelly's eyesight was poor when she came, and she sometimes had trouble navigating. Mercy would sit quietly when Kelly passed; sometimes Kelly would be surprised, then hiss and lash out, and sometimes Mercy would lash out first. But after a time, they found their separate spots.

But they both wanted my lap. Mercy had gotten used to stretching out on my legs when I put them up on the coffee table. Then Kelly took to giving me hugs, and her tail would be on my legs. There was much sturm and drang. Mercy wanted the lap, and Kelly would growl and not give ground.

115

Finally, it came to pass that Kelly got my chest and Mercy got my legs. I had to make strong claims of my own at times if I wanted to use my lap for a book or my laptop. Kelly would curl up next to me, or on the back of the couch, or on an arm. When I was gone, she would sleep on my side of the bed or on my spot on the couch.

And when I came home, Mercy was always in 'feed me' mode. Kelly would come to be fed, but then she'd want snuggle time. I begrudged it at times, but I treasure it all now.

Kelly's eyesight continued to fail. She would meow loud at times, sometimes to find me, sometimes just to navigate, I think. In the last week, her health took a turn for the worse; worst, in fact. She started to lose muscle control, and she stopped eating. She took to sleeping in my sock drawer, where she was warm and supported. And I held her. Even when she had almost no control at all, she would purr in my arms and relax, still enjoying having her ears and chin stroked.

But after three days of not eating, it was time to help her go, to let her go. We took her to a nearby vet. We held her while she went. She was loved. She is loved. She will be loved.

Come on, answer it! When a drowsy voice mumbled "hello" I burst: "Sally, you won't believe this! His cat just died and he. . ."

"Cat? Whose cat?"

"Sultan's cat."

"And?" Suddenly she sounded wide awake: "Is he in mourning now? Does that also include not having sex? In any case, we would like to think so."

"Listen, and he wrote her a eulogy. I can read it to you if you wish."

"He wrote her a what? You are kidding!"

"No, her name was Kelly and she came to him one day after her previous owner went away for school... And there is this other cat, Mercy, and they used to fight for him..." I read her a paragraph about *sturm and drang* on his lap.

"Wait a minute..." I could almost see Sally's gaping into the receiver. Something big was about to come: "Two cats . . . sitting in his lap . . . fighting for him ... the guy is a polygamist!"

"It's the cats we are talking about here ... Although he does mention *her* by name and is using a *we* form, not a royal we I'm sure ... Here, for example, he says '*we were there to hold her*', and then at the end he says, '*we took her to a vet*'."

"Yeah, and he gets the best of both worlds: *she's* holding his cat and he's telling *you* about it. And writing her a eulogy? That is just too weird. Now I'm not gonna be able to sleep—and if I do fall asleep, I'll be dreaming of cats in his dumb-ass lap." *An image of a cat is haunting me too* I then remembered.

"Anyway, that's why I haven't heard from him."

"And it would have been much better if he didn't broadcast that eulogy thing."

"I knew it; you are simply never gonna give him a benefit of the doubt." She may have said something about a "lifetime" in response, and "If I were you, I would save the eulogy and have a good laugh at it after a couple of days."

Monday morning. The corners of *Sultan's* lips had a dry drivel residue and the crease between his eyes appeared longer and deeper. Whitish cat hair was scattered around his black turtleneck and he was slouching in his chair, slowly lifting his body with elbows pushed against the armrests and turning his head toward me:

"I'm sorry," I said.

"Thank you," he whispered. "It was time for her to go... She was old and ill... I will have to go to my class soon... My colleague tells me that the students you tutor are doing much better in her class. Seems like you are making so much progress with them . . . it's almost unbelievable."

"Thanks, um, are you too busy today?"

"Kind of. . . but I'll make some time. And thanks for rating these essays for me."

I was watching him waddle through a long and narrow hallway, remembering a few other occasions of his inadmissibly late scuttling to his morning class after my missing to appear in his office to say my sultry "hello." Then I would be watching right around the corner, a couple of yards behind him, resisting the temptation to run after him and give him a quick hug; almost vindictive, as if wanting him to experience the same longing for me as I longed for him.

Between the walls of my home later in the morning all vindictiveness dissolved in suspense—*Sultan* was supposed to come over every minute. He sneaked in through the front door, apologetic for being late, or for cutting a life line with me for so long, or for a eulogy and *we* statements, or who knows what other reasons. Then he carefully took his cowboy boots off and timidly sat on the sofa. I nestled myself in his lap and positioned my cleavage, framed in a lacy top underneath a light V-neck sweater, right underneath his chin. He absentmindedly kissed my neck, stroking my back along the spine and then meandered around the tailbone in cursory motions.

"We don't have to have sex," I said.

"But we are headed in that direction," he mumbled. We went through the motions of the foreplay, ending in his taking my sweater and my pants off. In the bedroom his motions appeared frazzled at times, replaced by his subsequent trying too hard to bring himself to a climax. When it finally happened, flashbacks of an act carried a compelling resemblance to an outcome of a battle, with the bed, or our bodies as a battlefield. *Your body is a battlefield* said a placard from the sixties (now a relic of art history books) at the peak of feminist struggle for equality and freedom of choice. I, however, did not only relinquish my body for my own pleasure, I consigned it to my superego, directing its each move toward winning *Sultan* over, luring him into my allure, hankering his courtship, his undivided attention:

"Can we start everything over?" I smiled, raising my eyebrows in a half-teasing, half-serious grimace. "And if we do, would you buy me flowers, take me on a trip?"

"Where could we possibly go?" He paused and lowered his voice to an almost inaudible murmur:

"For travel—I don't have any money." *What about France?*

Body and words do not always speak the same language. Words coming out of my mouth changed from a banter into a plea, while asking *Sultan* about those *we* statements in his eulogy that did not mean the two of us, but *we* I dreaded the most. He said, with some hesitation,

"The woman I live with and I."

"What?" I hissed, the entire world imploding once again into a jumble of unfinished thoughts and abject attempts to bring my composure back. Over and over again I realized that hell was not a place of eternal damnation in the hereafter, but a state of mind one travels to and reaches it as if passing through an invisible wall, a point after which different means of survival apply. A point where one knows that outside world exists and is aware of her distinct place in that world, but none of it has any relevance. Physical pain of the hell we were told about is replaced by a mental anguish, causing a wish to exit one's own body and return once everything is over. Meanwhile, *Sultan* was saying something:

". . . and if that is always going to be so, then I have to go."

"What are you trying to tell me—that you're telling her everything and her *life with you better than life without you* response gave you an excuse, a permission for this kind of behavior?"

"I have to go," he said, putting his leather trench-coat and his cowboy boots on. An impulse to slap that face and erase an image of a distorted, hairless cat emerging in front of my eyes again was suppressed in exertion and after I glanced at the glasses hanging on the bridge of his nose. Instead, I touched his torso, slightly pushing him through an open door, and said:

"You have just killed me."

XIV

*T*he Third World War has already started—it is a silent war, not for that reason any less sinister. This war is tearing down practically all the Third World. Instead of soldiers dying, there are children dying; instead of millions wounded, there are millions unemployed; instead of the destruction of bridges, there is a tearing down of factories, hospitals, schools and entire economies.

—Luiz Inacio da Silva[7]

Did the infatuated boy's enchantment with his girl end in a sexual act or did it deepen by his telling her the most guarded secret of his life? My Sultan, she held her eyes wide open and her thoughts spanned in an endless chord, hoping for him to mend his words, to strengthen their union in a romantic whisper instead of talking about death. In their oasis, their village, an illusion of life continued and she began to enjoy it, ignoring an ongoing strife, overlooking a changed landscape of their land, scarred by trenches of demarcation lines and refilled with cannon-meat, men with fiery hands. His mother, a healer, saw many of them in the aftermath of a battle with their limbs scattered around them in a bloody mash and she promised to herself that she'd do anything to keep her boy safe. He'd tell her these stories he heard from his mother if she'd try to point out the senselessness of the war, at the factories in a nearby city gaping empty, though guarded by uniforms, or if she scorned the leaders who "brought it all

[7] in *Pedagogoes of the global: Knowledge in the human interest,* ed. Arif Dirlik (Taylor and Francis, 2002), 113-132.

about." "Do not talk like that in front of me," he'd warn her. She was not able to articulate a response powerful enough to make him listen to her. Deep in her soul, however, she knew that the forces larger than she could ever imagine were pulling the strings and were going to spank their belligerent chiefs once they reached the point of no return—once they bury the paths of civilized progress, ready to submit themselves, their territories and their markets to imported goods and imported laws of colonial world.

Instead, she'd confide in him about the arguments she'd hear in the small hour between her cousin and her husband. They came to live with her aunt and uncle when the war started and soon after he was drafted. He'd come home after weeks in the trenches, trying to wash out the filth and humiliation with the schnapps—one of the few domestic goods produced and consumed in unlimited quantities. After hours of his silent rebellion at the kitchen table, he'd start an argument with his wife—in a slurred speech and occasionally slamming the table with a fist. He'd also win every time since in the moments of the most heated arguments he'd simply put his gun machine to his wife's forehead. The aunt and uncle would start waving their hands and beg him to stop, followed by aunt's cursing her daughter for not keeping her mouth shot. At some point he would go to sleep and start his round of rebellion all over again the following day. Though he played tough nothing could change the fact that he lived in his in-laws' household. The villagers minted a scurrilous nickname for him— 'daughter-in-law'.

Her cousin and her husband were not an exception, but a rule (with slight deviations) when it came to domestic quarrels. Tolstoy's words from the beginning of Anna Karenina *made perfect sense to the girl, "Every happy family resembles each other and each unhappy one is unhappy in their own way." After a while she realized that every unhappy family in the village resembled each other; wherever she went a husband sat at the table with the bottle in front of him and a wife would be manufacturing a biweekly supply of baked goods for her warrior. Children would be crying in the corner until she'd find some time to change, feed, or simply tell them to shut up. The kitchen appliances stood there unused and useless for the village would get the electricity only for a couple of hours every few weeks. Those diligent women splintered the wood, set the fire in the furnace and cooked, heated the water for washing and bathing and never once lamented over their fate. This was another war, a silent one, the one not reported in the media, the girl thought. These women had no weapon to shoot from, yet fought all the battles their drunken men lost—and gossiped and poked each other. "You know, our neighbor M., she's a whore," the cousin confided in the girl once.*

The girl and her boy befriended a married couple in her aunt's neighborhood; they were young and lived by themselves. For an outsider, a person only observing ups and downs of matrimony in extraordinary conditions in which they all lived, this couple's wrangles were mostly amusing to their visitors. Like her cousin's husband, he'd sit at the table (a coffee table) with the bottle in front of him, trying to recuperate from the time spent in the trenches. He didn't rebel, he found a recourse in escapism. While his wife was changing their toddler daughter and watching over the pastries in the oven, he indulged in a conversation with his visitors. "Have you heard of 'Enigma,'" he'd asked them. Of course, they heard of 'Enigma'—they learned about everything that was happening around the globe, they soaked it all up in those couple of hours when the supply of electric energy was not cut. Their host especially liked 'Return to Innocence' and 'Mea Culpa'. Did they know what 'mea culpa' meant, he asked. "My sin. . . my fault," he'd answer his question as if in trance. "That's a good song . . ." The girl was wondering why his wife never sat with them, until her shrill voice ripped the air, "Are you paying any attention to what your daughter is doing? How can you just sit there?"

Their visitors, unburdened by the daily toil of raising a family and running a household, were simply amused and the wife's grumble did not stop them from stopping by their house every time the paterfamilias was home.

The aunt became critical of their whereabouts. To go to other people's house when they are busy or wanted some time to themselves was not wise. "But . . . her husband has all the time in the world when he's not out there . . . in the trenches," the girl protested, not thinking that once home he could be spending his time differently. His wife was her age, twenty years old, and already burdened with the household upkeep and childrearing. But where did the girl belong if not in the company of her age group? They had to find a different place to hang out and the school playground was the only choice. Besides, her neighbor's husband became soon a convalescent after stepping on a landmine and losing a leg. They visited with them one last time, but his joy of life was sucked out of him, 'escaped' through the wound of a cut limb. "Every time they change bandages they have to cut some more of the dead or infected tissue," he told his visitors, "but it'll heal eventually…" he concluded, indifferent whether it heals or not since he knew that the part of him would never heal and come to terms with a life of an invalid, as they suspected he now thought of himself.

Suddenly, the companionship of an infatuated boy became a topic of gossip among warriors' women in the village. Their bond was not sacred to anyone; not to her relatives, not to their peers and not to the local redneck coxcombs. One of them had his eyes set on the girl. Though he lived with his girlfriend, slightly older than him, and her child—in her house, he somehow considered himself a 'bachelor', fit to make his moves on the girl, by making pretend-business visits to her uncle, ogling her and making lascivious comments. She heard her uncle once telling him, "Well, you are not quite a bachelor and she's not quite a bachelorette." If they were riding in the boy's small car he would sometimes follow them

*in his tractor and push the horn. One night the car ran out
of the gas in the middle of the road and the boy had to walk
her to her aunt's house. When he came back to the car the
following morning, the back bumper and the trunk were
severely damaged by a blunt force. No one said much about
it, but everyone seemed to have known what happened. The
girl could feel the neighbors' looks scrutinizing her and felt, in
to her unexplainable way, exposed and responsible.*

*The redneck coxcomb never talked to her again, but the
boy raged over what, everyone knew, he did, threatening that
he was going to go to his "stupid girlfriend" and voicing that
she should "throw him out of her house." The boy's mother
overheard the coxcomb once, looking after the two of them
passing in the car, saying "I could fuck you both."*

The elephant in the room of our society was that holidays were for some
the most disturbing, the most depressing days, among all other disturbing
and depressing days in a year. They usually did not have this effect on me,
but this time I was consumed by *Sultan* and our love triangle, so much
that we were gradually transforming into a Greek tragedy. I found myself
continuously tracing the steps back to the beginning, where this theater of
absurd started in his untidy windowless office. No meaningful elucidation
followed my apparently futile yet laborious efforts to reset the time or at
least to understand our actions. *He lured me into his swamp!* I repeatedly
told myself after each one of those excursions that always somehow halted
at the moment *Sultan* suggested a handshake and then stroked the palm of
my hand. His stroke, a flap of a butterfly's wing, swiped me off my feet and
then, in an equally absurd way, grounded me into a quicksand pit. Was I
defeated? Moreover, was I defeated secretly and in silence? Sally would say
that I didn't do anything to win him over... In her unspoken reproach I
was neither firm nor deliberate in confronting him about *her*. I would add
that I also did not have the patience to continue with her presence looming
over. Meanwhile, the demands of an everyday life continued to multiply.
A man increasingly present only in my thoughts and in my writing could
not sustain my more palpable existence. In my everyday life I had to be a

mother, eat, sleep, drive, produce final papers—none of which proved to be an easy task.

The last week in one of my classes I presented a group project with my partners Viktoria and Sergio. Sometime during the week, while working together, I confided in her about the episode in the cafeteria and Sergio's *booty call.* "Be careful," she told me. "I know his kind," she frowned. "I guess it goes both ways," I replied, "I would need more than a few compliments, and a booty call, to fall head over heels in love." *Hmm, would I?* "It is his machismo I am talking about," she scolded me, as if I have forgotten a common enemy. "Sometimes I could just scream in frustration just by looking at Sergio," she said. "Is there a possibility that we are constantly misreading, or inflating, the cues from others?" I wondered. "Are we even capable of being *rational* and *objective?* If only I didn't make that phone call by accident… Is it possible that he somehow feels rejected?" I looked at Viktoria as if her answer were some cure for our human deficiencies: in conduct, in communication, in listening, giving, receiving… "He'll get over it," she said instead. "I know, but I don't like misunderstandings and his sort of a contempt for me… Why did he have to say all those things about his life…"

"We'll pick on him some more, I promise," said Viktoria in response, "he deserves it." Sergio, on his end, announced the last day of class that he had a surprise for us.

"He never shared with us in any detail what his part of presentation was supposed to be," I whispered to Viktoria. We learned soon enough. The first slide beamed at us for a few moments, promising a succession of pictures of various royalties from the colonial era and their bureaucrats assigned to educate those colonial subjects. "I didn't know we were supposed to talk about this," I glanced at Viktoria, "speaking of someone not being ready for graduate school," I scoffed. "What is this, a slide show?"

"I won't be talking much," Sergio announced after a few slides, "five minutes tops."

"What is he even presenting?" I turned to Viktoria again. And after a succession of various royalties of colonial world, as if he was somehow crediting them for educating the indigenous, a black and white pixilated image popped up on the screen.

"And here is the picture of my two friends," he triumphantly pointed first at me and Viktoria, then at the image on the screen: two women in caricatured poses, one of them with crazy hair and laughing with her mouth wide open, beyond doubt resembling Viktoria and me. "He must have photo-shopped the picture he took of the two of us," I whispered to her.

"These two," he continued, "much contributed to my education and that is why they are a part of my presentation. That would be all from me." A couple of classmates laughed and applauded.

"One thing you were right about," I said before taking my turn to present, "it didn't take longer than five minutes."

Subsequently, someone touched base on the movie we watched, "The Country Boys," posing a question of how a mother could leave her children to cohabitate with another man. Something boiled in me and I reminded him, oh yes, it was the other ex-military man, that it takes a village to raise a child and that she didn't simply abandon her kids; her mother, their grandmother, was taking care of them and we couldn't possibly know what her long-term goal was. I may have called him a chauvinist, possibly by pronouncing only half of the word and followed by, "Sorry, but I don't believe we need to be so judgmental." The guy did not deserve my rage, he would usually sit quietly and was having difficulties with the content and getting his point across. I reached out to him the first time we met in class; I listened and responded to him, even though much of what he said did not make sense to me, especially when he stated that "the borders should get closed." However, his reminiscing of the past and how he connected it with his present reminded me of my *epic* character. His grandma worked in cotton fields, but never spoke hate, he said once in response to our group's heated discussion about racism. He asked me to help him with an assignment; while I proofread his paper he was telling me, "You know, I would go with my grandma when she'd clean other people's houses and played with the toys, never realizing at the time what she was doing there and why she was doing it. First time a sixth-grade teacher touched my hands I could tell the difference between the touch of a soft and rough skin. My grandma's hands were always so rough, but I had nothing to compare it with."

After class, Viktoria asked me if I were OK. "Yes, it's just this damn weather and the time of the year and..." I stopped.

"You need a getaway..."

"Where have I heard that before? Hmm . . . another friend of mine told me the same thing."

"See, now you need to consider our advice and . . . go someplace"

She was interrupted by Sergio, rapidly approaching us, obviously having difficulties parting ways with his "two friends."

"Are you coming back next semester?" he asked us.

"Sure, I am graduating next semester," I said.

"And then you'll have a huge graduation party... Am I invited?"

"Yes, and a bunch of other male friends I have."

"Can I then bring a bimbo along?"

"A bimbo?!" Viktoria and I shouted in unison. Some professor was passing by on the way to his car, glancing at us. When he was at a safe distance, we resumed,

"How dare you call women bimbos?" we cawed at him and Viktoria approached him from behind, mimicking a motion of kicking him in the butt.

"Make sure you find a soft spot," I suggested.

Sergio turned around and made a motion with his hand, as if trying to consolidate his audience and announced, "But she is a bimbo, I will show her to you in all her *bimboism*." He started browsing through the pictures on his cell phone and finally exclaimed: "Here it is! Look" He made a half-circle with his phone, centering it finally into what he deemed a middle point between Veronika and me, compelling us to get closer and lean over a picture of a topless, middle-aged, sturdy woman with the soap-suds smeared over her cleavage and breasts.

"Look at this udder," he grunted.

"You're disgusting," I blurted and in the next moment we both started departing from him.

"This is some way to say good bye, Sergio's way," Veronika and I exchanged glances, forced to hear one more of Sergio's *faux pas* in an onomatopoeic "moo."

We stood on a parking lot for a while, letting the sparse snowflakes melt on our coats, hair and faces and letting the occasional car illuminate our silhouettes, blinding us for a moment with its headlights. Sergio made his departure known by blinking the headlights and snatchy honking.

"This is how some people deal with hurt pride," I said. "You know, I never intended to go out with him, or to make that phone call. It was not meant for him… Sometimes I think that life is a series of misunderstandings."

"Hey, why are you saying that?" She looked at me and the moment our eyes met we exchanged all unsaid clandestine and naked truths about ourselves. I lived in turmoil, restlessness and disturbance for the past couple of months without ever telling her a word and she knew the moment the first tear made its way halfway down my cheek. She clasped my arms, stroking them occasionally, and then pulled me closer to herself in a wordless, soundless, endlessly comforting embrace. For the first time in months I felt at peace with myself and others.

"Now, are we gonna get serious about life: living it, enjoying it, cherishing it?"

"I don't know about that," I grinned.

"You don't know? You'd rather let Sergios of this world to defile it, to convince you that you don't deserve better?"

"How do I know what I deserve?"

"You deserve what feels good for you—you deserve best."

"'. . .*and you're up to save the world*'," I hummed 'Metallica's' 'My Friend of Misery'.

"And they say, '*Misery, you insist that the weight of the world should be on your shoulder… You just stood there screaming*'," I mimicked a low-pitched shriek, at which we both chuckled, releasing each other into a cold, dark night.

"Call me," Veronika threw shouted *in lieu* of a good bye.

It took a long while to merge into the traffic on a busy, steep street by the campus building and each car's light was hitting my optic nerve as a mild electroshock. The most difficult of all tasks in my state was to pretend to the loved ones that nothing changed—the routines and priorities were still the same. When no one was watching me, usually late at night, I'd curl up on my bed and freeze, one outlet, an old lifeline with *Sultan* left open, through which still poured my passionate *conversations* with him, without stopping, without exhale.

She told the boy she was being looked at as if she was a whore, wondering at the same time silently what happened to all her relatives' encouragements to go out with him, praising his clan and reminding that he, the boy, 'helped her'. One of the units in the building in the city, where he used to live, gaped empty and windowless and the soot of the thick smoke gushing at the time of the fire through the window openings left a black trail on the façade above the window. It gave the entire building a threatening, surreal outlook, making its onlookers wonder where the civilization went and if the time present were the reality that would never promise hope beyond the visible and invisible demarcation lines. A need of creating normalcy within an abnormal and hostile world, a place under the sky, a place where she would feel comfortable and in control kept invading the girl's thoughts. Even if that place was right underneath a spooky, windowless and burnt unit, burnt down to its bare concrete walls, along with all the memories of a life flourishing within those walls, along with paintings, posters, furniture and laminates—she could create an oasis right underneath it. It was a resistant building, like most of those in the city built for some futuristic times, times like the ones she was experiencing, an apocalypse swiping away life as they knew it. The editing office of the newspaper was located on the ground floor of an equally, even more injured and desolate building and a couple of staff members gave her a 'tour' through the numerous drafty units, naked, silent, without life and without secrets.

The life in the village, carried on in its own way by the warriors, their females and their offspring, stratified and with each stratum exhibiting irreconcilable differences, was gradually ousting the girl. She was passed the age of innocence, in her fertile yet barren state, ripe to bear children yet missing the path of other counterparts, spending her, otherwise petulant, evenings at the school playground in the company of an infatuated boy and among the crowd of other boys and girls. And she felt in her heart that was where she should have belonged, not in the brutal world of matrimony. She needed to be initiated, the boy had told her. They all had their "petting partners" if they happened to hang out at someone's place and after the (candle) lights go out. His "partner" was a blonde, seventeen-year old girl, but "it was all in the past now." The boys and girls had other 'rituals' as well: someone was regularly supplying them with amphetamines and pot. Though the younger ones among them never tried it, the older ones did. One of the "initiation secrets," delivered as casually and as carelessly as any self-understandable, normal occurrence, did not come as a surprise to her. It explained the boy's red eyes and belated motions. When the truth came out he asked her if she wanted to try it. His out-of-town cousin had a supply channel and was visiting in a couple of days. The adventure, she thought, would be a one-time excursion of her curious mind, nothing else. And it was—for her.

She was properly warned by his cousin not to smoke the whole joint since it was her first time and instead have a couple of smokes from their joints. She looked at a starry summer sky through an open window and at that moment the world transformed into a comedy with her boyfriend and his out-of-town cousin as some of its main protagonists. The aftermath of her mind's excursion seemed like a slow-motion film, devoid of feeling, devoid of sensation and meaning, and the cousin's face, as in a horror drama, reincarnated in her distorted mind into something devilish and evil. The girl was lying next to her boyfriend when the devilish face asked if he could "have some." She was not yet aware of her boy's blind loyalty to his cousin, though the traces of her mind picked up on who was a leader and who a follower. Hence, she was not aware yet of how big of a sacrifice the boy had made when he said "no" to his cousin and walked her home.

One step of her 'initiation' was out of the way. The following evening, they were hanging out on the school playground again. The out-of-town cousin turned out to be an absentee star and the group of youngsters surrounded him as bees encircle their hives. Almost everyone from their group took turns of going behind the school building with the out-of-town cousin—except the girl. As a consequence, she began agonizing about the previous evening, thinking at times about his young and good-looking face that appeared so devilish to her for a moment, about his preposterous 'proposition' and lastly about his out-casting her in front of everyone. Sometime before midnight she became aware (not without a dismay) of her soberness among people appearing to speak in tongues while dwelling in a world of which she was not a part. Her boy would look at her and she smiled at him, pretending that she was enjoying the company of a drugged crowd, but silently begging him to take her home. She reminded him about the curfew her host was trying to reinforce, fearing while the curfew or her pleading would bear no meaning for him, now under the spell of someone more powerful than she ever was—and more insidious. The boy walked her home, both dragging their bicycles after realizing that both tires on hers were slashed. She had to do some explaining to her relatives in the morning...

The group at the playground resumed their routine after the spectacle delivered by an out-of-town visitor and the girl's 'half-initiation', or what was supposed to be a full acceptance into their circle. The rest, however, transpired in one of the teens' house when no one was home. She was sitting next to her boy, holding his hand, but in the darkness, they suddenly drifted apart. She thought she saw a blonde head pasted onto his, but did not have much time to think about it. Someone's hand was stroking her back and for a moment she felt comforted and secure. 'So, it's him', flashed through her mind right before his gentle lips touched hers. Never was her sense of belonging to their group so strong and a little enjoyable petting was a small price to pay to gain a much-needed sense of belonging and acceptance. She trusted her 'partner', one of the few in the group she thought had the integrity, honesty and—a very young girlfriend who had a very early curfew. On the way home with her boy, his words "Now you are one of us" had a significance greater than anything that transpired that night, greater than the comforting embrace of her other partner and his silent yet immensely meaningful approval.

Her late-night absences, despite warnings, were not welcomed. The reality, different than the one she constructed, surged at her, leaving her choices of 'returning home' as a prodigal daughter, or further pushing the limits, trying to live as an adult she already was. Her attempt to explore a return to innocence and spend the dark evenings and pitch-dark nights at home resulted in her boy's hanging out with the group at the playground by himself until one evening he came to her with the bloodshot eyes, an epitome of, she later learned, of a remorse. He did it again with the blonde, and without her present. He was terribly sorry . . . His demeanor spoke beyond words—he was woeful indeed and she believed him. She forgave him, but did it go too far? Did they have sex? He indicated that they may have had and any further question to clarify it felt as a stab in the fresh wound, leaving him to wallow in an ever more unintelligible jumble of vague and contradictory answers. Then he started bashing the blonde in a yet new hate speech, convincing the girl that nobody compared to her and begging her to forgive him. The next morning the blonde and her friend were on the way to school (it was almost mid-June) on the same bus the girl was taking to work; they both looked at her in a sort of forbearance. The girl knew then that she traded her forgiveness for a moment of utter control, a proof that she was in the driver's seat of her life, a proof that she did not have to prove herself anymore. However, her boy tainted her right to defend what's hers and a resulting pride and possessiveness by aberration of the truth. The girl's sublime and solemn sorrow was spoiled by the boy's lie about how far his adventure went, or at least what she was told was a lie, which finally put an end to nocturnal cuddling of ad hoc partners. It also ended a magic of summers' nights and a twisted, childish construct of a collective soul.

The reality, as seen through her prism, however unpredictable and admonishing of life's fragility, seemed corny and without content if she attempted to go back to the beginning, back to life without this infatuated boy in it. 'I have a way of getting under a person's skin', he told her once. She let him in because she knew before he did that she was a fair game. War skirmishes in the trenches, schnapps and poisonous tongues of warriors' wives appeared as trite as the existence of a cocoon in comparison to a life she could have, if only she were not forced to live in other people's house and abide by their humiliating rules offensive to her dignity and sense of freedom. Freedom!? Dared she demand freedom in an environment that was all but free? A nexus with different worlds existed at the newspaper editing office in a form of articles churned in the informational labs of the world's most famous agencies, all of which purported to 'know' how little war games fit into a large picture and what needed to be done to stop them. They created narratives that played movies in one's head, full of big words, important events and atrocious actions, but not a single sentence said anything about an incarcerated existence and systematically destroyed dignity in a silent war, war in 'internment'. The world's tacit agreement to censor the silent war created room for a black and white picture they were painting, a picture that did not threaten to denounce history and humanity.

The girl's job was to carefully select scant comments defending her cause even though she was not fighting for it with all her heart and soul, but those words had patina, they came from faraway places thus acknowledging her existence among others, promising a foster home after an eternity of abuse, reassuring (indirectly of course) that schnapps, trenches, homelessness and incarcerated existence were a part of a fight for the cause, not the reason to loathe those carrying it through. Her 'field trips' into history, or makings of it, interchanged with dreary days at her hosts' house and intensified with every subsequent escape into her boy's embrace. Letting him go would be another defeat, the one that would not bring redemption and reconciliation with patriarchy she betrayed, but her opening a passage to scorn and schadenfreude of warriors' wives.

They looked at the building's windowless opening, gaping at the passersby as if personifying a toothless grin, black soot trail on the façade resembling a twisted mustache. "How would you like if we lived together?" the girl said. "You mean, here, underneath this wrecked unit?" They climbed up and entered the place where he grew up; only walls were the same. Pieces of furniture were scattered around and rugs wrinkled and pushed to the corners. "This city was taken over two times before it finally ended in our hands... That's why it looks like a rumble now," the boy said. Upon seeing that abandoned unit she immediately wished to turn it into their little oasis, their escape from the world of surveillance, scrutiny and collective thought. They started cleaning, first by wiping the filthy floors and straightening the wrinkled rugs. Fire in the unit above messed up the plumbing and electricity supply, the former given the urgent attention and the latter left to rest for electricity was a luxury anyway. Was that how the greatest decisions in life were made—as a spur of the moment? the girl wondered, but she desperately needed space and she'd do anything to create it.

The issue of space was not as difficult to resolve as the issue of implications of its creation in a larger world. Now that the boy and the girl made their lives a separate entity in the larger world, the larger world needed to define it, give it a meaningful fit, a familiar frame of reference. Therefore, for most villagers, their new (or old) neighbors and the girl's coworkers they simply had gotten married. Cohabitation was not a part of an established practice and was deemed equally shameful as any other fornication. "Do you live together?" they asked and the girl conceded. "That means you are married." But they were not and the girl knew best how thin of an ice she was walking on. The pals from the playground would at times step in to 'defend' their version of a life together if a family member or a fellow villager inquired about their marital status and one of them proudly shared her explanation with the new cohabitating couple: no, they were not married since he could tell her to leave as he pleases and without much fuss. This was perhaps the most accurate explanation of cohabitation one could think of. In occasional visits with her relatives the girl learned that the explanation of cohabitation such as this one did not please them. "I just wish they'd leave us alone," she would comment.

In the mid-summer the first café-bar opened after a year or longer hiatus and the town began resembling a familiar place again, on the surface populated by humans who wanted nothing more than some leisure time and a peace of mind. Underneath the surface the drifty devastated apartments and rumble at every corner relentlessly reminded the forgetful inhabitants of a ghost-city that the chain of human sacrifices in the trenches continued and they shouldn't dare to forget it. War profiteers, as they were called by the locals behind their backs, bought or plundered their way out of the frontline and perked the female crowd in those bars, while others had no choice but rot in the dugouts sharing their food supply with rats.

"Put your best clothes on, we're going out," the boy told his girl, not without resentment at his playground companions who, on the other hand, resented them after the latest hearsay episode about what happened with the blonde during the most recent collective nocturnal cuddling. The café-bar swarmed with the crowd of high school wannabe adults and adult male wannabe big shots. A well-lit place itself, ornate with mirrors and cold marble, sent the adrenaline rush through the veins of the visitors almost used to a life of a mole hiding in trenches, though the aesthetic stimuli were heavily aided by alcohol. Some members of the newspaper

crew were there too to indulge in a miracle of the city's 'return to the future', however temporary, and they all greeted the new "cohabitating partners." The newspaper collective was going through the same micro-turmoil, as the ones lowest on the hierarchy scale, in the social hierarchical food chain, were eaten alive without excuse and without hope for upward movement. But for what it was worth, the editing office provided a place where the girl could feel alive as long as she was a part of any chain.

Chain-smokers holding glasses of fancier liquor than omnipresent plum schnapps were almost stepping on each other's toes while trying to push their way in or out of the place. To hold a glass of hard liquor in a café-bar meant to be alive. The girl's vodka, even though diluted with orange juice, once again propped her in belief that life was nothing but a comedy—a belief further reinforced on the way home. Not far away from their building her feet gave way and she found herself face down on the ground. Her boy was telling her to get up and "what if a colleague of hers saw her lying there," but she felt good in her inexplicable blackout since those two juice-vodkas were sufficient to knock her unconscious for a moment. She drank because everyone else did, but some mechanism inside her kept reclaiming her strayed spirit and in whichever vice she'd wallow she would be back to her old self—resilient, childish, innocent. "This must be just a freaking exhaustion," she mumbled apologetically after grabbing the boy's stretched arm and lifting herself up. Deep in her soul she knew she never needed any of the life enhancers her surrounding abounded with and right there she was different than everyone else. She didn't need and she couldn't stand what everyone else in her surrounding enjoyed.

XV

With or without *Sultan* present I manufactured my stories for him, as I scattered my pearls in front of his blind eyes—even when he had an opportunity to see. Strange movies began playing in my head; Juliette Binoche walking on a deserted street in Paris, meeting a stranger and taking him with her, home or to a hotel room I couldn't remember... She gave him the best of herself—her touches, her kisses, her sex and she wanted to keep him. "I'm a pure gold," she said. He wasn't listening and she went after him repeating the same in a whiny voice... Was I this version Juliette Binoche, giving away excesses of my *goodness* to someone whom I appeared not more than a fling, or even a figment of imagination? Pure gold is only found in hard-to-reach places, not at the stretch of a hand. Was I narcissistic in my conviction that a middle-aged mother of four could not compete with me, or was *Sultan* too twisted, too sick and infantile, or all together, to like me over her? "You're faster than I," he told me once and the thought of always having to catch up with me must have been unbearable to him. I was going to see him once more before the break, but not before the rest of a long week was over. Resentment, panic and most passionate feelings for him took turns and, depending in which state I was, I wished either to go to his girlfriend's house, slap his egghead or send him the most beautiful, the most romantic thoughts and love. "We'll figure something out," Sally was comforting me, dispersing one after another quick fix she had at her disposal. "But, what are you hoping to accomplish by talking to her?"

"I don't know," I looked at her sheepishly. "Maybe he didn't tell her, maybe the *life with him still better than life without him* was a figment of his imagination."

Cup of coffee in one hand, a cigarette in another, Sally was grimacing and wailing in a distorted voice:

"Life with him better than life without him . . . You see, both you and *Sultan* are very imaginative people, he must've had made that up... I mean, how could he simply tell you her response and then act as if nothing ever happened?!"

"But that's exactly the point—*she* gives him such a freedom, which in turn gives her a sick hold onto him. And no one knows how to do it better than those old school mistresses. But I am still going to visit with her, just to see the look on her face..."

"How are you going to visit with her? Do you know where they live?"

"He told me once . . . it's a little town across the river, maybe twenty minutes from here. I was shocked when I heard where he lived, I mean, being a department chair and all... A friend and I were driving once to some trivia night at a church in a neighboring city and we got lost, so she ended up in this one-street appendix of a town... She told me then we better get out of there soon because that's where she was chased by someone with a gun years ago..."

"Careful if you decide to pay them a visit, the same guy may be there chasing *you* with a gun."

"That was funny, you know."

"I don't think you should go without me," Sally now seemed genuinely concerned.

"Why not?"

"You don't know her, you don't know them for that matter! Maybe her four kids are in a gang and on a lookout for uninvited visitors."

"There are no kids in the house, only a guest of honor, *Sultan.*"

"But still, don't do anything before you clear it with me." She paused. "Are you going to that wedding this weekend?"

"No, I can't. I'd feel like a total loser."

"You mean, here are the bride and the groom and everyone's happy and drunk except you. Why are you letting the society's clichés to get to you?"

"Maybe I am, but then why do I have to participate in those clichés? Just a couple of weeks ago I was helping Alexandra with a review for a history test and there it was, among her notes, America labeled as a couples' society. Honestly, I never thought they'd learn anything critical in the way

I think of it and this "couples' society" label stuck with me—the way any *painful truth* does. We know how much insincerity and power imbalance is involved to keep a couples' society afloat and the disadvantaged party, here still has not much chance to change it. We have our washers and driers which were, say, revolutionary in the fifties and no wonder domestic life reinvigorated its appeal at the time, but what is there now?"

"Porn?"

"But who does the porn benefit—men or women? Who is exploited in sex industry—men or women? And we fall for the same tricks over and over again, like, now we have freedom and opportunity to become like men and that's all it takes... *If you can't vanquish them, then join them.* Justify the status quo in whichever disguise is the only reasonable, only possible outcome of sex wars."

"You have nice theories, but where does all your theorizing put you? What's the dynamic of your and *Sultan's* relationship? Why can't you apply some of your *equalizers* into your own man slash woman relations?" *Relationship!* The word clung to my wounded soul and my wounded pride as a balm—courtesy of Sally's quick fixes.

"Relationship? The truth is, and now I have to come to terms with that, I wouldn't call what *Sultan* and I have a relationship anymore. Part of me wants him to face the consequences of what he did and if you ask me he violated every single rule of the work ethics there is. I know, I know, I'd have to own up to my own actions, but it's too painful. . . I told him what I did not want . . . and thought that, when he called me that Saturday, he accepted my terms. You have no idea . . . there are times when I think I'm dying for him and then all the yearning is replaced with anger and bloodthirsty vengeance. I don't know which feeling is worse."

"Let's sleep on it," Sally suggested. "Possibly in a nice hotel downtown Chicago. What say you?"

"Alexandra is having a sleepover with her friend tonight . . . they could spend the following day together too... Oh, what a hell, let's go."

On rare occasions when I would find myself with a group commonly viewed as *my people* I'd look at their faces realizing that all of them had been carved with what was commonly called nostalgia and nostalgia fed its insatiable appetite with the sounds of familiar tunes and by urging the individuals in its power to never-ending cycles of pilgrimages to places of their origin. And if nostalgia, a common denominator of all voluntarily or involuntarily displaced ethnic groups around the world, didn't kick in within a reasonable time frame and if an individual de-puttied herself from what was supposed to be a homogeneous mass of cultural compatibles she'd never be able to experience the same joy of a collective trans when the familiar music kicks the eardrums and shots start gliding down the esophagus one after another. Sally would play some of those songs to me and I would beg her to stop—this *country* or what we called *folk* music spread the same sentiment regardless of the place of origin. The same joke would apply to all of them; if they sang backwards they would get their significant other, their house and their dog back. Sally and I were two paradoxes: she couldn't get enough of anything that reminded her of *who she was*, even in the slightest way, and I couldn't try harder to desensitize myself from what I called petty sentiments. Yet she was the one sailing through her new life without bumping into insurmountable hurdles of everyday life, never looking for much and never questioning much.

I, on the other hand, denounced everything *local* and distinguishable in my persona, everything traceable back to my origins only to find so many aspects of my new life indigestible. *'And you're up to save the world'* I was mocking myself. "I am here to change the world," I told *Sultan* at *La Trattoria* and he looked at me almost afraid and then told me about the etymology of the word *sinister*. In our everyday language it meant something evil, harmful and wicked, but originally the word *sinistra* meant *left* or *left-handed*. So, he conjectured, it had significance from a conservative or in *Sultan's* mind dominant and more powerful point of view that lefties were liberals (they were *sinister*) and rightists were right. And when I said that change would take place eventually he retorted, "Don't hold your breath." The resignation in his voice bothered me, prompting me later to the same unanswered question: what did he ever do to call himself a liberal, except for living in a bad neighborhood which didn't count for it was a rent-free cohabitation.

My severing of my *home-girl* and *recognizable* personality traits did not make me less *exotic* and more *generic* in my new environment, but that was not my goal either. The idea of hybridity appealed to me and I thought that nationalism and nostalgia were in the way of reaching a state of mind where one could become someone else and keep her old self, her old schema. I agreed to go to Chicago with Sally, though I knew what kinds of images and what kinds of emotions would our trip evoke. Chicago was a city with thousands of faces on one street, each one of them not concerned much about the other ones. The polished appearance of the Magnificent Mile on Michigan Avenue almost concealed what was underneath the surface and Sally and I were determined to scratch it for whatever it was worth. We booked the room in one of the Courtyard Marriot hotels and I, nostalgically, remembered Alexandra's and her two friends' joy when we stayed at the same hotel on the New Year's Day almost a year ago.

"Hey, I'm going to the gym," I told Sally on the way out, a remark at which she threw herself on the bed and grabbed the remote. I decided not to call any of my family members to avoid their cross-examination about the reasons for not meeting with them at the wedding reception and going to an obscure ethnic bar instead. Later in the evening the glamour of downtown gradually faded as the Irving Park Road set into a neighborhood of plain two-story carpentry buildings and the swarms of people disappeared from the streets as we were driving farther to our destination. I liked to attribute such desolation to a cold December night, but my previous whereabouts at the *Bohemian* (that was the name of the bar-restaurant) were not fraught with a queue of people waiting in front of it or simply walking around. Those nostalgias I thought were like leprous—hiding their "disease" and hiding from the day light. The night was the time to cut a yearning for homeland loose.

"Have I told you that some thug hit on me at this place once?" I asked Sally as she was circling around the block to find a parking space.
"No, and how do you know he was a thug?"
"He made a confession the second time I saw him. Apparently, he was supposed to get arrested *over there*," and I looked at her in a conspiratorial way for we both knew at least what "over there" implied, "but he somehow

escaped and was waiting for the charges to expire. The *Bohemian* was his second *home*."

"Gosh, what did he do?"

"I don't know much, but think that he was part of the group that killed one of the bodyguards of that (in)famous folk singer, Svetlana. I got curious about it and he was a real self-disclosure "slut" . . . I knew someone calling this the people who couldn't resist the urge to confide in strangers… Anyway, a group of dawdles was hanging out at the gates of the singer and her husband's house when one of the security people asked them to scatter… A couple of years ago, on my *nostalgia trip*," I chuckled, "Alexandra and I happened to have driven by Svetlana's house, after her husband was assassinated too, and it struck me how all those mansions were close together and didn't quite look like a gated community here, or at least my idea of it. And in the middle of the residential block there was the building of *your* favorite TV station…"

"And which would that be?" Sally glanced at me while trying to parallel park, or rather squeeze her car into a small space on the side of the street.

"TV *Pink* of course," and not waiting for her reaction I continued, "but that's the spirit of our former metropolis; even though the gap between the rich and the poor is widening rapidly and enormously the city itself is not so segregated, with its residential and business sections intertwined and hundreds of thousands of people dwelling near in apartments the size of a box. You know, I never thought that those half-mile long apartment buildings would appear to be a landmark of communism, but that was exactly the impression of a person coming to a visit from a western prairie…"

"What happened to the criminal?" she laughed at my usual verbal meandering.

"I'll tell you inside . . . if the singer and the amplifiers let me."

As we entered the dimly lit and muggy premises of the *Bohemian* a sharp tobacco stench invaded my nostrils and I switched to breathing with the less-than-a-quarter of my lung capacity. I said to her, "I'll never be able to explain my dislike for tobacco and the opposite, irresistible desire to smoke on certain occasions. I've been fighting this urge to smoke for the past I-don't-know-how-many days."

"I wonder how they get away with permitting people to smoke after passing a non-smoking law," Sally remarked, "but it works for me," and she lit up a cigarette. "Want one?"

"Sure," I reached for it in a manner of an addict. The waitress was approaching us through the haze of fresh and old fog to take the order.

"Finish up before they start singing," Sally poked after we ordered our margaritas.

"So, the bodyguard demanded that the group leaves because they were making a lot of noise and "Svetlana's kid was sleeping" and that was when the strife started. Nobody was going to tell *them,* a trigger-happy gang, to shut up—they shut up the bodyguard, forever. I don't know how *my* criminal managed to escape the country, but he's been hiding ever since. And what kind of dirty business he was involved in when he took half a million dollars and squandered it in his hideout here within only a year or two. Scum like him dared to say he loved his country after robbing it and infusing the one he couldn't stand with the fresh flow of cash. You know why he couldn't stand it? Nobody gave a damn about him. He worked as a laborer for some painting company and for him life only made sense here at the *Bohemian.*"

"Were you involved with him?"

"Not really. But he managed to make me listen to him, didn't he? And I did. I even asked questions. He read the *Bodyguard* by V. Čolanović and one more book with the similar topic. That was it as far as the books were concerned. You know me: I'd ask anyone such a question—what books did they read. He must had been bending over backwards to get into my pants. Talking about books!" I paused, "He also managed to make me feel . . . dirty. I let a common megalomaniac criminal to buy me a drink and to kiss me without even . . . letting a vibe, a chemistry to take its course. His kind... To think that he could take anything, touch anything without permission, without pardon. This place reminds me of him."

"Can't you relax for once?"

"OK, I'll try." I looked around and saw faces as if transposed from one place to another, inoculated to thrive or be thwarted, to blossom or wilt in the new climate.

The singer started her first number and we drifted away along with others, drowned in margaritas as others were drowning in beer and shots of schnapps. In the interim Sally bent over to me:

"Humans are at their best when hunted or hunting," she made her last sober statement that evening at the *Bohemian*. "I heard this in one of the episodes of the Star Trek. It's good sometimes to pay attention to the things you normally ignore." I almost jumped up from my chair.

"I remember that episode! *The United Federation of Planets* was trying to populate some technologically highly developed planet with the nineteenth-century-kind-of-people saved from a certain death after their *rock* was about to blow up. The former gave up sex and started cloning, while the latter still did it the old-fashioned way...The cloning nation was facing the extinction due to *replicative fading,* so they had to switch to good old sex—with the primitives!"

"Remember Dr. Pulaski's recommendation: to create a viable population each woman needed to have at least three kids with three different men. And, technically, the polygamy had to be legislated."

"Do you think we are so overcrowded now that we have to head in the opposite direction? Become asexual? I mean, what is the strongest tie that keeps the two people together? Kids—everyone would tell you that. And the *hunt* doesn't make much sense now, in what we call a *developed* world, unless we redefine it.

"Then we must be transitioning from hunting to procreate and even hunting for plain sexual gratification to a different hunt," she winced.

I slightly bent over to look at the bottom of my glass, "However, I did feel after that episode as if a part of my painful evolution was over . . . leaving a couple more decades to go... The suspense of a hunt or a chase is supposed to be the lure of places like this, but the culture of TV prophets makes them degenerate. You know, the paradox those TV preachers disseminate is in their general message to *procreate*, but under some inhumane and sterile conditions. It makes you wanna escape sex altogether. I'm sure that many people do . . . they just masturbate."

"How is that not sex?"

"It's not—the real sex is also about power—one party is always hunted. Maybe that's how the feminist movement arose; women got pissed at being fair game all the time."

"Would you say then. . .," and she was careful choosing the words, "that what you feel for *Sultan* is anachronistic?"

"Guess I could afford some more anachronisms. A third of my life was anachronistic, but with *Sultan,* I'd say it's an atavism. And we had a lot of sex, but I didn't want him for sex . . . if that makes any sense."

"It doesn't."

"I wanted him for his words; that's what kept me alive. Sex was just the side effect. They say now the biggest sexual organ in humans is the brain. Think about how such a *discovery* transforms the notion of a hunt. In a few centuries we'll be able to talk to each other and have multiple orgasms in the process..." I said this as the population at the *Bohemian* started multiplying, or my vision made them so, sending me a signal that it was time for me to ease up on margaritas.

"You think we should take a taxi back to the hotel?"

"No. I know what I'm doing. In twenty minutes I'll be back to normal."

"That's another law we are breaking tonight," I warned her.

"Along with a bunch of other people... You know, not so long ago there was a law against witches. Just because there was a law it didn't mean the witches were real."

"But the alcohol in our blood is."

"Says who? Could the inspection tell we were smoking in here once they turn the AC on?"

"How exactly you think we could *purify* our blood? Oh, I'm too drunk to argue with you... And I know I'll regret my actions tomorrow..." I slurred. Someone may have bought us a round of drinks and I thought I would have appreciated it in another life time, but in this one I just wanted to go back to the hotel. And "to go" was the right expression since driving involving Sally (or me) did not have much appeal now. However, in the leap of a moment we were back to the hotel and, for the first time in months, I drifted into a deep, dreamless sleep as soon as my face touched the pillow.

Nothing! Back home. I turned the computer off and put the shoes and the coat back on. Then I took them off again, remembering that

Alexandra should have been home soon. *No, Sally should not be a part of this. It's between me, Sultan and her. I have to hear this 'life with him' phrase from her mouth.* I sat on the sofa and in the next moment went back to the computer. My narrative was waiting for me, waiting to be told . . . with passion and dedication.

XVI

*M*arko... *The boy became jealous of everyone in contact with his girl. A young freelance writer visited the editing office once a week. He was coming from a city, mostly hitchhiking, some forty miles away. A young enthusiastic man in camouflage uniform lifted the spirits in a stale editing office, though the pawns posing for a political game, or a rather obvious one called outflanking the commoners' trenches, showed mostly indifference at the sight of fresh blood in their news factory. The boy, and it was time to say his name—Dean, developed a rather quick dislike for Marko, resulting in barking and cursing him every time he'd open his mouth. The girl, and her name was Diana, felt embarrassed and wanted to alleviate Dean's outbursts somehow. She could relate to so few people in this ghost-town and Marko appeared to be an epitome of civility and kindness. With him around, Diana felt alive and normal, as in a long-forgotten time of peace. Yelina, from their playground circle, had a crush on Marko and Diana naturally became a liaison between the two of them. "Why she?" Marko asked, gesturing a large circle around his body to allude at Yelina's "weight issue." "She likes you," Diana would respond adding, "Give her a chance." "I can't," Marko would smile at her almost remorsefully, tumbling eventually to Diana almost a blasphemous question, "Why don't you give me a chance?" Diana shuddered at the very thought of betraying her boy. Even if she didn't want to admit it to herself or anyone else, she let Dean crawl underneath her skin or even more than* *that, and it was something she feared to articulate even in her thoughts—she let him take control over her life.*

The first couple of weeks at their new place, right underneath a spooky, windowless and burnt unit, felt delightful. On rare occasions when the city had the electricity she would turn the steamer on and vigorously clean the dirty carpets they found rolled up in the corners. She scrubbed the floors, the bathroom, the kitchen and she was exhilarated at how much work she could do in one day without getting tired. "I'm bored," Dean would tell her every day she'd come home from the editing office. "Is there anything for me to do at that office," he'd ask. "I don't know, I can ask," she'd reply. Male personnel at the editing office, however, did everything to present their position as irreplaceable. Every other impression might have been understood by the authorities as a sign that the not-so-irreplaceable could be drafted and used to replace their fellow citizens, now increasingly reluctant warriors in the trenches. Everyone was rather replaceable there, in the trenches. No, the male personnel held their positions firmly and there was no place for Dean there, as she was told after her inquiry. The pressure from Dean then became directed at her leaving the place—if they didn't appreciate her enough to let him work there. "If you love me and if you care about me, you'll quit! So, why don't you approach your boss in that way?"

She did and her boss told her without a blink that she's welcome to stay, but Dean had no place there. She had to think and think fast: what did she have to lose if she came back to Dean with such a response? Possibly a place to live at… Steep price to pay. If she quit she could prove her love and loyalty to him. And she left. Her boy sat on the bed and listened to his battery-operated radio when she came back. It was still early in the morning. "So, what do we do now?" he mumbled. A couple of days went by and Diana secretly hoped that she would receive a phone call from the newspaper and an offer to come back. At times heavy silence lingered between her and Dean. "Maybe you should go back and ask them to give you your job back," he suggested once. After all, the newspaper office was her lifeline with the world, a confirmation however weak that she was alive. The days without money, without electricity and without freedom dragged one after another without purpose and without meaning. She didn't have anyone to turn to and instead established a volatile and dangerous lifeline with the boy who gradually realized that control over her, above all proclaimed love and emotions, was a destination at which their relationship embarked.

The answer at the newspaper was no and a no followed by an announcement that they found a replacement for her—a newly arrived journalist eagerly welcomed into the small news manufacturing community. After all, Diana was given a chance beyond her qualifications and she gambled it away. Dean decided to go to visit his out-of-town cousin, to soak up a carefree life of partying and weed smoking among his old pals and with his beloved, alpha-male cousin—the supplier. She had all the time in the world among the walls of her new confine. "You have no idea how those trips make me feel," he shared with her the night before he left. "It's like the world belongs to me and no one else! It's like Andrew and I and our gang are invincible! We go around the town and no one even dares to look at us. And if they do, they get what they deserve." Those words resonated in Diana's mind and every consecutive remembrance of Dean's speech estranged her more from what she once was experiencing as a reality. Life became like a living in a matrix created by someone unknown and dictated by forces she couldn't control. She trembled at the uncertainty of what her next move should be. Moreover, she trembled in expectation of Dean's next move.

The second morning of Dean's absence she crawled out of the bed, carried by the remnants of her old determined self, took a deep breath in front of a mirror, splashed her face with the squirt of cold water and stepped outside. She plodded *down the stairs, stopped at the landing to glance at a steaming pot on the wood stove and to say good morning to a woman in a night gown. The wood stove on the landing, sending smoke through the broken glass, gathered the tenants of the building the same way the fire in a cave gathered and comforted those first humans in prehistoric times. These tenants were equally powerless facing the forces that could take away everything they had and everything they needed and the smoldering fire they kept nurtured their hope that life could go on, even if darkness extinguished the rest of the world as they knew it. Those gathered around this wood stove marked the territory of the new clan of survivors, the ones who successfully made sense of their new reality. The woman's gaze followed Diana down the stairs, the woman's gaze asked Diana to join the survivors around the fire, but she didn't belong. She couldn't handle their questions and she couldn't share their purpose.*

Outside, the chilly air of early fall sent the new impetus into her stride and infused the new hope of her old self from the old times. The school building stood a couple of blocks away as a sanctuary, inviting her to attempt her new metamorphosis, to offer herself and the knowledge she believed she possessed. As with the newspaper editor a couple of months ago she bravely stepped in front of the principal and told him that she could teach. She went to college, she traveled, knew languages. He offered her a position at the two schools in the surrounding villages to which she would have to commute on the designated days of the week. Before she could grasp that the principal offered her a new reincarnation, the meeting with him was over and he was escorting her to the personnel office.

Dean came back full of impressions and full of stories, mostly about séances of smoking marijuana and street fighting with those who glowered at them. "Funny thing is," he said, "one of those punks ended in an emergency room where Andrew's mom worked as a nurse. You should have seen the look on her face when she came home. She said she was going to call my mom, but I don't give a damn. We had a fun time!" She told him about her new job, but wasn't sure if he was listening. Someone called him on the phone and in the next moment a group of his friends (his childhood friends as he called them) came in. He started exchanging his stories with them, while they were taking the cigarettes out of the box and then emptied the tobacco into the ashtray. She knew the ritual and had seen it a few times lately. One of his buddies took the plastic bag out of the pocket and emptied the contents on the table. The same one started to suck in the dry cut marijuana into the empty cigarette socket and when he was finished he twisted its tip to keep the new filling in. In a manner of a sacred ritual he placed the lighter underneath the twisted tip and lit the joint. He had the honor of inhaling the first smoke and, keeping his breath for as long as he could, passed it on to the next one in the circle. "Want some?" Dean asked and Diana said no.

After a while the room was filled with heavy stench and loud incoherent talk, interrupted by occasional outbursts of laughter. Diana went to the bedroom and later in the night Dean joined her. Muffled voices were still coming from the living room. "What about them?" she asked. "They'll leave eventually," he replied half-unconscious. Minutes, or hours, before they left Diana's tension intensified to a point of a sensation that her mind was floating above her body, listening for every real or imaginary sound, then falling into her body again—alert, stiff, nauseated and scared, until she finally heard the entrance door opening and closing. Some of their hauling voices scratched the night's silence outside and Diana quickly left the bedroom to lock the door.

The traces of previous night's raving were seemingly invisible on Dean's face when they woke up. He appeared cranky and quiet at first. "Why don't you make us a breakfast?" he demanded. Diana's body stiffened remembering her mental anguish from the night before. With her pride and feelings hurt, she refused. That morning she met a new

Dean—Dean that didn't hesitate to use force to get his way. He threw a potato at her missing her head by an inch or two. "You will make breakfast if I tell you to!" he shouted. "No Dean, I won't. And don't you ever offer me marijuana again." She appeared calm and spoke softly, yet every muscle in her body achingly stiffened as she spoke. He looked at her for a long moment, she shifted her body weight form one leg to another and the suddenly relaxed buttock started trembling uncontrollably. He came on step closer to her and then stopped. She leaned on the sink, waiting for his next move, thinking that she was going to collapse if he makes one more step toward her.

The phone rang. His mother. Heard what happened during his visit, wanted to talk to him. Dean made some dismissive comments and hung up. One of these days, on the way to school Diana thought, she was going to talk to her. Diana then decided to tell her everything, to ask for her help.

My narrative to *Sultan* started developing a life of its own, expanding into an uncharted territory, prompting me to feed and enliven it for its own sake. I write, therefore I am. Time is bearable, the soul doesn't hurt as much. Is he worth it? Is anyone worth it? And as if programmed, the anger and anguish took turns until I fell into a restless oblivion of sleep. A couple of nocturnal hours of writing helped me recuperate some of my composure and soothe the anger and anguish plaguing me. The following morning, I was ready to act. I didn't need Sally's help, I didn't need Sally's approval. I was going to find the place where he lived and visit with his matron. Several addresses appeared in the yellow pages, none of them in the nearby town where he told me he lived. Then it downed on me that such an address wouldn't be listed as his since it wasn't his house. *Wait a minute!* There was some online form for a marathon sign up and his name and address were listed for additional information. Bingo! That was the name of the town where he said he lived! I wrote it down, carefully folded the piece of paper and put it in my winter jacket.

After days of comatose anguish, I suddenly felt energized and adventurous. The daring determination to undertake an enterprise such as this one didn't subside after another two-mile run through the frigid air. Every step forward brought my intention closer to its realization. Afterwards, cold, exhausted and with the face crimson red I sat in my living room thinking that the crisp cold air sharpened my judgment even further and all my senses started pushing me in one direction—to her house. There was no time to waste and no time to call Sally. This was my business and my business only! I briefly looked at the MapQuest and scribbled a couple of directions. It seemed that her house was located on a main street, amid all traffic, used dealerships and small businesses. I knew that part of the town.

It wasn't easy to see the house numbers clearly in a poorly lit street and the weak beam of light from the sparse street lamps lost its battle with the evening shadows on the porches and in-between the dwellings. A couple of times I had to bring my car close to a stop to take a closer look at the numbers and to annoyance of a few drivers behind me. A plain white house stood beside the road with a dark number painted on its front side: 605, that was the number I was looking for! I felt an invigorating rush through my veins as I looked for a parking spot. The house was now behind me, blinds shot and a silhouette of a lamp reflected on a window seal. *So, this was his domestic sanctuary, or no, his den!* I quickly corrected myself while slowly approaching the front yard. There wasn't actually a front yard, the house stood only a couple of yards from the street and the front door was on the side. For a few seconds, necessary to reach the front door and push the bell, I shut down a part of my conscience that usually gauged right and wrong and as soon as it started to threaten me that this action might be wrong. Slow steps approached the door. There stood the girlfriend, short, round and smiling. Her oversized sweatshirt reached almost to her round knees. She looked at me with an expression of a curious child.

"I just wanted to know if he ever told you about me..." I stopped. Another silhouette trotted out of the darkness and the girlfriend docilely withdrew into one of the side rooms.

Sultan's corpulent guise took up the space of the door opening in turn: he stood there, his height three steps above me, in his domestic realm, wearing a short, upholstered gown tailored like a miniature two sizes too small kimono and tied with two miniature strings in the middle. The crease between his eyes, the crease that I loved and that used to give his egghead an intellectual aura, seemed as if it cut right through his skull.

"What are you doing here," he hissed. "I told you to wait till Monday."

The nerve he had.

"Why Monday?"

"Because that's what we said."

"No, I don't remember making any such deals—it was your arbitrary decision. As if you could put me in and out of the closet the way you find convenient." For a moment I saw the girlfriend pacing in and out of the two rooms across the hallway, with a demeanor of a trapped animal.

"Do you remember how it all started? Do you remember how you said on the phone *'let's see where this is going'*? I didn't ask for it after I told you I didn't need the friendship or anything else if I couldn't have you! And when I told you we couldn't be what you called friends with benefits, you called me the following morning and started your blabber about our connection and that it's "strong" and blah blah!" I almost lost my breath.

"But it's over now!" he retorted. "You're draining me. . ."

"I'm draining you? Because you did something you were not supposed to!?" And there it was, lingering in the air for a long moment after, a rude awakening call, an accusation whose sole purpose turned out to be killing a frail fabric of magic I carefully wove to fall back to in case the outside world or this *other woman*—not myself—become too much to bear. *I killed the magic,* I kept telling myself as I turned around and his voice followed me as if reverberating in waves across the mountain peaks,

"It was consensual, it was consensual…"

"You did what?!" Sally screamed out of my receiver.

"I visited the girlfriend."

"But why? That wasn't how we planned it! That's not how you keep a guy."

I lifted my head resting on my hand, asking in resignation, "But really, how do you keep a guy?"

"Not the way you tried … You have to swallow a lot of pain, cry yourself to sleep and wait. Why couldn't you wait?"

"Wait for what? Godott?"

"Oh, you never told me about *that* one … But, how is she?" Now curiosity overtook her surprise and I described a woman to her in the exact same way and in the exact same words we both, though jokingly, did before.

"So, what else is new? Did she say anything to you?"

"No, not much."

The girlfriend's turn to talk came the next day when I received a courteous phone call. She wanted to meet and I suggested the library. This time I wasn't going to meet her straight from the workout—it was my time to shine. I put on my designer coat, designer pants, high heal boots and took *Sultan's* letters with me. *Could even a Judgment Day be any more serious than this?* She appeared in a long black rain-slash-trench coat, jeans and a red cable-knit sweater. Breathing slightly laboriously while approaching me, I thought she exhaled a painful sigh. We went into the building and sat on two comfortable faux-leather chairs by the book shelves.

"What would you like to tell me?" she asked.

"I don't know, I thought there was something you would like to tell *me*."

"I knew about you long before he told me," she lowered her eyes. "And I tell you what I tell him: life with him is still better than life without him" *What!?*

"Why are you so forgiving? What did he do to deserve it?"

"He told me he wanted to stay with me." *Where else can he go?* "I've been both ways: I made scenes, I cried . . . and at some point, in my life—I just realized that the outcome is the same or better if you let things go… I've been . . . the *other woman* too. Always sneaking around, always alone for the holidays…"

"I didn't feel like the other woman," I protested. "With us, it was rather public. We went to restaurants, to *La Trattoria*, his favorite…"

She cringed. "I'm surprised he took you there . . . It was our favorite restaurant." She paused again. "What do you want?"

I showed her some of the letters he wrote, "See this at the end, it says My Bella, that was one of my nicknames... He said he wanted to see where things go, that we have a strong connection..."

"But he'll stay with me... That's where he wants to be. That's love. We are so—a good fit."

"That's also what he told me," I retorted. "I found it a little strange that he would share with me the details of your intimate life . . . everything . . ."

"Yeah, I know he talked about that to some other people too..." She blushed. I gaped at her.

"He told me about all these great plans he had: change job, start doctoral studies . . . That's not gonna happen, is it?"

"No," she said in a voice a mother talks about an irrational child. "See, I've been through a lot in my life. I got pregnant when I was sixteen, got married just to get away from my mother... There were times when I wanted to run my first husband over with the car and some other times when he held a gun against my head. So, it ended. My second husband was a ladies' man. He traveled a lot, but I stayed home. That's who I am—loyal I guess."

She was telling her life story at a public library to a stranger. And she swallowed her pride and dignity to meet me here and to ask me for a favor— to exit, and exit quietly. She brought tears to my eyes and I didn't know why. She was telling me silently that she deserved to have her man, that she should get to keep him, however faulty and fake he was. He was weak she said and I had to be the strong one. I just looked at her and let her suck me into her world of failed marriages, female loyalty, and a desperate need for companionship. I even let her take me for a coffee into a nearby restaurant.

"I feel like giving you a hug," she said while walking out of the restaurant with me. I felt tempted, but then remembered how I imagined her arms—as the tentacles. She made me listen to her and I was left with no one to listen to me. I needed to talk with *Sultan,* to clarify this whole episode, to check if I was dreaming. *Listen to me, I called him silently!* Another story unwound again that evening. As if someone else performed my actions of the previous night and day, I wiped them all from my memory, sat in my chair and recreated the magic, continuing my narrative for him and him only.

XVII

D ean's mother listened to Diana in disbelief. After the war started she moved to their vacation home in the village where the mother and her daughter lived to escape the hardships of a city life and deprivations the city dwellers were subjected to in these troubling times. Diana was on the way to school where she now worked and decided to stop by. "This can't be real," his mother was gripping her hands. "You both need to come and live here," she finally suggested. The following morning, she came into the apartment, raging at Dean and, as mutually agreed, telling him that she heard about the drugs from the police who were watching one of his companions, suspecting him of drug dealing. It was a matter of time, she threatened, before they come over and arrest them all. "Do you even know what a life of a drug addict is? They steal, they sell themselves and always need more. Finally, drugs become the only thing defining their life. I couldn't watch you do that to yourself! I couldn't watch you shivering and bursting into a cold sweat on a hospital bed!"

The place Diana wanted to make her home, place she wanted to cleanse of all impurities while armies took turns in vanquishing the town and leaving havoc behind, that place now smacked of another impurity, breathing coldness into its walls, and ousting from her life in yet another way a so much desired need for domesticity and harmony. The following days Dean would go out early in the evening and come back late at night, telling her that he was just "hanging out with his friends." She would lie in the darkness of a cold room and listen to the sounds of a city's night life, infused by fear, debauchery and alcohol. It was another one of the nights in which those muffled, half-anguished, half-animalistic moans came from the unit next to her. Dean and his pals called it a widow's apartment. A widow became a special category of women in these times of war and, unlike the reputation of an unfortunate matron she enjoyed in some times past, became synonymous with epithets of 'easy', 'available', and 'sluttish'. Sacrifice and martyrdom of their husbands did not usher her, the widow, into an honorable realm—to the contrary, she was assorted into the market of easily available goods and became an object of countless jokes.

The "widow" arose interest of the crowd gathering at Dean's place. Drunk and high, they would stand in front of her door and eavesdrop. On some nights unnatural and exaggerated moaning was coming through the rickety door— hallmark of the times marked by burglaries and plunder while the city was in-between its takeovers. "I think she's having a threesome," one of the drunken visitors-voyeurs remarked, adding that he saw two soldiers at her door on his way to Dean's apartment. Much later, as the drunk and high 'audience' departed into the night, Diana wondered in the solace of the dark bedroom if anyone moaning like that could actually be enjoying sex.

She saw her a couple of times in passing, usually while both were passing each other by on the stairs. Dean was spending less and less time home and by the time she would come back from school he would be already gone. A sturdy blonde in tight leggings and a leather jacket stood in front of her door, maneuvering with the key while holding a flimsy doorknob, when Diana came home the night after she became a reluctant audience of her neighbor's night life. The girl was in her mid-twenties, but looked older under a mask of heavy make-up. Diana glanced at her, trying to erase the traces of judgment that was heavily passed on by other neighbors and multiplied by the girl's recently acquired status of a widow.

"Hi," *Diana said, not expecting the answer and not even expecting a glance in her direction. The bewildered look she gave her in return said more than words, as if asking Diana not to bother her with the common courtesy when she knew very well what everyone thought of her. But, there was something else in that look: a sadness, remembrance perhaps of who she once was, and Diana caught a glimpse of that remembrance, long gone before she was finally able to unlock the rickety, squeaky door. In a split of a second the widow's face became a mask again and she quickly slid through the opening.*

Abandoned in the apartment that became a scene of drug séances, Diana developed a strange curiosity for her neighbor. Dean's mother would say about the war widows that they were angry with life, with God and with themselves, telling the world and men to go to hell along with them. It was an early afternoon when Diana saw her coming toward the building at her usual time. Where does she go? What does she do? Diana wondered. The next day she stood in the hallway around the time she spotted the widow coming home. Minutes passed and she felt equally perverted as she thought those drunken eavesdroppers were, although she only wanted to see her and possibly get to know her. Minutes, that always seemed longer if one waited, passed without the clunky sound of her neighbor's ascending the stairs and Diana went back to the living room. What was she trying to accomplish anyway?

Suddenly she heard the steps and soon after the key turning in the lock. Rushing to the door she grabbed the doorknob and then stopped. Let's make this a chance encounter, she thought. In the next moment, Diana grabbed a half-full garbage bag and swiftly slid through the door. Her neighbor turned around at the sound of the door opening. "Oh, hi", *Diana smiled.* "Hi," *the woman replied.* "We meet again," *Diana broke the ensuing moment of silence.* "Small world," *she heard a response.* "Look, if you have a moment, we could have a coffee or a drink at my place. I'm Diana," *she offered her a handshake. After a moment of hesitation, the woman shook her hand, briefly and as if in a hurry. "I'm Dana," she said. "So, what do you say, coffee at my place?" "Not now," she said hesitantly, "Maybe later, around five?"*

"Agreed."

Diana rushed back in the house, carrying the garbage bag she wanted to take out and, after noticing Dana's puzzled look, slapped herself on a forehead mumbling that she "forgot about the garbage." On the way back to the apartment she started speculating about Dean's potential reaction if he ran into their unexpected visitor. What were the chances that he'd be home at that time anyway, she consoled herself. Dana came in carrying a pack of Pall Mall and a lighter. "So, who are you living with?" she asked.

"A boyfriend," Diana replied. "This was his parents' apartment before . . . everything happened…"

"I see . . ."

"I teach at the two rural schools not so far away from here… And what do you do?" She sighed.

"I was a singer."

"You were a singer?"

"Yes, I was, but it's hard to sing after someone you loved died. Come on, you know about me. People call us widows, which is the first thing they'll say before anything else. And the next…"

"The next?" Diana repeated as hypnotized.

"The next thing they'll say is a joke . . . about widows. You heard them, don't pretend you didn't."

"I suppose… Your husband died in a combat?"

"Yes. They were guarding their positions in the trenches, doing the usual, hollering at the enemy on the other side, when the order came that they needed to break through the enemy lines. The positions the enemy held were of "strategic importance" so they needed to push them farther back. Can you even imagine how it looks like? Getting ready to execute your own death sentence? They were told that if they didn't

do it, the enemy soldiers would and then . . . I guess the bullet in one's back is worse than a bullet in one's chest."

"I am sorry . . ."

"Thank you." She continued while lighting her first cigarette, "Do you know how many men died that day?" Without waiting for an answer, lowering her voice, she said, "A hundred and fifty. For nothing. Or because someone thought that the enemy occupied a strategically important location." She emphasized the "strategically important" as if blaming it for the death of her husband. "Nothing happened of course. When the military superiors concluded that part of the enemy territory in question was unassailable at the time they simply gave orders for the soldiers to retreat. And what do you know about it?"

"Not much. You know, I worked for a while at the local newspaper and know how much fabrication and falsification was going on. I knew from the moment I heard on the news about the "enemy attack" that it couldn't have been the whole truth. And all the lamenting about "brave defenders" who resisted, rebuffed and guarded our holy ground . . . until most of them were killed. Yes, they are honored in haste eulogies delivered by petty officers at the funerals and remembered by sorrowful families, but nobody seems to be asking why they were sacrificed to begin with."

"True... Anyway, after the death of my husband I was lost. Don't you find it ironic that I, a singer, have lost means to support myself after he died, whereas I supported both of us when he was alive? Yes, he kept telling me to quit singing in those barrelhouses, but what else could I do? It was working for us just fine. I mean, he wasn't around to see occasional butt slapping and some soldiers' trying to slip a bill into my cleavage, but that came with the territory. After he died . . . they all just came after me as vultures, as if they only waited for that to happen, giving them a green light to hunt me down. I am at the mercy of drunken soldiers and occasional local bureaucrat of our "holy" national party."

"But, you have your rights! You are a widow . . . sorry, you are a wife of a fallen soldier!"

"A wife who was married for not even a year and who didn't have any children!"

"So what? You can't continue living as if nothing happened. You couldn't continue singing."

"Unfortunately. You know what, I have seen enough while working at those places—our mayor's mistress sitting in his lap and calling him a 'horse'."

"What?"

"I guess he pissed her off about something... Or maybe she was pregnant . . . again."

"But he's married!"

"Where do you think you live? In love and war everything is allowed. Some famous writer said that once . . . Anyway, it was nice talking to you. Maybe we should do it again sometime."

"Sure. I am here by myself most of the day…"

"So, where is that boyfriend of yours? Why is he leaving you alone? I think I saw him a while ago with a group of men strolling down the street. He is not drafted yet?"

"Well, his mother is pulling some strings and he is still fairly young, but I think it's only a matter of time…" Diana felt slightly embarrassed at her wish for Dean to go on the front line, she felt embarrassed that he was abandoning her and scared that his association with local thugs could cause her harm. After Dana left she washed the coffee cups and cleaned the ashtray. Dean would not tolerate his docile girlfriend's association with the woman commonly known as a whore. His reputation would be irreparable and Diana knew that she was walking on a thin ice.

Dean realized soon after they moved into his parents' apartment that Diana had nowhere to go and that compromising with her how the two of them should live their life together was not necessary. If she objected to his leaving her alone or spending time with people known for drug *trafficking or simply as users, he would coldheartedly respond that she should go back to her relatives. This is not right, this is not life, this is not love anymore, Diana repeatedly told herself every time Dean would remind her of her position. The night after Dana's visit he came home with a couple of users. They appeared to be in a good mood, laughing each time someone would mention "Are there any pot smokers here?" Diana retreated in the bedroom and, intrigued, later in the night, asked Dean if they were laughing at some jokes or what. On an occasion she tried to establish communication with him, terrified that his mood swings, an instability as she often thought, and her ongoing retreat into her own world and not acknowledging him could lead him to rage against her. Traces of love she once felt were giving way to fear and subordination.*

"Oh, we were laughing at one of our buddies. He told us about that stupid refugee girl that came into a café a couple of nights ago and asked, "Are there any pot smokers here?" He started giggling... "And?" Diana asked in anticipation. "Nothing... Crazy Ned got up and said "Yes, I'll show you the smokers!" He took her to some abandoned building . . . ha-ha . . . and, you know the rest."

"But why would he do that?" Diana insisted.

"And why not? Crazy bitch came into a café asking about 'smokers'!"

"Would anyone do it to you if you did the same?" She left unsaid the comment about how potheads have their ways of finding each other and the girl was no different than him or his companions... And didn't need to be raped to be put in place! Dean interrupted her moment of silence, spitting a short and dismissive "What do you care anyway?" She cared. Not primarily for the individual she didn't know, but for the non-existent dignity and rights of women in this godforsaken city. It struck her that it wasn't only war and devastation that brought the most inhumane in men in her surrounding, but something inherently brutal from the time she had her first

memories and even beyond. One anecdote became etched in her memory, a testimony of sorts that roots of misogyny and violence went much deeper than what came about in the bloody years of war.

Diana was in her sophomore year in high school, surrounded by rowdy boys and a few girls in one of the most notorious technical schools in her home town. The boys would gather during recess to tell their fat jokes, pick on someone or tell stories the exact same way Dean and his dawdlers did. In one of them an out-of-town girl showed up at a party and received her ration of sex, alcohol, and rock'n'roll as soon as the male attendees learned that she was an out-of-town, provincial visitor. She pleaded with them not to hurt her, yes, that was mentioned in the story, but who cared! Her being an outsider, though one speaking the same language and living the same dreams as those who hurt her, was a reason enough to be violated. A few years later, where Diana embarked in a whirlwind of a bloody armed conflict, people like her were no more desirable as any outsiders from any part of the world. One other word evolved into an extremely derogatory epithet at the time, and it was the word refugee, as if they trespassed onto a sacred territory of their brothers in faith and were not exiled, tortured and threatened to leave their hearth.

"We first heard a loud pounding of multiple steps on our stairway, intensity of sound multiplied by stomping the military boots against the concrete and then inevitable banging on the front door. We were getting ready to spend another sleepless night cowering under our bed covers when the deafening sound on the door hit everyone in their corners of the house, paralyzing them in fear. I don't remember who opened the door, possibly my mother, when the uniforms invaded our hallway."

Dana was sitting on the sofa, absentmindedly holding a lit cigarette in one of her hands and a cup of coffee in the other. "I am not judging you," Diana said to her in the hallway after one of their subsequent "coincidental" encounters. She wanted to add, I am trying with all my heart to not cross the line beyond which you are walking right now and join you, and you cannot even imagine how close to it I am, but voiced another one of her invitations for a visit instead. This time Dana did not appear as suspicious and as hesitant, she accepted her neighbor's invitation followed by something that Diana interpreted as a sigh of relief. She told her then that the place where Dean and she lived was not much of a home and she was there mostly by herself, but having someone to talk to certainly felt closer to home. This time Dana didn't wait until later in the afternoon—she pulled her pack of cigarettes and a lighter out of the purse, dropping it then on something that could've been a night stand hidden from sight from the entrance door. Small talk with her left Diana in the same state of anticipation and suspense a calm before a storm would and she knew that those short comments about the prices of dairy products on the market were not the topic of the day. Diana agreed with her, adding that the farmwomen on the market knew that what they came to offer to the fearful and helpless city rats was irreplaceable and in high demand; therefore, there wasn't much room to negotiate.

Coffee tasted more bitter than usual since Diana's supply of sugar reached a new low and replenishing it did not depend so much on her next pay check as on Dean's mother's good will. She could only buy so much for the money she earned, with a rapidly increasing inflation. Bitter taste in the mouth could be washed off, but nothing could assuage the bitterness in the soul after another story of immense human suffering. They started out by exchanging the usual courtesies, laughing at what appeared their sealed fate of being known only as refugees in this godforsaken city, Dana's widowhood, and sharing stories from school days and where each one of them was when the madness of the war started. Though living a few hundred miles away from each other before, the war scenario followed a similar plotline—they were left behind by their brothers and sisters in faith, surrounded by enemy neighbors and enemy soldiers. For a while they thought that everything would fall into place, that they would be liberated by "theirs" and that the enemy that threatened and tortured them would be defeated. After only a couple of months a painful realization awakened them—they were on their own, at the mercy of enemy's criminal paramilitary forces and the hostile neighbors.

Diana created a special memory compartment, sealed and almost inaccessible even to herself, so that anyone asking questions whose answers she'd have to search in her sealed memory would leave with a superficial and short recount of many times regurgitated narrative of her exile. Dana, on the other hand, seemed to have reached ever new stages of self-liberation with every new detail in her saga, every new expected or unexpected turn. She seemed to have abandoned one's usual guard, one's mental shield in interactions with relative strangers and Diana was a stranger to her. After Dana's first confession she didn't know whether it was empowering or humiliating to her; did Dana think that sharing her secrets was safe with her next-door neighbor because she sensed something extraordinary in her personality or because her next-door neighbor was lonelier and even more powerless than she was? A mind of an ordinary person with ordinary experiences might be more premeditated in if, how, when and to whom they were going to tell their carefully guarded secrets and stories, but for a reason Diana couldn't explain or grasp, all the guards were off and her and Dana's encounters crossed into a realm of extraordinary the moment they decide to have a coffee together.

"Could you have jumped through the window and run into the woods? Unless they surrounded the house…" Diana heard herself asking in a subsiding voice that ushered Dana

into a new crescendo of a saga with never-ending cycles of pain and suffering.

"I thought about it... The balcony in my room was ten feet from the ground, and when the first machine gun handle hit the door, my mind started telling me with a speed ten times faster than the speed of light to head to the balcony, grip the rail and ease myself to the ground. Jumping four feet in that case would have been easier than jumping ten feet and risk breaking a leg. But no matter how fast I was thinking those uniforms were faster than me. One of the soldiers barged into the room where my sister and I were hiding and ordered us to take our clothes off. 'Look at you! Look at your short hair! Want some drugs?' He shouted at me. I didn't know where he got that idea from. I never took any drugs and how would he know it anyways? My sister started crying hysterically and the uniform told her to shut up or he was going to cut my breast off. He wasn't joking either since the blade of his patent knife touched my skin when my sister stopped crying abruptly. Another man came in and my sister started pleading with him to stop this. I felt paralyzed, as if having a bad dream. In the next moment the other man took my sister out and the one with a knife ordered me to suck his dick. When he was finished some other uniform came in and raped me..."

"Dana, you don't have to tell me the rest . . . I understand how it must have felt . . . In the house where you were born and raised... How did you escape?"

"That night we went to our neighbor's house. They hosted a refugee family . . . an enemy's refugee family if you wish. That was the only way to stay somewhat protected until they forced everyone out... Ethnic cleansing was largely reciprocal—men taken away and women and children harassed to a point of "voluntary" departure to "theirs," "the other side," or else face homelessness and starvation. On the days of exchange, organized by local war lords, people were bought and sold as any other merchandize. My family was *not sought after on that market. After months of incertitude and mental anguish we were left to be handled by small scale war profiteers, who went door to door and had their own channels to do the exchange for less money. That's how we ended up on "our" side. Don't laugh! You know what I mean; were we really welcome? Embraced? The most common objection you hear from the locals, even at the slightest hint of an accusation of being left behind, not even a hint, but something that locals like to interpret as such, is 'Why didn't you fight back?' 'Why didn't you conquer your own territory?' Like in the dark ages! How is one supposed to conquer their own territory? You think things will stay like this? I don't think so!" Dana inhaled deeply and exhaled another cloud of cigarette smoke when the knob on the front door unexpectedly clicked. It was Dean.*

Diana tried to cover up her discomfort and surprise, but unsuccessfully. Dana was taken aback too and, standing up, said, "I better get going." In the hallway she crossed her path with Dean and they both mumbled something resembling a greeting, followed by Dana's swift slide through the front door. She couldn't have helped me even if she wanted to, Diana thought. First, she noticed Dean's bloodshot eyes and an expression of a hunter about to hunt down his game.

"Since when is she visiting my place?" He hissed.

"I really . . . It was just a coincidence…We both came home at the same time and then . . . she asked me something . . . if she could borrow something . . . and I said yes."

"So, why didn't you just give her what she wanted and close the door? He raised his voice up a notch. "Or why didn't you tell her to go to hell? Do you really want to be associated with a common whore? A whore! That's what she is! Or are you maybe the same as her? That didn't occur to me before, but I can see now… You are just like her! You are a whore as well!" By the time he finished his tirade his voice resonated like a thunder in Diana's ears. He squeezed her arms and shook her paralyzed body, all the while repeating, "You are

a whore! You are a whore!" and "Don't you dare having her over again!"

"Let go of me, please!" Diana started shaking and sobbing and Dean finally released her from his grip, pushing her away as if she were something despicable. She didn't dare to ask where he was and why his eyes looked the way they did—at that point it would have been equal to pronouncing her own death sentence. Instead, she sat at the end of the sofa and, with the chin on her knees, cried to exhaustion. Several times that night she felt the urge to open the bedroom door, share with Dean what she learned about Dana and beg him not to judge her so harshly. The next moment she almost laughed at her own silliness, thinking that Dean might even share it with his junky friends as another interesting anecdote about the "widow." No, she'll keep Dana's confession to herself... But what about his forbidding her to visit with Dana? She panicked. He can't do it and in the next moment she surrendered again... He could do anything he wanted to. This revelation froze the blood in her veins. How did I get there? She lamented, asking herself where the love was he swore by only months ago?

The clock in the corner of my computer screen showed two o'clock in the morning. I created something, something larger than just a silly chit chat, something that I and only I can nurture and grow into a story to be shared with the world, not only *Sultan* and especially not him now that I killed our magic, now that it was trivialized with his girlfriend's involvement. Why did she call me? To buy *me* with her story, to have me sympathize with her and to leave her man alone for all those reasons? She stretched her tentacles toward me the same way she did it with *Sultan* and why was I wasting my time with her? Why did she make me cry? After all, she must have thought that she accomplished a mission and with the upcoming winter break and inevitable separation from *Sultan* she must have thought that time worked in her favor as well. In a way it did. I was going to see *Sultan* one last time tomorrow before we go on a break. Unless… And this unless was equally unpredictable as the outcome of my recent visit to his dwelling was. I didn't exactly know what I was hoping for, directing all my rabid thoughts only to him and procrastinating everything I needed to do dangerously close to the deadlines.

Why can't he be with me? I asked myself over and over again. I asked him the same question the last morning we saw each other. I asked him if we could talk. After a long hesitation he said yes. He said he was going to be at a tavern in my neighborhood around noon. While getting ready I looked through the window—the winter hit hard this year. Thick, heavy snow was accumulating fast. *It's worse than I thought*, I told myself while trying to maneuver the car on a slick, snow covered road. The restaurant was only three blocks away and a thought that I could've walked occurred to me as I was sliding on the road. However, a U-turn at the stop light to go back home, now almost at the restaurant's parking lot, appeared equally dangerous as the left- and then right turn to reach the destination. Hesitantly, I pushed the gas pedal slightly at the green light and started turning the wheel. I made a left turn successfully, but before pulling into the parking lot the car swerved and, carried by a layer of ice and snow underneath, the left rim hit the curb of the driveway while I was attempting, unsuccessfully, to contain its movement and to slide it through the driveway. The impact stopped the car. I straightened the wheel to avoid the oncoming traffic, and slowly drove to the parking spot. Without even looking at the tire, I stormed into the restaurant.

Sultan was sitting at the bar. "Come with me, I want to show you something… Something happened!" I exclaimed in a low pitch. He slowly stood up and trotted with me outside. "So, how did you do this?" he asked looking at the indented rim.

"I was trying to make a turn and the car hit the curb. Do you think that the tire is losing air?"

"No, doesn't seem like it. You got lucky, girlfriend! You are gonna be able to drive home."

"This is all I needed now…" I whispered.

"It happens," he said, adding, "Let's go inside. The snow is wet and heavy, we'll be soaked in no time."

Inside, *Sultan* kept his distance. The crease between his eyes deepened as he talked about a character strength and how he was able once to ride his Yamaha for eight hours uphill and through the thunderstorm. While concentrating his mental energy at the tips of the fingers on his right hand, clustered together in an upward moving gesture, and repeating "I did it, and that's all that mattered," the bartender, a young bearded fellow, glanced at *Sultan* as if wondering about the state of his mental health and then at me—tacitly asking what I was doing with a man on the verge of crying and gesturing as if conjuring up a spirit. In any other circumstance I would be flattered by the attention of a handsome bartender, but at present I only wanted *Sultan* to stop gesturing and talking in his half-whiny voice. I wasn't interested to hear about his accomplishments on a Yamaha in one stormy and rainy night, I wanted him to talk about us—me and him and the eternity. The bartender's occasional piercing glances would tell me, if I paid enough attention, that the *eternity* would end for *Sultan* much sooner than for me, but those unspoken reproaches were only worthy of a dismissal as trite objections of equally trite people. After all, the age discrepancy, as long as the male was older than the female, was one of those *respectable sins*. The inequality associated with it did not fit my idea of a union and *connection*, so I wouldn't consider a possibility that I might have lowered my feminist bar. And here I was facing a paradox of my own creation: while not accepting the other-woman-ness with the patience, the way Sally advised me to, the way it was conventional if I wanted my other-woman-ness and the relationship associated with it to last, I wholeheartedly accepted the rest of the package that designated me as a second-class female looking up to her desired older *lover,* though with the absence of *patronage.*

This lover, now visibly calmer and in a sort of a cathartic state of mind, was gazing at a cup of tea sitting in front of him. The face of a cat, unpredictable, cunning, came back into my thoughts. The bearded bartender now looked slightly relieved. *Sultan's* decision to leave the place came unexpectedly and right at the moment when I decided to deliver my speech to him. I blabbered incoherent parts of it while we were standing outside, interrupted by waves of snow gluing to my face and then oozing down to my chin in a weak stream and leaving an ice-cold trail that almost paralyzed my jaw and the ability to speak. "So what if everyone else thinks that we don't belong together..." A heavy snow flake hit one of my eyelashes, forcing me to close my eyes and cover them with the palms of my hands. "So what if everyone thinks that this is a fling, destined to end—it is my cross to bear and I'll bear it!" The main point of my speech, churned out in a warm interior of a tavern, was greatly misarticulated outside and I wasn't even sure if he heard all of it from the howling of the wind and the noise of the traffic, or if he even paid attention since both of our faces were slashed by the frigid and heavy snow, half-freezing and half-melting on the skin, so that after only a couple of minutes outside we both desired a warm, comforting and dry air of the indoors. *Is that it?* I frantically thought. *Is that how love and affection is gone with the wind*— I found the dramatization of the moment perfectly suitable and perfectly appropriate in my whirlwind of thoughts gathering around one rapidly emerging and almost unbearable thought: this is the end . . . if he doesn't promise that we'll stay in touch, that we'll see each other, that we'll talk and hug and touch... Yes, touch: the most unbearable of all was the future in which he wouldn't be touching me anymore.

As if reading my mind and knowing how powerful (and how poisonous) the touch could be, *Sultan* wished me a farewell without reaching out for my hand, without embracing me and without a promise of intimacy beyond a vague "We'll talk." He also added, after inspecting the damaged rim one more time, "Doesn't seem that your tire is losing air... You got lucky," he repeated. "Otherwise, it's not a big deal, I would've replaced it with a spare tire so that you can drive home. Drive safely... I better get going... This snow storm is getting worse..." *Sultan's* departure on the last day of the semester, on the day of another snow storm in one of the harshest winters remembered, left me injured in ways I could not anticipate. Even this injured car in front of me was punished for, however impossible, association with me. My faint smile froze on the almost immobile face. He departed... Will he ever hear my words again the way I wanted him to hear me, the one and only way that maintained my life support after a sudden collapse of its independent sustenance?

How did this collapse happen? Are we all destined for it if, by certain point in life, we don't make the right choice? The youth is seen as a culprit for all foolish decisions and a course of life that older and *wiser* would never take. Those older and *wiser* seem to keep forgetting that youth has the resilience to take any burden, and face the consequences of any choice that might be fatal in mature years. Older and *wiser* seem to be preoccupied with a word play in renaming what can only be experienced as fear, deterioration, and despair into *caution, stability,* and *predictability.* In my mid-twenties (and it appears that the youthful resilience starts to give in around that time—in my case at least) I used to indulge in a popular magazine where the readers could have their questions answered by a pop psychologist. Most of the time I scorned their mediocrity and lack of self-reliance, but the psychologist hung a Damocles' sword above my head one time when she responded to one of her mature female advisees. I don't remember the exact words, but the overture and the rationale of her advice imprinted in my memory admonished that at some point a youthful resilience must give way to an obsessive need for stability and control. The psychologist was telling her one-shot client that we never fully recover from a failed relationship in our mature years. What youth can shake off in a split of a second, the deepest scars set in at a later stage of life. Those failed relationships in mature years leave only desolation and despair, she said. Be careful who you choose in *those* years, she advised.

Sultan convinced me that the *right* man was a scarce good and that he possessed all the attributes to be one. That is why he was so desired. *"I understand why she wants to hang onto me..."* he said. *"She wants you because she's desperate!"* I protested. *"Life with you better than life without you?! That's bullshit!"* I expended my attempt at another kind of linguistic virtuosity, the blunt one. I called his common law wife desperate (though I couldn't tell what she was). But even as desperate, and this was devastating, she was a better choice than me. As he told me once, she was something known, something predictable, and something that wouldn't go away. And I will not be forgiven for not coming from a familiar milieu, dear to *Sultan,* and for not reaching a point at which fierceness turns into caution and fickleness into predictability. Senescence had a prophylactic effect on a mind as an affect numbing drug and I, though my clock was ticking in dissonance, was understandably far from its sway, under the effect of highs and lows of a poacher.

Youth. Celebrated and desired in a culture denying the presence and truth of death and deterioration, yet loathed and feared by a senior clique. Youth was beautiful and pleasant, yet not more appreciated than a case of bipolar disorder if not brought under the ruling thumb of seniority. If one escapes the mind numbing drug of mature years there is a steep price to pay: for all enormous highs and subsequent deepest lows. It's nothing biological I persistently thought: emotional lows are a socially constructed punishment for escaping the norms governed by a deteriorating, senior mind seeking familiarity and control. Yes, I enjoyed the same emotional (though benevolent) thrill a couple of times in my youth, but the aftereffects of those past thrills were nothing in comparison with the emptiness of my present state. If it were for the sake of proverbial self-reliance I would have defeated my current state, but as the years passed I, as everyone else, was molded in a conventional melting pot into a being inextricably tied to a web of interdependence and interactions that inevitably carried some side effects. In the process, there was just enough space and strength left to weave narratives about and strive for freedom, with its ultimate strength—independence—taken away. The remnants of human inherent independence are traceable in the youth and it was exactly that sense of independence, a conviction that I possessed independence as a human being, what guarded me in the past from a feeling of current helplessness and disempowerment.

Now in my mid-thirties, rejected by someone I named *Sultan,* a person who was, unlike me, in control, who successfully gave up the self-reliance, independence and emotional entanglements for an ultimate *life with you better than life without you,* I was disarmed by life itself and by imminent mature years, lurking to get my attention in teaching me a final lesson that there was no such thing as independence and freedom (of choice or any other). Though strengthened by the regime of a societal booth camp, able to navigate it and survive its harshness, I was much feebler as an individual, warned once again by forces beyond my control that this and every future downfall will take away more and more if I don't give up an illusion I thought each one of us was born with—that I was free, strong and independent.

However, in need of *Sultan,* in need to narrate to him and thus revive, I opposed him at the same time, his dwindling aspiration to be greater than himself, greater than the small town where he grew up and the prairie surrounding it, greater than his duties of a musty department chair and greater than a man tied to a middle-aged mother of four. *To hell with you,* my old youthful self would say, but that old self was thinking at one time that somewhere, far away, maybe in the prairie where *Sultan* came from, life was better and more meaningful. If our minuscule life could be conceived of as ever expanding, the way some conceive of the universe, life would be beautiful indeed, but I came to realize that there was nothing beyond prairie, the one where I placed *Sultan* and myself, thinking that my Maslowian quest for belonging must end here and now. Sally told me all she thought I needed to know about him; he's a phony she said, but even if I believed it what did then my affection for such a *phony* make me? I tried to suppress and redirect my feelings after witnessing his indecisiveness and sluggishness, but one line from him would reopen a magic world I created with him at its center. For now, the unsaid words would flow in that world, my expansion backward if not forward, to the original state of hope, hope for belonging and union that I so tragically attributed to *Sultan.*

XVIII

A folder secretly named "For *Sultan*" grew steadily. The more pain I thought he inflicted on me, the more dedicated I was in expanding my narrative to him. *Diana* and *Dean* shattered the invisible walls with which I surrounded myself, the walls that hitherto ended the expansion of life, even an expansion of cosmos for me. More importantly, they stretched a thin and frail *life-line* between me and him. Was there even a need for communication that could've been heard and articulated? I articulated my narrative for him, however, and it helped me enhance a sense of purpose I imagined with him, taking our human existence to heights unseen.

A relatively pleasant Indian Summer, one of the rare pleasant occurrences that year, or the previous, or perhaps even of the years to come as well, was giving way to the colder, sunless and windier days of mid-November. Diana's neighbors in the building were stacking logs, some of them alongside the wall facing the parking lot and some others on the small lawn, shaped as giant, somewhat amphoral anthills. Preparations for the winter were of no concern to Dean, as long as he could spend endless afternoons and evenings in the company of his idle buddies with a shared penchant for pot and amphetamines. Diana had a strange mixture of aversion and fear of them. She had no money to buy the firewood and the electricity, even though the electricity came back in longer intervals than during the summer months. It was still far from a reliable source of energy. Closer to the end of the year the inflation struck hard. Foreign currency, primarily German mark, was the only reliable source of monetary security and the exchange value changed by the minute. Diana received the value of the whole ten German marks for wages in November, but by the time she was going to exchange it for a stable currency it was not worth the third of its original value. Disappointed and hungry she stepped into a kiosk in an array of the small, mobile units along the passageway to the local marketplace, handed the salesclerk a bundle of worthless banknotes and received two pieces of candy in return. Outside, first turning left and right for fear that someone might notice, she gobbled both pieces of marshmallowy, chocolate covered sweets, reminding herself indifferently that she just ate her monthly wages. What about the next thirty or more days? The passersby didn't seem to have the expression of despair on their faces, which made her think that she was simply the unlucky one and there was no one to complain to.

Going back to the cold apartment set an ache in her heart, so she decided to go to the marketplace and aim endlessly between the rows of tables with various goods from the local small farmers and the black market. She almost regretted spending all of her earnings for that month on sweets, instead of buying something more nutritional. A sight of small, whitish brick wall-like structures of home-made cheese on one of the tables made her drool. A wrinkled face of an energetic woman, covered in a colorful bandana tied underneath her chin, was yelling through the dwindling crowd, "Freshly made cheese," and "Hurry up, only few left." The "few," however, could have been understood only in relative terms. If she had a hundred of those little white bricks, then yes, only a few left would be a true term. Diana suspected that the woman, in all likelihood, sold only few and wished she had the money to buy a piece. But even if she saved her monthly earnings, eaten by a raging inflation, she would have been short of a few thousands of those worthless banknotes. A certain emotional numbness overcame her: she knew very well that she would be going to bed tonight with a growling stomach and that the few remaining sellers would be going to their homes almost empty-handed, but was unable to develop any feeling she could wrap her mind around, blame anyone or anything for life that wasn't life, but slow dying. "You look awful!" Dana told her on the stairway. Was she now watching when I was coming home to waylay me the same way I did it a couple of times in the past? Diana wondered. She wasn't exactly disappointed to see Dana, but wasn't looking forward to meeting her either; she had nothing to offer her, except Dean's insults and his prohibiting her to see "that tramp." Embarrassed, she only hoped for Dana's lack of insight and lack of concern for her troubles. Nobody needed to know anything about me, she told herself. "We can hang out at my place if you wish," Dana uttered without a usual small talk introduction. "I don't know," Diana replied, but instantly bit her tongue after saying something that could have been received as the highest insult on the other end. One does not listen to another person's life story and then tries to avoid any contact with them. "I apologize," she corrected herself, "this hasn't been the best of a day for me."

"And why is that?" Dana attempted a quasi-sarcastic overtone. "Is it because the winter is coming and we don't have any firewood, or because the inflation is eating all of the money, whole friggin' ten German marks, or because a bomb could drop on the building any moment and kill us all?"

"All of the above," Diana attempted a smile. "But I feel a little better now. I'd be happy to visit with you."

Inside, Diana was surprised that Dana had a monthly supply of Pall Mall sitting on the kitchen table and a bag full of groceries, waiting to be put away.

"Let's see here, how about a can of tuna fish for dinner?" She cheerfully invited Diana to join her at the kitchen table, handing her the can of fish and an opener. "I have some relatives on the countryside," she answered an unasked question about a huge loaf of home-made bread she pulled out of the cupboard. "Not that I couldn't make it, but I simply

don't like standing in line when they distribute the monthly ratios of flower to those families of fallen soldiers… I can't stand some of those women—as if they were the only ones who had a martyr in the family! And those old men in charge of distribution! Ogling the younger widows and acting as if they were giving away their own possessions.

"*Look, maybe you should save this food for yourself,*" Diana finally said. "*I really shouldn't…*"

"*Nonsense,*" she interrupted. *You know, I am doing something that pays a little more than ten German marks. I sell cigarettes on the black market. How do you think I can have such a huge supply of cigarettes for my own self?*"

"*No idea.*"

"*See?*" She paused, *There is this owner of the gas station, the one right off the highway, ha-ha, the only one in town as we know, and he has his channels of supply and all I need to do is to resell them for a price slightly higher than what he paid for. He doesn't pay any tax on neither booze nor the cigarettes, so I don't really have to pay him an arm and a leg for a box of cigarettes. And they sell, they sell like nothing else… What's the matter? You don't look well.*"

"*I'm sorry that you had to leave so abruptly the last time…*"

"*Oh, forget about it! Tell me what's happening,*" she insisted. "*Is everything OK with you and Dean?*"

"*OK? How could it be OK? I am a prisoner in his house, but don't get me wrong, I am not trying to dramatize here. Can't help but think that I am a prisoner of my own free will. Nobody forced me to move in with him…*"

"*Nobody forced you?*" She pierced my eyes inquisitively, as if trying to pull the secret content of my mind. "*Who were you living with before you moved in with him? Relatives?*"

"*Yes,*" Diana confirmed. "*I just felt I didn't belong with them anymore,*" she confessed. "*My uncle didn't approve of my absences and Dean kept telling me that he didn't care what anyone else thought and that he was going to do whatever he pleased. I didn't know that he was capable of such a—transformation! He followed me like a dog wherever I went, waited forever in front of my aunt's house until I was ready to meet him, idolized me . . . until he was sure I wouldn't go away. And I didn't even want to be with him. I pleaded with my aunt to tell him I wasn't home when he'd show up at the door step. But you know those villagers; he was a bachelor, from a well-off family and the fact that we were both almost children did not matter. . . I am trapped, but it's all my fault. My entire damn fault!"*

"No, it's not," Dana reasoned. Maybe your relatives could've shown more good will than simply trying to foist him on you, to pimp you out to a first interested male. Of course it would make you feel unwelcome. Your reaction was as typical and as expected as waking up in the morning. There was no way back. Even if you complied with your uncle's wishes Dean would have found a reason to prove that he was in control. And once again, everything would be your own fault. You wanted to protect yourself, not to expose your vulnerability and your relatives didn't support you. Dean knew that; it was your vulnerability that he has mistaken for love, something he could control, not the good intentions. And what does he know about good intentions anyway? A spoiled brat like him? You know what: I also heard that one of his companions raped some girl…"

"I know. They actually talked about it as if it was some kind of an anecdote, a joke."

"Like they are telling jokes about widows… I heard about it the same way you did: as an anecdote, not without a moral-of-the-story lesson to all women who dare to think they have the same liberties as men. It's all about power and control. You think I don't know that every time I…" She stopped.

"Dean's mother said . . . sorry…" Diana remembered that the remark she heard and was about to blurt out could offend Dana.

"What? She said what?"

"Nothing... I wasn't thinking."

"Thinking what? That I might feel offended? I'm beyond feeling offended. I am numb to insults and offenses. Anyway, she must have mentioned something about why women like me live the way they do . . . Yes?" Diana nodded in agreement.

"Funny thing is that those simpletons give us more credit than we deserve."

"How so?" Diana gaped at her.

"First of all, they think it's a matter of choice, a vengeance, something that would make us feel better about ourselves and the world. I say, pardon, I know it's not a matter of choice. There is no such thing as a choice. Those of us floating higher above the water are creating all kinds of illusions and telltales, but those in an imminent danger of drowning know it's all bogus. Eventually, our circumstances may become more favorable and we may be given some more opportunities in life, but meanwhile it's all just a battle for survival in an extremely hostile environment."

"But if there is no choice, why are we not running around with the guns or doing drugs, or plundering abandoned homes?"

"Because the opportunity was not created for us to do so. Society is a strange and dangerous mechanism. You think that those "righteous," "civilized" people had no impact on what is going on here. We are all conditioned by our environment, smaller and larger, and our "choices" are tailored over time to resemble some kind of "free will." And if we knew who's pulling the strings the whole illusion would dissipate as the soap suds, but we don't. And it's OK that you don't take me seriously, or that my words don't provide comfort to you because they are not supposed to. We can't make each other feel better, though we can try. I can't do anything in your situation with Dean…" She chuckled, "But you can get the taste of my world tomorrow evening when I am going to pick up the merchandize," she gave Diana a meaningful look *before continuing, "We are going to the gas station. Some local war lords might be there. Don't you find it exciting? That gas station is the heart of our community right now."*

"Depends. In which way is seeing a war lord supposed to interest me?"

"Well, you'll realize that they are not gods walking on the earth as some might think."

"I know they are not gods—they die—some of them at least."

"Everyone dies . . . but should we say in a less dramatic way. What I am trying to say is," she paused looking for the right words, "You can forget about that feeling of absolute powerlessness and subordination as soon as you hear them open their mouths; they are dummies, Diana! But try not to cross them, OK?" They laughed for the first time that day.

"Are you afraid that some of those people might harm you?"

"How? I have nothing to lose, nothing to gain. I am not opposing anyone or anything. And if my survival skills don't work out for me, then I'll die. Hopefully fast. Tell your bachelor you will be visiting a coworker or something."

Diana could not foresee what kinds of consequences her lie could produce, that is, if Dean ever found out where she was going. This. . . .adventure with Dana could bring some action in her life of home captivity. Her life wasn't completely uneventful; she feared starvation and physical abuse, but thinking of those things wouldn't send an adrenaline rush into her bloodstream. At times, after overhearing his conversation with his mother over the phone, she wondered where and when Dean was eating. His mother must have asked him what he'd bought for the money she gave him since he replied in his usual annoyed way when talking to her, "Yes, I bought what you told me, why do you keep checking on me?" Whatever she told him to buy did not end up in the fridge, *now that the electricity was back more often. It was a matter of time when Dean's mother would grow suspicious again, Diana thought. He asked her for the money more and more frequently and recently none of it was spent on groceries. He must've been going to eat to his mother's place she concluded since he stopped going to the market and grocery stores with Diana. He needed money for something else…*

"Let's walk to the gas station," Dana suggested. "It's only a couple of miles."

"That's fine with me," Diana replied, though not in complete compliance. She tried to put on a cheerful face, as if they were going out to a café or a restaurant. It just occurred to her that none of the restaurants were in business for almost two years. While rushing through the streets for a couple of minutes, Diana broke the silence, "You know, it's strange how the atmosphere of the war and devastation settles in your soul, even when there are no visible, tangible reminders that we are living in a war zone."

"What, you don't call these rubbles we are passing by a 'tangible' reminder?" Dana chuckled.

"No, I meant that even when you are home, or at work, doing some ordinary task one would do in a peaceful time—which seems to have existed eons ago. There wasn't a single explosion, except for that deranged soldier who blew a barrelhouse with a bomb a couple of months ago…" Diana smiled.

"Oh, I've heard about that. And why exactly did he do that?"

"My aunt said it was because the owner gave him a hard time; he was already buzzed and kept provoking him, so the owner decided not to serve him schnapps that evening."

"See, one good thing comes out of wartime: if somebody gives you a hard time you can always get back at them by blowing their house. That psycho was a soldier, 'defending our homeland', nobody's gonna go after him…"

"How do you get back at someone if you don't have a bomb, or if you're not a soldier?"

"Then you have to know your place," Dana replied. *"Even if you're violated, even if you'd witnessed horrible things... These locals here attribute it simply to luck or lack thereof. If you're lucky to have lived at the right place when the ethnic division started you have nothing to complain about. Otherwise, it's your fault. Hey, we're already on the corridor. Only a mile or so to the gas station!"*

"Then I suppose these people living around the corridor are the lucky ones."

"Yes. Our entire state depends on this road. The corridor is its artery. Immensely more important than a village called Kravice (little cows). Why would anyone call a village 'Little Cows'?"

"Is that where you come from?" Diana asked.

"It was one of those godforsaken neighboring places in the hills, close to a borderline, river Drina. I mean, the new borderline... On Christmas morning a group of paramilitary savages rampaged the village, slaughtering everything that was moving in it."

"I didn't know . . . that." Diana stuttered. *"Why doesn't anyone talk about it?"*

"Because it's an unpopular truth. It happened to the villagers of a stigmatized ethnicity. You can't change the logic of a war that has been pre-made for us. Those counter-narratives have to be treated as glitches that nobody would and should care about—in a grand scheme of events..." At that point Dana sounded learned, intellectual, almost powerful, greater-than-life older sister. Diana looked at her in awe, wondering somewhere in the recesses of her mind about misfortunes that force that same mind to relinquish her dignity.

"And they were the members of a nation accused of all evils in the war," Dana continued. *You see now how that complicates daily news and possible generalizations and*

good-guys-bad-guys pop-narratives. On the other hand the mentality, the mindset of these locals here says it all: those who don't fit in the grand-narrative were the unlucky ones—or the guilty ones for not fighting back. But for God's sake not everyone was in the situation to fight back! What do they even mean by that?! The war is not a game, it takes strategic planning and an army of trained soldiers. Those places where innocent civilians were killed were written off from the start. You can't just live on the 'corridor' and despise the unfortunates who died since they didn't live on such a strategically important place. And that's the thing about the war: if you die, it's your fault. One needs to be born lucky, not born with rights that can be taken away any moment."

"Now that you mentioned it: I feel inadequate so often here for no other reason but simply for not having the same luck as some other people surrounding me. They make you believe that this war situation is something that should concern only people like you and me, but they, they are just fine. And you know what, I think that can't be true. It's not the apathy, though apathy is part of it, but it must be something much more. There must be some deep embarrassment that everyone feels, an embarrassment that life in general has deteriorated so much and that there is nothing anyone can do about it, or give to one another."

"Deteriorated? Are we in a good mood today?" Dana was trying her sarcasm again. "It's much worse. What we read in a censored book a few years back became reality. An entire village slaughtered on a Christmas morning!? Only two years ago we believed in such a possibility as much as we believed in fairies. I left my house in a trunk of a car. We had to pay a hundred German marks per person and those people," she faintly smiled reminiscing, "Those people that took us through the check point in two different cars were nothing but war profiteers, and yet I can't think of them as anything less than saviors. If there were more of those and less sadists, those people that were slaughtered . . . and raped could still

be living. And who says that human life is priceless? The price ranges anywhere from a hundred to a couple of thousand marks. If you are young, a girl and relatively undamaged... Even when this is over human trade will not stop here. It's just started."

"How do you mean?"

"I've seen enough. Almost every village has a brothel house. And it aren't the local girls—it's the ones from farther east that are being traded. And why do you think no one is making a big fuss about that? It's another one of those unpopular truths, or fortune versus misfortune! In either case, there is no need to discuss it."

They both fell silent for the remainder of the trip. Neither one of them felt a need to say anything more. The silence of their surrounding was only broken when a rare car would ramble by. Diana was trying to decide if it was the silence or the sound of an occasional car that created something unhealthy, something unnatural in the atmosphere. A couple of those cars were pushing the horns as they passed by, which set a feeling of uneasiness and discomfort in Diana. Dana was acting as if nothing bothered her.

"Seems like M. and his buddies are here. You heard about him? Who didn't—he's a local hero. Let's sit over here..." The gas station was like an oasis; everything was there, from an improvised warehouse for the black market merchandize, to a café-restaurant. Dana said they would talk to the owner once the place clears up.

"I know M.," Diana whispered. "I've seen him with the newspaper editor on a couple of occasions. I only remember the office gossip that he had a couple of mistresses," Diana scoffed. "My former coworkers used to say that he'd take his wife out and both of his mistresses would be at the same place and at the same time. Not that he cared . . . In war and love everything is allowed. Who said that?"

"I don't know, but I sure know it's true."

Some uniforms approached Dana and she indulged in a chat with them, interrupted occasionally by loud voices coming from the bar. At first the uniforms glanced at Diana occasionally, and the longer they stayed in Dana's company the more liberty they took in fixating on Diana, ogling her from head to toe. She couldn't believe they found her attractive; she didn't find herself attractive anymore. Dana didn't find it necessary to introduce her to her interlocutors. Someone in M's group at the bar slammed the fist against the counter and the gas station owner, in a role of a bartender that night, recoiled at the unexpected turn of an already overly energetic conversation. He seemed overly alert and not quite at ease since they first saw him and the new developments justified his attitude. No one could tell what exactly was going on at the bar, but it alarmed the group of soldiers in Dana's company to act. All of a sudden, the uniforms talking to her literally lifted both girls from their seats and pushed them into a small corridor toward, what appeared as, a storage room. "I don't think you'll get your merchandize tonight, Dana," one of them hissed at her. "And what the fuck is she doing here?" he pointed at Diana. In a whirlwind of the succession of seemingly disconnected events, Diana managed to articulate an unspoken question, 'How did I transform into persona non grata in one minute?' There wasn't time for her to think further—the soldiers were pushing them through the corridor with a force of a tornado.

"Open that door!" One of them ordered Dana at the same moment she hit the door with the shoulder and lost balance. Not waiting for her to recuperate, he pushed Diana out of the way and opened the metal door into a dark storage area that smelled like moth balls and gun powder. Another one of the soldiers pushed both of them through the opening and they stumbled across a box sitting on the floor. "Up, up!" The uniforms now barked in unison and as if beside themselves from panic. Then the deafening sound of a shot coming from the bar stopped the time for a moment and *paralyzed their motions. It only lasted a split of a second, but to Diana it seemed as if her entire life unfolded in front of her eyes—as they say happens right before death. She thought this must have been it, the death.*

Someone was ordering them to get up and move or else some of those bullets might be waiting for them. They stood up and tried to move along the soldiers' steps, the vertigo and nausea pulling them dangerously close to the ground again and again. Another door opened, the back door to the building leading to a small paved driveway, an opening to many backdoor transactions of the war lords. One of those transactions seemed to have been closed only moments ago.

"You saw nothing here; in fact you were not here!" the tall dark haired uniform instructed Dana, placing his heavy-looking arm dangerously tight around her neck. He didn't have to repeat the same to her companion: his momentous diverting the attention from one to another and ominous look he now placed on Diana did it for him. Diana felt some strange contractions in her stomach. "Don't go back to the main road," he added after a short pause and before disappearing, along with his companions, into the darkness of the building.

"Run with me and don't look back," Dana quickly whispered while rapidly moving toward the barbed wire fence that was dividing the property of the gas station and the adjacent field. She grabbed the wire between the spikes and lifted it in an attempt to create a bow large enough for Diana to slide through. "Watch your hair," she warned her once Diana was halfway through. They took turns in helping each other through the fence and once on the field they started running in a direction leading to a cluster of suburban houses, or what was left of them. For a couple of long minutes they could only hear their accelerated and laborious breathing and rustling of the stiff grass stubble. The injured and hollow walls of the once houses gaped at them once they had gotten

closer, no less threatening and hostile than the gas station they left behind. Another barbed wire fence.

"Let's see if we can go around it," Dana suggested. It's rather dark already and it doesn't seem that anyone is coming after us," she added.

"Dana, I'm afraid of wandering around this neighborhood, especially getting close to any of these once houses. Don't you think that there might be some inactivated explosives?"

"Don't worry. We'll stay away from those backyards as much as possible: once we are on the roads it won't be as dangerous. You know, we have to get away from this open space—we might still draw attention. Not that we wouldn't draw attention of a possible patrol in a spooky neighborhood, but we could pretend that we were just using a shortcut from the train station. Here, the fence is broken here. Let's go in between these two houses."

They finally broke on the remains of a gravel driveway, watching each step through a frostbitten weed as if walking on the eggshells. They followed the driveway to the neighborhood's main street, deserted and mottled with the dark imprints of the grenades.

"These have been activated, no need to watch your steps now," Dana attempted her black humor.

"I'm not . . . I just need to . . . rest for a moment," Diana cried while holding her knees and still out of breath.

"What can I say? Se la vie, or death, depending on the perspective."

"I didn't know this city was destroyed this much," Diana straightened laboriously while looking around at the rubble.

"Well, different armies took turns in taking it over… Look, I didn't know any of this would happen… Otherwise, I wouldn't have taken you with me. I just thought that, maybe, you could start earning the real money… You are working for nothing and nobody is taking care of you."

"But what do you think will happen now? Will you be able to go back and face whoever is alive at that place? What if they killed the gas station owner? Who is going to be your supplier? What if they. . . .don't want any witnesses?" As soon as Diana uttered the question hovering over their heads since they were extruded through the back door, they both stopped.

"I can't think that far right now," Dana retorted indifferently.

"Is it like you are getting used to whatever happens, without much fuss or any desire to change it?"

"Something like that," she said and continued, "On the flip side, if staying alive is a sign of luck then we are the lucky ones over and over again."

"Will you be talking to any of those . . . people that escorted us out of the building?" Now Diana was trying to sound humorous.

"Possibly, but only if they visit with me, though I'm not sure if I'm looking forward to their visit. We need to know what exactly happened—people on the market will talk I'm sure. I still have some of my supplies left: that's it!" She exclaimed, excited for no apparent reason. "I'll go to my usual spot on the market and listen to what others are talking about. Bad news travel fast."

They continued meandering through the streets of the devastated neighborhood until reaching one of the side roads leading to the city center. Dana made a request that first occurred to her companion—to part ways before reaching their building easier. A heavy, inexplicable guilt set in Diana's heart, as they made the rest of the trip to their building as if not knowing each other. It was almost an unnecessary precaution since the street lamps were shut down and there were no passersby in sight.

XIX

"**M**ost societies think they operate by something called morality, but they are wrong. They operate by something called law." Oh, how avidly I devoured anything, regardless where it came from—TV, literature, school, that carried a hint of an attempt to explain life and actions of humans. A seasoned professor of law, greater than life (and everyone who used words in such a virtuous manner would be greater than life on my scale of human values) and embodied by equally so Al Pacino, made this statement in front of a group of select students in Germany. I ached *Sultan's* presence, I ached to share with him that I just watched a good movie, "The Reader," and was dying to share my impressions with him. That one time at my place, when he was holding a Bible in Gothic script that belonged to one of his ancestors, he told me he was proud to be German. He said it to me on more than one occasion. Was there a need for such a declaration? Weren't we beyond national and nationalistic sentiments?

My defense of small nations resisting a post-modern colonization in service of the new world order, as I was trying to explicate in a paper for one of my graduate classes, had nothing to do with the pride, but with the small nations' elementary right to remain who they are, to keep their dignity and still receive their share of wealth and wellbeing. Globalization should certainly not entail imposing some kind of a global identity which, even if imposed, would not be a *neutral* identity of a computer technician, the kind we hear every time we call a customer service located somewhere on the other end of the globe. This new identity would be imposed top-down and I thought I knew something about it. "Blame the Lutherans," as the young Hmong girl said to Clint Eastwood in "Gran Torino." True, churches are the main sponsors of immigration and to say that they are only doing it to help the government would not be a whole truth. Churches have their own agenda, but sometimes their congregations and leadership are in a gray area of what kind of liberties they can take in imposing their religion on immigrants they sponsor.

On a global scheme, scattered around the world, some small nations are suffocating under an increasing pressure and the burden to give up the laws they lived by, to fall apart and blend into a sea of the new nameless and once again enslaved populations. An intellectual would defend their inalienable *moral* right to remain who they are, but those moral rights are awfully inconvenient for this rapidly changing world. The issue of small nations, of diversity, of whether they are entitled to preserve their way of life and identity is not all black and white and every time when I'd like to side with either of these extremes, I question my choices. The one most commonly brought up dilemma, the one I struggle with the most—is if the different groups should preserve their customs and traditions even if they violate the gender equality or any other set of rights, commonly accepted as basic human rights. Advocates for human rights forget in their righteousness that imposing those rights by a military intervention, that is top-down, has little to no effect and makes one question the very motivation for a pre-emptive war. As those scholars of ethics usually state, those values have to be taken as one's own and even then it's not always easy. Until now, "the greatest impediments to the credibility of the defense of universal human rights have been the double standards in policies applied by the most powerful countries in the international community."[8]

In any case, the world needs laws and, as the said seasoned professor of law so glamorously stated, "the laws at the time." The question of private and public wars all over the world is not a question if they are moral, but if they are legal. And here is where some of us stumble and fall. Who decides whether it's legal? Working at Auschwitz, I thought of the professor again, was not illegal according to the laws at the time and between an intent to murder and simply working there the line was conveniently drawn to

---

[8] Caterina García Segura, Rethinking world society and cosmopolitanism in international relations. Theoretical approaches and political models. *European Standing Group of International Relations, Paper Archive, 2010.*

separate ordinary, law abiding citizens from war crimes. The stigma and guilt even of those "ordinary citizens," however, lingered for a while—until they were able to recuperate and until a number of their descendants started to deny that any of the crimes ever happened. One would think that truth can never change, but truth is not in symbiosis with ethics and morality; truth is in symbiosis with the law—and power.

The more complex and multifaceted the law becomes, the more intense the power struggle for simplified and generalized truth is. The arch enemy of those convenient, cosmopolitan truths are the uninvestigated, unannounced, unpopular truths held by disenfranchised and disempowered yet outspoken peoples. A *cosmopolitan* would not dig into those unpopular truths and would not announce that something declared "evil" or "true" by powerful fabricators of so much needed simple truths and desperately wanted bad guys, might not be so. Thousands of silent voices swarm in my head, some in a form of obscure movie characters, and some the voices of the very oppressed I have personally heard narrating their unheard stories. When the professor started telling about the law, a student asked, "But isn't that . . . narrow?" to which he replied, "Oh yes, the law is narrow." The student protested: "I don't know what we are doing here anymore. You tell us to think like lawyers, but there is something . . . disgusting about this… Six women locked 300 Jews in the church and let them burn. What is there to understand?! Then you choose 6 women. You put them on trial, you say, they were the evil ones, they were the guilty ones. Because one of the victims happened to have written a book… Do you know how many camps there were in Europe?"

I would like to join him and ask: Does anyone care to know what was happening in Europe at the end of the 20th century, beyond what the convenient, *general* truth holds? Does anyone know how many camps and mass graves there were in Europe at the end of the 20th century? Has anyone heard of the village Little Cows? Only because the laws of a state were violently invalidated and the open season for another human slaughterhouse announced. How were the victims really victims if they were supplied with ammunition and were able to organize, shoot, torture, incarcerate, rape and victimize the same ones they claimed victimized them? And the

Holocaust and its victims abused over and over again, by comparing the victims who also victimized with the victims of the Holocaust. But *truth* works in mysterious ways—or are those ways mysterious anymore? It's about power and control, not the truth. The "glory" of the truth is taking us on a virtual trip to the time of Charlemagne—I conquered, therefore I own the truth.

While conquering territories and drawing the demarcation lines between the nation-states is now viewed as a reactionary move of dying nationalists, the foray that matters has to do with the conquering that takes place in a parallel, cyber world, world of information. It is a stratified process, however, and one could say that anyone with enough brains and sufficient needs could cut into a cake of virtual world's wealth. The highly structured domination over cyber space, justified by globalization, is "legal," whereas others mischievous, small-thief scale intrusions, are not. On a small-thief scale a computer-savvy outlaw in Africa, with a laptop, can rob a bank account of a working class American. They don't need to risk their lives in an armed struggle with the police when they can do it from their own village thousands miles away. While some of those cyber thieves are as honorable as Robin Hood by taking from the rich and giving to the poor, others simply take from the poor and make themselves rich, or survive, whichever is greater.

I was thinking globally—as the advertisements for "success" promoted. However, this thinking global did not bring a sense of empowerment in navigating a changing world; it made me sick. Part of the reason I could also attribute to procrastinating the work on the final papers and not having a valid excuse. Faults of the new world order? Broken life line with *Sultan?* Broken car? Of all real or imagined problems I created, the one that received the least attention from me was validated by one of my professors. Frazzled, almost deranged I showed up at the professor's office door and asked her for a two day extension to turn in the final paper. How was I supposed to finish it now that my attention was dangerously divided between the indent in my car's rim and, what I dramatically named, an indent in my soul without *Sultan* in my life. As I dramatized, he was murdering me and my voice since I thought he didn't find me amusing anymore. A possibility of other explanations did not emerge at the time—a possibility that he would spare my life on account of my narratives and that he, who was my creation after all and not completely imposed on me (a characteristic that granted the primordial Scheherazade the beauty of her fatalistic vulnerability) would not only spare my life, but set me free. The shrill sound of the phone interrupted my silent speculations, "Hey, are you still alive?" Sally was hollering on the other end. "What the fuck are you doing?" she scolded someone before I managed to say, "Yes, I am alive. And what are you doing?"

"Oh, not much. Playing poker... I am on the roll tonight. How about you?"

"I don't know. Busy. Can you talk?"

"Not really; just wanted to see how you were doing. You haven't called for a couple of days."

"Seems like we're both busy. Let's get together when I finish my final paper. I'm kind of late... Next week sometime? My place? Then we can do lunch."

"Sure. Later." Then she added, "Don't wanna ask, but can't resist..."

"Don't ask," I interrupted.

Sultan and no one and nothing else were feeding my relationship with Sally for the past months. Now, she wasn't part of the *conspiracy* anymore since I have completed my *mission* without her knowledge and without her approval. My other missions were also completed: the final paper turned out much longer than intended, but I was satisfied. The new interim between a fall and spring semester, as many others in the past, started out with a slight panicky concern of how I was going to spend the time not filled with mandatory readings, discussions, papers, even though I anticipated (as always) to have established my leisure time routine after a week or less. The first days of not having to do much mental work were the hardest and during those first days Alexandra was still in school. I arranged to meet with Sally on a day when she had the afternoon off. In the weeks of extraordinary stress, but also in the first days of unduly worries over not having enough stress, namely in the first couple of days of my winter- or summer break I would envy the cashiers at Wal-Mart and various grocery and convenient stores, but this time I expanded the list to certified nursing assistants, including Sally, thinking that they all must've had care-free, steady lives without much turmoil as mine. If a doctor from Mexico is able to come to terms with the life of a taxi driver, or a pharmacist with the life of a nursing assistant, what higher purpose was I striving for?

I looked through the glass door overlooking a guest parking lot. Rare automobiles were parked on a few spots, some of them covered with a thick snow-blanket. Beside a regular movement of a workforce, a few people would visit with each other on a day like this. A gloomy day and its gray light greeted me on a creaky deck, followed by Sally's cheerful "hello" soon after. "Stay there," she ordered after probing the entrance door and attesting it wasn't completely closed, "I need a smoke." Her insatiable need to smoke, as if her physical survival depended on it, made me desire a cigarette once in a while, against my decision to uproot the habit completely.

"You are a bad influence," I told her, trying to snatch a cigarette she already lit.

"No, you can't have mine," she swiftly motioned away from my hand. "Smoke another one."

"No, that's not in accord with my . . . new year's resolution! Not to smoke, not even occasionally—zero nicotine by the end of the next year."

"But smoking my cigarette, that you can do. Cheater!"

"Maybe it's because I wanna be like you... Sally, sometimes I envy you."

"What? I need to sit down for this—let's go inside!" She extinguished her half-smoked cigarette in a thin layer of snow by the wooden railing, busying around it as if she were roasting a marshmallow and then, following my previously set directives, threw it in a flower pot filled with a nub of frozen dirt, dead plant and a dozen of other cigarette butts that I forgot to pick up and throw away.

"Brrr, it's cold outside! Freaking winter: I never liked it and I never will. Can't wait for spring. Anyway, what were you saying, you envy me? She pronounced the words "envy me" with a few octaves higher pitch, possibly to scare me away from such thinking. Then she added, "You should, I am on a winning streak with my poker buddies. You brought me luck the other night when I called you."

"Good to know. As long as I can make someone happy… Oh, forget it. This will prompt me to speak of . . . you know who." I suddenly laughed at the thought of an expression I could apply to *Sultan*—the one we don't speak of. "*Those we don't speak of.* Remember the 'Village'? Now he's the one we don't speak of," I said aloud, amused.

"Ha-ha, to what does he owe his new status?"

"To my imagination of course."

"He owes much to your imagination, all kinds of ascribed endowments, from spiritual to . . . well, physical."

"No, I never bragged about his physical endowments, that wasn't important… Sally, I can't talk about him right now… Maybe it's the time that I . . . let go."

"Just like that? Without a fight?"

"It is not exactly without a fight…"

"But if you really care for him, you shouldn't give up so easily. What have I told you: patience is how you need to play…" She thought for a second, "Did you do something else—foolish?"

"No," I said. This was a semi lie and only in case if what I did and was doing was really foolish, but who was to decide? "Our conversations should not always center on him: there is so much more to talk about. You, for example. How did all the drama in your life go?"

"Which drama? Marriage? You know about that."

"I don't mean your marriage. You seem to have, how should I say this . . . come to terms with your new life. That's why I said I envied you."

"You're joking, right?" she looked at me incredulously. "What makes you think that?"

"Well, you never question anything, you seem to be fine with . . . where you are and who you are… Of course, this is my impression and it might not be so, but . . . if I am so much wrong that's because I don't know you so well. I expect this . . . linguistic virtuosity from everyone I talk to and not everyone is able or willing to spill their beans in front of me . . . as we know…"

"We can talk about *my* drama. It would be just a variation on the theme, but…"

"It's the variation that creates the difference."

"OK, after the *Storm,* you know what I mean by *Storm,* right?"

"Yes, the Croatian military offensive that technically ethnically cleansed the country in 1995. . . ."

"Yes, we had to escape along with hundreds of thousands of others and look for a refuge in our *motherland*. You know that, by motherland, I don't really mean to praise the land that gave us the food and shelter?" She continued without waiting for me to respond. "There is nothing glorious in being a refugee as you know. Everyone is sick of you after a while, or maybe even from the very beginning…"

"There is a certain glory, a biblical right to dignity as a refugee, a persecuted one if you wish… At least I see it as such, not because it's biblical, but because of the words that give the exiles a sense of importance, a *mission,* as in Matthew 5:10—I looked it up—Blessed are those who are persecuted because of righteousness, for theirs is the kingdom of heaven." Sally started laughing at my last words.

"Why are you laughing? I didn't make this up and I can't pick and choose where I will find the beauty and creativity. And you can't deny the beauty and the purpose in the "persecuted because of righteousness!"

"No, I can't!" She interjected in-between the laughter. "Didn't you say that *you are the salt of the earth*?"

"Oh, that. Well, we don't take such words as the absolute truth, but as the inspiration. Why wouldn't I be able to interpret it the way I want?"

"Because the earth is over-salted for my taste."

"Over-salted? Well, hm, . . .that's creative too…I trusted that my outlook on the world could be appreciated for who I was personally, not taken together with what group I belong to. Especially if your belonging to a group is used to invalidate you and your position."

"But you can fight back—as I always do. I am what you call a nationalist, always was and always will be."

"I thought I was a cosmopolitan . . . a citizen of the world, but that was equally naïve as your standing for some ideals impossible to defend. I could now laugh at my idea of a citizen of the world. How many of us would like to be the citizens of the world, but need visas to even step foot into a neighboring country? How could I have known in my childish naiveté that cosmopolitanism either assumes social action or elitist snobbery—neither one suitable to a person without an elementary freedom of movement. By the way, who do you think would publicly support your nationalism?"

"No one has to support it publicly, it is my private right to feel what I feel."

"I'd defend a nation's right to preserve the language and cultural treasure, or a cultural sovereignty since I think it's something beyond banal politicizing. Language is always a servant of ideology, but its real importance is in preserving our biological survival..."

I was careful not to mention the name Skutnabb-Kangas, the name that would only make her raise her eyebrows, but as that particular name popped in my memory another vivid recollection found its way to remind me of my *never-ending conversation* with *Sultan.* We played with the words and the names of various linguistic and other, to us, known personalities as naturally and as easily as one gossips about the notorious celebrities, and the more exotic the name we used the more enticing our conversation was. I had *his* attention, not his scoff, after showing him an article explaining why linguistic diversity is important. He was curious about Scutnabb-Kangas; *Sultan,* a middle-aged tenured faculty with a master's degree who did not have to study past Cummins and his linguistic theories. I appeared to transmit a knowledge beyond cognitive linguistic, a field where he left off in his remote studies, interdisciplinary, international and . . . *cosmopolitan* knowledge! I contrasted once in *Sultan's* office my altruistic cosmopolitan aspirations to those *narrow, tribal, nationalistic* and *empty* slogans and, while listening to Sally, nostalgically remembered our past conversations. Skutnabb-Kangas revealed the truths I had to pass onto him since he was the only one there to receive them, to understand them:

> *"Linguistic and cultural diversity are the storehouse of historically developed knowledge; linguistic and cultural diversity are connected to biodiversity." "Interesting," he responded. "I never heard of Skutnabb-Kangas. . . . I'd never think of the correlations she draws . . . Hm..." "Linguistic and cultural diversity on the one hand and the biodiversity on the other hand are correlated—where one type is high the other one is usually too. . . . the two types of diversity seem to mutually enforce and support each other..." "Now that I think about it, it makes sense... My students would*

sometimes embark on the discussions about words they could never identify in English and I couldn't help them because I couldn't find the meaning either... She quotes someone here . . . says that indigenous and minority communities are, 'reservoirs of considerable knowledge about rare, threatened and endemic species that has not to date been independently accumulated by Western-trained conservation biologists'..." Then we both agreed with her that the "strongest and most stable ecosystems are those which are the most diverse," and that "uniformity can endanger a species." "Read the last sentence," I urged him and we both leaned over the last page as worshippers would over a holy scripture, pronouncing, to us sacred words, "The future belongs to multilinguals." Our bond was never stronger, never more beyond the ordinary, never richer.

In an ordinary world I was classified into a certain group, whose real, partially known, invented or imaginary *qualities* Sally tried to defend to herself and the others.

"You see, I don't have a philosophical perspective on how I see things, but certain comments will elicit responses from me by which everyone will know who I am and what I stand for."

"I am not saying that certain comments would not provoke me to react the same way... We are entangled into a web of relations we were placed into and any intentional disentanglement smacks of betrayal. We cannot accept the extraction of inextricable and are willing to pay for the sins of everyone knotted onto our net. Some of us do it without any justifications and some of us create these elaborate, glorified accounts of the past... But sometimes I am tired of all intellectual hodgepodge only to steal some living space for myself, where I can feel at ease and in harmony with others. Harmony is a big lie: look at our surrounding! In a state of collective dementia yesterday's culprits are organizing a witch hunt on today's offenders. And with each consecutive hunt the accounts of the past are more diminished and distorted. Sally, my burden . . . the waste I have accumulated and am carrying around has become so heavy that I . . . I don't want to filter my words through an intellectual hodgepodge anymore… I want to scream at the top of my lungs "you imbeciles!" at a talking heads on TV . . . for only to me known reasons…"

"Imbecile, asshole, whatever, but doesn't an . . . imbecile like that push you to defend who you are? Especially if we know that all about us personally and our past experiences screams victim, not a perpetrator? Or is it a matter of perspective"

"It is more and more evident that the more we try to distinguish between good and evil the more we become a blend of the two. Today's *Dark Age* is not different than the Dark Ages of the crusades, reincarnation of Barbarossa—I mean . . . Hitler's *Barbarossa* . . . Our memory of being victimized and a global dementia about events that call for the reinventing of history, along with my wish to join the dementia create an ever-growing sense of powerlessness that I don't know how to overcome… Entangled in the national ties was never how I saw myself…There is something utterly insincere about how we are lured to root for *ours* and even more insincere when called to *embrace* or *accept* others. You know, many are now rediscovering . . . Karl Marx . . . remember Karl Marx?"

"Yees," she nodded slowly and mocking suspense."

"The nations are not something eternal. I wrote this paper. . . about our country… I think its disintegration in the present historical moment had an ideological purpose, but also in a larger perspective, in light of the claims that nations had their beginning and will have their end, such disintegration, only to create a number of mini nation-states, was premature and reactionary. What role do newly created mini-nation-states have in a global world?"

"Pawns? Drug trafficking oases?"

"Well, yes… Although none of the political moguls would ever admit they supported and acknowledged the independence of a small nation-state because of its strategic importance in drug and human trafficking."

"No, but knowing how flawed, how criminal some of the moves of the global powers are . . . inspires me to hold onto my . . . flawed or not . . . convictions."

"If it were only so simple . . . I almost think that I lost the battle for my convictions. Remember Max from Andric's "Letter from 1920"? He leaves, as we left, but will carry a memory of the place he leaves as one long, terminal illness. The narrator asks him why he leaves and he says the cause of everything could be brought down to one word: hatred."

"I almost agree with you… But you are the only one who can make it simple or complicated, aren't you?"

I could not add anything meaningful to Sally's last remark; she respected my wish to not sift through my latest emotional affliction, but managed to remind me of the . . . *source,* yes, source—either of all affliction, or the one she was aware of. We couldn't agree about how we needed to cope with various afflictions, ranging from what we experienced as hostility and betrayal, to other-woman-ness. I was running away from my present, into the past that Sally could relate to if she wanted to. We both could have rediscovered the past in the stories—long before they came true. I looked at the final draft of the paper I wrote, thinking that there was so much more to add. I didn't write an homage to the country that there isn't anymore, accusing "foreign elements" and transnationals of "657 terrorist actions" in which "82 individuals were killed and 186 injured." That was more terrorism than any country populated by 22 million people could handle in less than half a century. I was raising a question of justifiability of violent and organized criminal actions against a sovereign land. Cosmopolitanism and *withering away of the state* are conceived on the foundations of old, never-ending hostilities and primal nationalisms, a backward process mistakenly interpreted as a *painful transition* from one mindset into another, an unfortunate interpretation that dangerously undermines the momentum of feelings any rhetoric appealing to one's sense of belonging produces. Even if nationalisms of *backward people* were going to be tamed, whose cosmopolitanism are we going to embrace? Anthony Smith[9] says, "Too often, the examples of global culture which are chosen to illustrate its growth turn out to owe their origins and much of their appeal to the power and prestige of one or the other of great metropolitan power centers and cultures of the contemporary world." He calls these cultural centers the new "cultural empires of modernity." How is then ideal of cosmopolitanism not subverted, as Smith suggests, "by the realities of power politics and by the nature and features of culture." In other words,

---

[9] Anthony Smith, *Nations and Nationalism in a Global Era.* Polity Press, 1995.

are these new cultural or cosmopolitan empires truly restorative to our wounded humanity, and if so where lies their healing power?

"Tell your story, because if you don't the others will tell it for you. Remember this? Have you read Mark Twain?" I admitted to this professor emerita standing in front of me, and whom I congratulated on an excellent panel about the civil rights movement, that I haven't read much of Mark Twain. The wisdom of Mark Twain or charisma of a seasoned professor at a conference a couple of years ago conjured this admonition hovering over me once Sally left and I tried to stay occupied with the final touchups in my article. I spent another hour debating the feasibility of unmasking of, what I saw as superficiality of one of Andrić's scholars, evoking Andrić's impeccable premonition and sophisticated insight into the nature of things others thought they knew. *Hmm, but would this be, is this necessary? This. . . Mary Kaldor, I could write another article about her ivory tower research!* Finally, I ended the debate with myself and decided that Andrić would inevitably *romanticize* an academic paper, but could not shake off the resentment over *others' telling my story for me* and their (re)defining the place I came from, the place where they saw cosmopolitanism and I saw hatred, more than anywhere else. Kaldor[10] says, "What makes Sarajevo, for example, such a vibrant place is precisely the fact that different cultures have survived side by side for so long—the mosque, the orthodox church, the catholic church and the synagogue are all within a few hundred yards of each other. A cosmopolitan is proud of such diversity." So, there was cosmopolitanism again, though this particular kind of cosmopolitanism ended in a bloodshed.

Sarajevo of Andrić, and if only of Andrić I sadly thought, was in my cultural schema where "The Letter from 1920" transcended into timelessness. I didn't want it to mark my past, present and the future, but I remembered it and dug it out of a pile of nostalgic paraphernalia. Debating over again whether the power of narration in the "Letter" or the rhetoric of a daily-political scribble ought to persuade my target audience, I once again decided to keep the "Letter" to myself. Moreover, I read the "Letter" to myself, astonished at surgical precision of Andrić's prophetic language,

---

[10] Mary Kaldor, *Human Security.* Polity Press, 2007.

exhilarated to have rediscovered this rare piece of a distant cultural treasure and deeply saddened at its tragic truth—truth reverberating in my memory as rhythmically and as consistently as Andrić's recount:

I was lying, next to an open window, in the room where I was born, Miljacka [the river] was flowing, whooshing outside, interspersed with an early autumn wind. Whoever spends a night in Sarajevo awake in his bed, can hear the voices of Sarajevian night. The clock on the Catholic cathedral chimes heavily and assuredly: two in the morning. More than a minute passes (seventy five seconds to be exact, I counted) and only then does the clock from the Orthodox church strike with a somewhat weaker but penetrating sound, chiming out *its* two in the morning. A little later the clock tower at the Beg's mosque sounds, with a muffled, distant voice, and it strikes eleven o'clock, eleven ghostly Turkish hours, according to the calculations of remote, alien parts of the earth! The Jews do not have their own bell to chime, but God alone knows what time is it for them, according to both Sephardic, and Aschenas reckoning. So, even at night, while all is sleeping, in chiming of the empty hours in the dead of night, that difference keeps vigil which divides these sleeping people who, when they are awake, rejoice and grieve, receive guests and fast according to four different hostile calendars, and send all their desires and prayers toward one sky in four different liturgical languages. And this difference is always, sometimes visibly and openly, sometimes imperceptibly and covertly, similar to hatred, often completely identical to it.

This, specifically Bosnian hate, should be studied and killed as a dangerous and deeply rooted illness. I believe that foreign scientists would come to Bosnia to study the hate, just as they study the leprosy, if the hate would be accepted, separated and classified subject of study as leprosy is.[11]

Later, when the drag of the daily routine came to close I checked my *life-line* with *Sultan* and, besides the already saved messages, there was nothing new from him. I almost expected nothing, I was almost relieved to find nothing since I now had another space where our conversation was never-ending and alive. It needed only a slight inducement, a figment of imagination, to continue its uninterrupted flow I opened my folder named *For Sultan* and continued the saga.

---

[11] Celia Hawkesworth, *Ivo Andrć: The Bridge Between East and West*. Athlone Press Ltd., 1984.

XX

*A*s Diana pushed the entrance door closed with her back, she leaned on it for a couple more minutes, not willing or not able to move across the hallway and into the living room. *I just witnessed a murder,* she chanted to herself, as if the repetitiveness of this statement could somehow trivialize the gruesomeness of its content and undo its effect on her. She stood there in agony, leaning on the door as the only source of support, forgetting that Dean's arrival and catching her in such a condition could multiply her ordeal. What was she going to tell him if he suddenly appeared? Was she going to be able to act as calm and as serene as she usually was in front of him? How could she hide if they looked for her? She should have rather opted for starvation than listened to Dana and had followed her. When the effect of an aftershock subsided to a degree that she could begin speculating about the potential consequences of her act, questions without answers continued to swarm and trouble her jaded mind. Still delirious, she peeled herself off the door, grabbled in the dark and dropped on the bed with all of her clothes on. While lying awake in bed she listened in the nocturnal sounds from the outside and, though she couldn't discern an intelligible speech in muffled noises she thought having heard, she could sense the commotion and uproar of, by then, in all likelihood properly notified authorities. She couldn't exclude the audio sensations of her overworked imagination either; somewhere else, a sound of a weapon fired with the intention to murder would alarm the entire neighborhood and the entire police squad would rush to the crime scene in a matter of minutes, but not on a place infested with deadly arms and heavy artillery in every corner.

She tossed in bed for some time, each motion as laborious as if the universe crumbled on her and she was struggling under its weight. This heaviness, however, had a miraculous soporific effect and after a while her eyelids became equally ponderous and unresponsive to her attempts to keep them open. She lay motionless for a couple of minutes when the sudden jolt brought her back to consciousness. Instinctively, she tapped around the bed, but Dean's spot was still empty. Good, she sighed with relief and then immersed herself in dreamless sleep.

The shrill sound of the phone first seemed to be coming from a great distance and then became louder and louder, until its persistence and loudness erased the last traces of sleepiness and urged her to prompt herself on the elbow in an attempt to rise. At the door her drowsy eyes met Dean's gaze—he was also walking toward the phone and she receded. "No, what!?" He was talking to someone and by the annoyed tone of his voice Diana assumed it was his mother. She was probably about to tell him the news. Diana didn't doubt that Dean's mother would be one of the first to learn about the incident at the gas station's café-restaurant. Her connections among the locals extended to the highest military personalities on one end and the mayor on the other. Her evening soirées, on the few occasions when she and Dean spent the night at the vacation house in the village, consisted of gossip séances with the mayor's sister, carefree and happy chatter of two white widows—that was how the villagers called those fortunate women whose husbands worked abroad and didn't rot in the trenches of a fratricidal war.

Dean was still mechanically asserting something his mother said on the other side of the line and Diana inferred that she was asking the usual questions of how were they doing and how were they spending the money she was giving him. Then she delivered the news: she could tell by a sudden *change in Dean's voice and a slight excitement when trying to obtain as much information as he could. From a seemingly disinterested distance Diana surreptitiously examined his body-language and intonation, which could become more expressive at any given point and his piercing eyes could land on her again if his mother happened to have said a word about Diana's prior evening's whereabouts. "I still can't believe M. got killed," Dean said in a somewhat more impassive voice. Diana slightly shivered—so M. was the designated target . . . the local hero, the liberator, a role model to any aspiring playboy in uniform! "OK, see you then," Dean finished the conversation on a friendlier note and in the split of a second between his turning around and addressing her, Diana's demeanor changed from a paralyzing anticipation into a suspenseful, well-acted curiosity before Dean started telling about M's murder.*

"My mother thinks we should move in with her," he announced flatly. "She's asking about the money and if we have food . . . but why should she be the only one to worry about it? Where is your aunt? Couldn't she take care of you?"

"She doesn't have to... She was here, a couple of days ago," Diana corrected herself.

"Listen to me, if my mother asks anything, anything at all, you will tell her that everything is fine. And don't make me share with her about the visitors you have," he raised the voice while pointing at her. "She's coming to visit today... Where is that whore? Friend of yours?"

"I don't know," Diana's esophagus contracted in an urge to swallow, while her mouth was becoming increasingly dry. 'It's only a matter of time until he . . . until everyone finds out', she frantically thought.

"She's not . . . my friend."

"Oh, yet she sits on my couch and drinks my coffee and..."

"Dean, what happened? I thought you loved me..."

"Loved you!?" he thundered, mocking her faint voice at the same time. "What have you done for me recently? You

don't like the people I hang out with . . . but they don't like you either . . . you don't cook, do you want my mother to cook for us all the time?"

"No . . . But . . ."

"What, but?"

"Does anything about me concern you anymore? I left that one job for you . . . and that was a mistake . . . I worked the entire month for . . . for . . . less than two German marks," she tumbled the words as fast as she could, fighting tears, then collapsed on the couch and covered her face with the palms of her hands.

Dean looked at her for a long moment, then turned around and said, somewhat more temperate, *"Maybe it's time we go back to my mother's. It's only a matter of time until I get drafted and the winter is almost there . . ."*

"OK," she said timidly, part of her rejoicing the prospect of not having to worry where the next meal was going to come from and another part panicking—what was going to happen to her and Dana. If this . . . offer . . . came only a day earlier, she wouldn't have gone with her, she wouldn't be in this agony now.

She had no time to say good bye to her reluctant friend, to commiserate with her and to speculate together what could possibly happen to them. *'But we didn't really see anything',* Diana defended them, already imagining the procedure of a long trial, trial that would never begin after arrests that would never be made. Dean's mother came into, once hers, residence without knocking and without greeting. As soon as she stepped into the hallway Dean approached her and she started talking to him rapidly, *"Why is it so cold in here? Didn't you say you were going to contact one of those lumberjacks whose names I gave you and order some firewood? Do you still have the money I gave you?"* Then, remembering why she really came, she continued in the same, now almost panicked tone of voice, *"Forget it, it's not like you are going to spend any more time here . . ."* She continued the *inspection of the house, "Oh, my God," she clamored, "there isn't a speck of food in the refrigerator!"*

Glancing at Diana, Dean declared, in a form of a rhetorical question, "And how do you exactly think the food would stay fresh in a refrigerator when there isn't any electricity, for hours, or days at a time?"

With a half-credulous expression on her face, she almost agreed with her son, but then, self-accusingly, continued her lament, "you should have made ice when the electricity is on and put the food on ice in the ice chest..." Instantly remembering that they didn't have any, she threw in another throng of self-accusations, one of them being that she actually didn't provide them with an ice chest and that it was "very inconsiderate" of her. Relieved, Dean began teasing her about her "unconcern." While she and Dean were having their mother and son moment, Diana stood by the living room window, overlooking the overladen tall and short buildings of the city's small downtown, smoke spouting from the numerous chimneys on the roofs and even from a number of windows of the taller ones. The grenades must have damaged the ducts, she thought absentmindedly, wishing at the same time to become invisible, to not have to go through the motions of showing her awe and a 'healthy envy', as she wanted it to appear to his mother, of her over-pronounced affection toward her son. When she first told her of Dean's gatherings with the wrong crowd, his mother was devastated and yet, surprisingly, not in a single gesture she showed any trace of disbelief. It seemed to Diana as if she instinctively knew what was going on and only forced herself to think about it if someone, potentially having a first-hand knowledge about her son's whereabouts, reminded her.

However, all the premonitions faded away in her face-to-face encounters with him and Diana was watching her face and her demeanor this time, as any other, melting into a gruel of admiration, any hint that something might be wrong, hint that might spoil the time she afforded to spend with him, intentionally pushed out of the way. Cold house? Who cared?! They were going to move in with her into her vacation house back at the village. Money she gave him? Three hundred German marks, a little fortune that, if converted into their worthless currency, would not fit into a suitcase? They must have done something with it. Diana suspected that it must have not occurred to his mother that Dean was the sole decision maker of how to dispose of her acts of generosity. Now she better say something, she better put on a mask of . . . normalcy in an abnormal time and place, Diana thought, lest Dean's threats to her come true. He was already glowering at her when his mother's attention was suddenly diverted by something else.

Smiling, but indeed wishing for everyone just to leave her alone, Diana approached his mother. In the split of a second their eyes met she realized in terror that his mother knew something . . . perhaps not the whole story. But what was there not to know? Hanging out with a notorious woman at a notorious place. Notorious place for women in any case. Men with open access to the gas station at the 'corridor' and initiated into the transactions away from the public eye were revered as little short of divinities, but also forgotten rather soon if fallen for any known and unknown cause. M.'s murder and the fantastic stories surrounding it will linger around the town for a while and, inevitably, will be succeeded by other dramatic and violent events. Diana wasn't worried, she couldn't worry about M.'s violent death. What could she possibly say to his mother? The social network she had at her disposal, seizing as far as the mayor's office, was stronger than any aspiring local media and Diana only hoped that she didn't bring up the subject in front of Dean. In the next moment she panicked again—who am I trying to deceive—she frantically thought. One after another, headlong thoughts precipitated before she was able to speak up, "I don't know where this all is going..." Dean's mother suddenly curiously gazed at her and attuned into the first words Diana uttered since she came in and, before Diana let her assume anything, she realized that her attempt at a conversation did not have to do much with the mysteries, dramas and legends their everyday life was full of, but only with a 'mundane' concern of mere survival. Dean's mother almost lost interest after Diana finished her statement—she just received her monthly wage two days ago and was able to buy a whole candy! At first as if wondering what her complaint had to do with her, almost at the verge of reproaching her for her ingratitude for all the money she generously supplied, Dean's mother remained silent and her face suddenly darkened. If a gaze could transmit a venomous vibe, then Dean's glower directed at Diana would have annihilated her as soon as she mentioned money, changing his mother's mood and attitude.

"Any updates on what happened last night?" Dean asked, changing subject and, apparently, trying to cheer his mother up by reminding her that M. had a mother too and that M.'s mother's distress was much worse than worrying over her son's squandering some money.

"No, I haven't heard anything more than I already told you," she said, adding, slightly too fast, "Why don't you pack your things and come with me?" We can leave everything here as is, lock the door and I could maybe ask our downstairs neighbor to keep an eye on it."

"Now, you want us to go now?!" Dean protested.

"Now is not soon enough," his mother replied. "I am already freezing and didn't even spend thirty minutes at this place. What were you two thinking?" Diana knew that the question was really directed at her son, but decided to play her obsequious game, certain that there was an accusation directed at her and hidden somewhere in his mother's exclamation, given that she most certainly knew . . . By the time Dean's mother rolled her eyes toward her one last time before they got up and started packing, Diana was certain beyond doubt that she must have known . . .

Carefully putting a couple of neatly folded sweaters in a plastic bag—after all, it was only going to be transported to and from the car—Diana tried to gain some time and figure out how to say good bye to her next door neighbor. Was she even home? She hasn't heard her rickety door opening and closing; the whole building appeared ghostly and quiet that morning . . . By the clock on the weekends, as soon as the morning light bathed the windows, she would hear a few housewives marching up and down the stairs, one of them certainly starting the fire in the woodstove on the second floor landing, another one inciting the faint flames until they firmly get a hold of a couple of smaller logs and until the thick smoke dissipated through the cracked glass and then they would all take turns boiling water for the first morning coffee, frying eggs and perhaps even bacon. Diana thought she could smell it a few times through the crack underneath the front door. At that time of the day Dean would be sound asleep, but Diana would lie wide awake and yearned nothing more than a taste of a strong coffee and a warm breakfast. The electricity in the building would be turned off until at least early in the afternoon, but the urge to have one normal morning would always be superseded by the urge not to mingle with her neighbors standing in line to handle their kettles and pots and gossiping. Maybe they didn't gather around the woodstove on the landing anymore because it was cold enough for them to start their own woodstoves, it occurred to her shortly after. The occupants of that building were chipping wood ever since she and Dean moved in, which would be a midsummer. That must have been the case, Diana concluded. They started their own woodstoves, which served multiple purposes; heating and preparing meals. I must be deranged, Diana told herself after elaborating on her neighbors' woodstoves in the midst of her trying to pack her meager belongings for the fourth time that year, pondering about what to tell Dean's mother about her visiting the gas station and, finally, her melancholic attempts

to find a way to say good bye to Dana—or to see how she was,
to check if she was even home . . . or alive.

Lack of commotion in the hallway and on the stairway
meant also that there weren't any suspicious movements by
anyone trying to get a hold of either Dana or her. She hasn't
thought of that, however tenuous, fortunate circumstance in
all her ordeal. Trying to brace herself with the last atom of her
strength, a part of her reasoning still intact by ever stronger
overarching fear, induced her to start prioritizing. I will
first pack, then go to that house, then try to talk to Dean's
mother, then . . . she chanted to herself, until one decision,
more determination, penetrated her mind: then I'll find a
way to come back here and check on Dana. With this last
thought she exhaled almost aloud and, now reconciled with
her destiny, wished that the whole moving process could go a
little faster. Dean wanted to first carry his stereo system down
to the car, but his mother dissuaded him by promising that
they would come back. All he needed now, she said, were the
clothes and whatever he had in the bathroom. She couldn't
stand that freezing cold place anymore, she said.

Would *Sultan* care to read it, would anyone for that matter care to
read this saga, conceived only to be dedicated to one person, but mostly,
and ironically, to divert my attention and dedication to that same person
who was abandoning me, rejecting me the way infants reject toys that can't
hold their interest. It turns out that this remark carried a subconscious
meaning for in Sally's world *Sultan* had always been an infant! I stretched
on the chair in front of the computer, feeling tired in a way that intimated
going to bed and perhaps even a promise of a good night's sleep, without
much tossing and turning—one a.m. Then, remembering to perform
one more ritual of checking a broken *life-line* I opened my inbox one last
time before going to bed. One of the subject lines read "You May Want
to Learn about This" and, on the verge to delete it along with other junk
mail, I glanced at the sender—it was from *Sultan! How could I. . . I would*
never forgive myself . . . and, feeling immensely fortunate, I opened it. His
courteous, yet somewhat formal greeting compiled the bittersweet feelings,

dangerously swaying into frustration at the absence of those soft, intimate characters of my mother tongue, however incorrect, however incorrigible… The ending was equally courteous and equally cold at the same time. *Do I even want to read it now? Maybe just read it, the response can wait until tomorrow, or the day after… What? Anyone could have told me this! What video?! Porter Stansberry? Do I want to know this?* Sultan was describing one of the, supposedly, most reputable financial analysts' assessment of the current state of affairs in the economy and his admonishing about what was very likely to take place in a country whose economy was allegedly on its last legs.

For a moment, I forgot my initial objections to *Sultan's* letter formality, engrossed in its vividness and increasingly interested in this Stansberry individual. Recently often busying around the computer in the small hour, lack of sleep (and peace of mind) now for weeks visible around my eyes and on my face, I decided that my lately established life of a night owl would not terribly suffer from one more sleepless night. In the end, I was grateful to *Sultan* for our *never-ending conversation*, with or without the intimacy of my mother tongue or … a hint … between the lines … that he was thinking about me. Why would I hope for a revival of his affection, it suddenly occurred to me, rather hit me in my fatigued face—I sabotaged our, however frail, connection by confronting his girlfriend. *But she wasn't supposed to be with him by this time,* I thought, the mute fury palpably rising from the lowest point of my abdomen, shattering the fantastic interplay of feelings I rapidly rewove from the moment he reappeared—even if only virtually. *Why would I care about this Stansberry person anyway?*

The answer, an indication of an answer came an hour or two later, in fact a succession of vague, repetitive hints, concluded by an invitation to buy his self-help financial advice book and subscribe for something I was too tired to remember. Stansberry accomplished one thing: he brought about an utter and most profound disturbance to my already distraught state of mind. And of all possible topics to touch on, why did *Sultan* choose the downfall of the economy? Was there significance? A metaphor? Perhaps he was equally disturbed, or innocuously transmitting a cooling out effect on a dying relationship. He should know something about cooling out, if he cared to learn what others say about a place such as the one where he works—his community college up on the hill. They promise students an array of degrees only to divert them from an ambition to finish a four year college, except for those smart enough to study nursing or some other vocation. *Sultan* even called himself a professor—a full-blooded professor! I realized now that a mix of awe and pity always interplayed in those first, crucial days (and weeks) after I met him, always eager to change the subject, to listen about something else, if he ended up talking about his teaching; teaching that ceded to matter or evolve the moment he received his ten-by-ten office of a department chair.

What kind of a promise he and alike were able to keep to their community college students? That they would supply indefinite numbers of financially starved adjunct instructors, have them work for slave wages, deny them benefits and keep the illusion going—that there is always a second chance at education and a better life. One can always catch the last train at a community college, even if the train goes to nowhere. And *Sultan* and a few fortunate ones had all the time in the world to sprawl on the chairs in their offices, intertwine their fingers at the nape of their necks and yak about anything and everything. *Oh, my God! Why did he hire me as a guest instructor? Whose daily bread I was taking?* None of the dozen instructors he managed were employed full-time and I comforted myself that there couldn't be any violations of rights if there were no rights to begin with. *"But disparaging those we love…"* Oh, I don't have time for *this! Why are my feelings constantly changing? Why am I mad in the one and crazy in love in the next moment? He can't fly as I thought he could… His spirit was catching the last breath and taking me with him very high, but then… I would crash in full force on the ground that wasn't going anywhere. I'm tired…* This must have been the last thought directed at him and in a long hour until finally sinking into the oblivion of sleep, but the fomented images of street riots and food shortages continued invading my imagination, courtesy of a web prophecy *Sultan* directed me to.

For the first time I didn't know how to start my reply to *Sultan's* latest letter to me. My struggle came from a simple realization that his message was least personal of all his messages, with almost nothing for me to hang onto, nothing that promised continuation or offered a reason for me to make an effort at communication. Yet I needed the communication, more than anything else. I was defenseless, disoriented and starkly confused by his actions—his conduct was worse than silence, worse than resentment. *What if I gave him the taste of his own medicine?* That was it: I'd write a nicely packaged and elaborate critique of those gruesome prophecies. I had all the time in the world; minus the cooking, parenting and the attempt to preserve a semblance of a social life with Sally. For the first time an aura of compulsion engulfed our *never-ending conversation* and I struggled for words, *"If you could've known how much grief this letter caused me. . .",* then, quickly deleting this first line, I replaced it with *"Hello, how are you?"* He never understood anything I told him the way I intended, but he was awfully good at pretending that he did. Now he wasn't trying to pretend anymore: this was real *Sultan,* epigonous, repetitive and . . . mediocre. At the time, gravitating to my chair at the computer as by a command, or with the avidness of an addict, I couldn't afford these liberating insights—I was still in his grip, as intense and strong as the sensation of pain in an amputated limb:

> *I was not quite sure what the intent of your message was, but would've appreciated a couple of comments, so that I have some idea where you stand on these disturbing admonitions. In my opinion, they surpass any known literary, read imaginary bleakness, not to mention reality and life as we know it. But that might be the catch. Anything that surpasses the life as we know it is not possible. This Stansberry person calls it a normalcy bias and it makes sense; I know something about it . . . If a disaster never occurred before in one's lifetime, then it will never occur in the future. This must be some kind of psychological defense mechanism, I mean defense in "normal" circumstances. Otherwise we are all in danger of turning into prophets of doom—right now the ones we know of have a difficult mission and we don't take them too seriously, if even considering what they say at all. What is interesting is that we are all fairly well-versed into terminology, but it doesn't help in practice. Isn't that ironic? Stansberry blames*

normalcy bias for New Orleans residents' non-readiness to act in the wake of hurricane Katrina and German Jews' disbelief in what was about to happen to them during a Holocaust. As I said, I suffer from my own various normalcy biases and already know what the consequences could be. The point is that there is no time to get prepared for a disaster and if you try to make the time then you would be doing nothing else. We used to think of those always forecasting a disaster as a special kind of people, eccentric and abnormal in their own way, but forecasting a disaster seemed to have become a trade for some and a very lucrative one for that matter. There is something very insincere about Stansberry, when he's trying to depict the government's inability to contain the imminent crisis, stop the "riots," food and water shortages" and other ensuing famines. He then goes on to say "but even if the crisis culminates in mild inflation, you should be ready..." And come out of its boiling point as a millionaire, or close to it. Oh, I almost forgot to mention—you have to follow his advice and purchase a couple of things from him and his team of analysts. If you are asking for my opinion this is a radical call to end a dying liberal democracy and finally start living the way ultra-right radicals always strived for: tax-free personal gain and personal gain only. If it has to be by expropriation, and what is the likelihood that it is not, or by outsourcing the wealth into the countless offshore banks, it's a small price to pay for the extent of liberation from the 'government'. Who is he kidding? While there is truth in his prediction that dollar will not remain the reserve fund currency of other countries in the near future and that the powerful, primarily non-Western ("non-democratic"), nations are doing all they can to disentangle themselves from of a dollar grip, his praise of Russian mafia's purchasing real estate all over Europe to evade taxes, or China government owned businesses' shopping for the over-priced realties in Latin America denounce his real nature and partisanship. He's nothing but a spokesman of neoliberals, the new caste in a dying liberal democracy, where everything is up for grabs. What is left of a democracy when its resources are expropriated and relocated, with self-interest as the only credo of its newly established oligarchy of neoliberals?

Welfare state, pride of wealthy nations is now a dirty word in neoliberals' vocabulary as the word communism once was for those red scare witch hunters. Yes, I used the verb "was" because we both know when and how communism dishonorably ceased its reign as a power-balancing force. As if any force ever departed with honors . . . I am scared to look into the future and it isn't the fault of any prophet of doom. I have my own premonitions…

I quickly sent it to *Sultan,* before changing my mind and asking about his feelings, or asking how he was going to spend more than three weeks of winter break. The winter, first announcing its long-term presence with ever new layers of incessant snow, hit the region with full force in the second half of December, dropping the air temperatures down to double negatives. The water in a nearby lazy river, the parts of it that were not frozen, vaporized for weeks under the frigid air, giving away an impression of a large hot spring. It was one of the nature's most perfect deceptions I have ever witnessed. It looked stunning from a heated car at a relatively safe road. The snow-cleaning crews plowed most of the snow from the main roads and the cars were finishing their job by spurting away the rest of the soiled, salty slush. Life had to go on; this most banal phrase I repeatedly chanted to myself on the way to a mechanic shop miraculously restored my vigor to a level at which I could forget about my *life-line* with *Sultan* for a greater part of the day. Life had to go on, run its natural course, regardless of personal drama and turmoil. It was most certain that the mechanic was going to replace the rim on my car and charge me a small fortune, but there wasn't a single act I could perform to alternate the course of necessary action to restore a much larger, personal breakdown. As Diane Keaton in "Baby Boom," I wasn't going to declare to various mechanics that I was sick of their plaids, "yups" and "nopes," of those apathetical price estimates while life around me was shattering into pieces, and pass out on the snow—no mechanic in real life could handle that much theatrics. I was only going to chant to myself a resigning *life has to go on*. Its unbearable fictional dramatization in most cases is a quiet despair of marginal protagonists in reality, whose coming to terms with their lives does not require extreme measures, a spectacle or a patent.

Sometimes, it's a handful of cherries, as in the Kiarostami's movie "Taste of Cherry" about a marginal character driving around the city, looking for someone to bury him after he commits a suicide. The one he finds offers a different solution: a handful of cherries his wife once saved for him, which in turn saved his life when he was in the same despondent state of mind. A character appearing at first as a simple, callous worker at a construction site extends the unadorned beauty of a cherry taste as an alternative to self-annihilation and suddenly transforms into a powerful and convincing figure, overshadowing the original gloomy burial plan with a most exquisite and yet simplest alternative. Most importantly, this alternative seems to be at the tips of our fingers and all one needs to do is to reach out and seize it.

At the shop, I quietly headed for a waiting room. The daily traffic smeared the tiled floor of the waiting area with the black slush while the waves of bitterly cold air swiped the entire room every time a new customer would go through the front door. An atmosphere of cold humidity settled in the room, frequently replenished by the newcomers from the outside and the mechanics' in overalls trafficking from the garage to the front desk and back. After a while, the manager approached me with the updates about the rim, adding alignment and other potential damages the impact of the car's hitting a curb might have caused:

"The measurements show that the alignment is completely off. Also, and I don't know if you have noticed, the front tires have no tread left and I would not recommend driving with those, especially in this weather… Anyway, my rough estimate for all this work would be around five hundred…"

"What?!" Now I had to seriously abandon romanticizing about the meaning of life, cherries and plaids—and react as anyone whose pockets were hit yet again by an indifferent, *I am just here to tell you*, mechanic.

"I've driven hardly twenty thousand miles with those tires, how's that possible?!"

"Maybe," and he scratched his head, "you've hit the pothole and the car went out of alignment prior to the most recent . . . accident? That can cause some extra wear and tear of the tires."

"No! I would know if anything like that happened. Is there a warranty on these things?"

"Unfortunately, no. There isn't a factory warranty on the tires…We, however, can give you a warranty on our tires…" I looked at him in disbelief: replacing a bent rim turned into an extreme makeover as if I owned a fifteen years old clunker, not a year and a half old *best-selling car of the year*. A car, whose tires were likely made out of chewing gum . . . . a car that needed a serious fix and the mechanic in the grey overalls was trying to communicate it to me in an equally serious, impartial way.

"If you'd like us to take care of this today, we could."

"And how long would I have to wait?" Another blow of frigid air was going to form ice crystals in my sinuses and I rapidly started weighing pros and cons of following the mechanic's suggestions.

"I certainly didn't expect all of this…"

"If you'd like us to do all the work, we can give you a ride home and pick you up when we are finished."

I waited a long moment before responding, not exactly trying to make a decision, but placing all of my thoughts in a mental void releasing me from the responsibility of making any conscious decisions. It was the only way for me to part with half a grand and after a long pause that I spent in my mental void, a sort of a mental black hole leaving the garage manager in a state of a slightly impatient anticipation, I finally gave him the permission to do the work. To demonstrate his appreciation, or pity, he personally took me home and, while I was thanking him on the way out, he threw in a warm promise of "we'll take care of it." Oh, but I had my escape, my *life line* in a yellow folder was beaming at me as soon as the old machine came back to life.

XXI

*T*he vacation house stood at the end of the graveled driveway the way a curious host stands at the door and greets the guests. Dean's mother knew how to create a welcoming little nest, surrounded by a small garden on one and a storage-summer-kitchen shack on the other end. The most welcoming to Diana was a splash of warm air racing through the living room door when his mother opened it and marched through. She even had a pot of stew simmering on the woodstove. Dean went upstairs, to the room through which they watched the stars and where she first tried to smoke pot. Never before a starry summer night made her laugh so much and never before the aftermath of an intense laugh was so dull, empty and meaningless. She did not understand Dean's desire to induce his happiness with an herb that would subsequently take more away from one's personality than it would be ever appending to one's good spirits. She remembered how Andrew's face appeared so devilish in the dark and how Dean looked up to him as some kind of a divinity. "Why did you make her laugh so much," Dean told her his mother asking him in the morning.

Now she stood there, his mother, not so gullible anymore, but still looking for an explanation that would make everyone look innocent in her eyes. Diana could sense his mother's struggle, a sort of a conflict of split loyalty, even though she did not expect much loyalty from her. On the surface, and through a lens of villagers' gossip, Diana's actions appeared as paltry as they were. Accusing Dean of squandering the money she gave him on drugs and alcohol would equal a *suicide. However, not telling her the truth as she saw it would never erase the mistrust and judgment that would eventually mar and smut everything she'd do. The villagers might have ascribed Diana some sort of free will, shamelessness and boldness, however far from the truth, or how she really felt, that was. And she knew that she would not be pitied or valued for witnessing what in some other times might have been thought of as a crime. She was already not pitied for being pulled into a vicious cycle of Dean's take on life—his drug escapades and testing a broken system, system that was bursting at the seams, would be forgiven because it was his world Diana entered so recklessly, not hers. After all, she might have appeared equally guilty in the eyes of people whose sense of compassion and humanity were abandoning them in a squeeze of debilitating, annihilating war raging around their little safe haven. And it was the likelihood of accusations that she made what might have been a rampant choice (as if she had a choice), thereby betraying Dean, his family and her relatives, that outweighed the possible consequences—Dean's wrath for her telling the truth—that made her keep quiet about witnessing a murder. Even the truth, she woefully realized, would never completely expiate the impermissibility of her mingling among men celebrated, and feared, for unscrupulousness with the enemy—and women. The locals would never give her the benefit of the doubt whether they knew the truth, or not. But Dean's mother had to know it, 'I owe her that much', Diana agonized.*

"The woman you call the widow . . . and other names . . . invited me for a lunch a couple of days ago. We didn't have any food in the house."

"How do you mean? Family of four could survive with less money than what I give Dean. . . ."

"I don't know what will happen to me if I tell you this; Dean said I'd regret it if I ever said anything to you . . . where the money is going... We've talked about this before . . . I

mean, I've informed you before… Please don't say anything to him—I don't know what he'll do to me," she started crying.

"He'll do nothing," his mother's jovial and benevolent character all but rejected the intentions her mind couldn't conceive of. Then glancing at Diana's terrified expression, finally communicating to her the seriousness of perceived threat, she said, "Nothing will happen to you and I will deal with him. I can't believe he's running around with those . . . thugs again." She paused, and it looked as if she was deliberating whether to continue with another equally uncomfortable topic, when Diana broke the awkward moment of silence,

"I went with her because that was the place where she picked up her black market merchandize to sell on the flea market. In this day, it's a rather honorable calling. We've h-eard," she stuttered, "we've heard a shot, but some soldiers forced us out of the building before the altercation started . . . That's all I know…"

His mother looked at her, expression on her face telling Diana that she had no reason not to believe her, but something in her demeanor seemed remotely unsettled, like a lingering, unasked question 'Why her, why in the company of the notorious widow'?

Diana wouldn't know how to answer it if his mother ever attempted to tap into that uncharted territory, but was telling herself that the interaction with Dana was the only one devoid of judgment and piercing looks. The only value and "tradition" she was trying to preserve was her own life and when one's life becomes one's only asset the rules of the game and the priorities change. Diana admitted that in many a restless night she tried to cope with an obsessive wish—to cross over into Dana's world. She didn't see a beauty or appeal of "freedom" that were luring her into that realm, but only a liberation from hypocritical mores and long dysfunctional quasi-sodality clamps. Clamps constricting some more than others… Her confession to Dean's mother did not bring a desired relief, partly because his mother would have to churn her interpretation of what took place to those who could stop Diana's further involvement or her becoming a part of a "no-witnesses" credo, popular in certain circles. She would have to confide in her friend, the mayor's sister, and eventually her own brother—an important military figure. Diana shuddered at the thought of mayor's sister and Dean's mother regurgitating her whereabouts and constructing their own fantastic design about the appalling event of Diana's visiting the wrong place at the wrong time—and with the wrong person. After sharing her side of the story, the kind of story that even for those misfortunate and unsettled times looked as if it came from a low-budget thriller, Dean's mother left her alone. She sat on the sofa with one obsessive thought that wouldn't leave her—that she didn't belong there.

Dean came in after a while and headed toward the steaming pot on the stove. "Anything else?" He put his arms around his mother's shoulders. "Crepes? Mmm, looks good." She didn't respond with the usual affection and, what he immediately deemed as her lack of unconditional love at that very moment, began to irritate him. She, on the other hand, had to be careful how she'd approach him about his torts, considering . . . a need for the source to remain undisclosed. Glancing at Diana's frozen posture on the sofa and avoiding her frightened and pleading eyes she decided not to say anything to her son, but her usual playful and jovial conduct with him was absent. "This place is boring," he said after a couple of unsuccessful attempts to cheer his mother up. "Do you have any money?"

"No, I don't have any money!" she burst. "Why do you need it anyway?!"

"Why do you care why I need it?!" he yelled back. "And why is now different than any other time?" He stood in the middle of the kitchen with a half-rolled crepe, tense and annoyed.

"*Because I don't have that much money to throw around! Do you even see what is going on around you? We are in a war! People are dying—some from bullets some from starvation... In a couple of months you will get drafted too... Don't you think that I need to save something for you when you are hundreds of miles away from home?! I am so sick and tired of your carelessness, your . . .*"

"*You are what?!*" *Dean interrupted her, thundering.* "*What is your fucking problem?!*" *He then carefully, for his apparently distraught state of mind, lifted the crepe from the plate and smashed it against the wall. It hit the wall unfolded and the strawberry jam oozed down the snow-white wall, leaving a blood- like stain. He left the room for the second time and went upstairs.*

Diana got up, her knees quivering, and offered to clean up the stain, feeling powerless to break away from a growing self-accusation that she contributed to a family wrangle. For them, she suspected, it was only a farce, a short lived sturm and drang because nothing could shake Dean's motherly love, but for her it meant that a last hope at reaching a safe haven burst as a soap bubble. Later in the day she relived another déjà vu while watching Dean and his mother's reconciliation and her subsequent slipping a banknote in his hand. Minutes turned into hours—hours of anticipation, tension and hope that she could snap out of her new reality as one snaps out of a bad dream. Then, when the agony prolonged, she only wished to be out of the house for a moment, even if she had to beg Dean to take her with him . . . wherever he was going. The barrelhouses in the village, or cafés as their owners and the locals called dimly lit rooms on the ground floor of a family house, with a couple of barstools, booths, mirrors, a counter and a host of bottles hanging from the ceiling, did not resemble their counterparts in the town only by one feature: these places in the village were the social scene of alcoholics more so than drug users.

In the room that was going to be their room from then on, Diana pleaded with Dean to take her with him,

"C'mon, I don't want to stay here by myself..."

"You didn't have a problem staying by yourself at the apartment; what's the difference?"

"I don't know . . . I was never fine with it, but I don't know if I can stand being here by myself...It's as if I am being scrutinized more by different people visiting this place, I don't have any privacy..."

"So, now, what my mother is doing for us is not good enough for you, you want privacy."

At the word "privacy" he slightly raised his voice and swung his hand as if he was going to slap her, but changed his mind.

"No, and please don't yell, I just . . . don't feel comfortable surrounded by all those people . . . that I don't know."

"Then stay in the room," he blurted. Like a prisoner, Diana added silently.

"Do you really want to be like everyone else around here? Living a cliché?"

"Hm, living a cliché," he scoffed. And how is not living a cliché gonna be better for you? You think you're gonna have the time of your life if you go with me? As you wish . . . I don't have anyone in particular to hang out with at any of those places anyway."

Diana smiled, grateful, yes, grateful to him and his willingness this one time to take her with him.

She headed downstairs to the bathroom. A blow of pressurized air shot through the faucet when she turned it on and shortly after a muffled sound of a laboring machine, what turned out to be a water pump, came from the basement underneath. She heard Dean's mother commenting once that the constant shortages of the electricity were causing the water pump to suck in air if the faucets were on when the electricity was out. A twenty-gallon plastic tub, filled with water, was sitting in the bath tub as a back-up in the hours, or days, *when they had to switch to medieval time-count and the life style. The water trickled out of the faucet, first wriggling out as a worm and then splashing into the sink in a series of short squirts. Diana waited until the water stream stabilized and let it flow into her cupped hands. It had a rusty smell and a slightly yellowish color, a quality of standing water, but she couldn't wait to splash and splash her face with this cool liquid until she thought she erased the tiredness and worry from her face. Her hair hung in disheveled curls around her now ruddy face and she went through the mini-cabinet on the wall in search for possible hair products. Dean's teenage sister was staying with her uncle in the town and was more or less just the visitor on the weekends, and Diana was able to locate an almost empty tube of hair gel his sister left behind.*

The doorbell rang and in the next moment the hallway was filled with laughter, simultaneous talk followed by an unintelligible whisper, diminishing as the voices moved into the living room. When she opened the bathroom door Dean was standing in the hallway with his green military jacket and boots on. The smoke of expensive cigarettes was lingering in the hallway.

"I just need to put something else on," she muttered.

"No, you don't. What's the point? Do any of your other clothes look any different than what you have on?"

"Well, you changed…"

"We don't have time. I'm not waiting for you here forever!" He headed toward the front door and Diana quickly put the shoes and the jacket on. Another car was pulling into the driveway.

"Doctor's brother," Dean scorned. "They both left the hills where they grew up—one to become a doctor and another to become a criminal. Everyone knows that, yet he can move freely all over Europe and the rest of us are trapped here in this shit-hole."

Diana's heart skipped a beat; it was Dean she forgot existed, Dean having a conversation with her—or at least talking to her. She didn't respond and he didn't expect her to. If she did it would have been a question about his mother and her companions. Why was she so unselective in choosing the people she associated with? Florence Nightingale for the villagers who all but waited in line in front of her house to sit down at her kitchen table and receive a remedy for various aches and pains they complained about; patron of the young nurses and young village brides, their discrete "older sister" for whatever secrets they confided in her during their coffee and cigarette séances; faithful wife to her absentee husband and, finally, protective lioness for her children, equally fending their sins as their virtues in her domestic ward. Though Dean received most of the fending, his mother would intercede on behalf of anyone close to him, but with the clear distinction of where her true love and devotion lay.

They walked quietly next to each other, cutting the way short through the backyards and reaching the railroad tracks. Diana strode from one rail threshold to the next, counting them for a part of the trip and then lifting her gaze from their hypnotizing monotony, attempting to make a conversation with Dean. Perhaps he'd realize that she didn't want to appear as a total burden to him. The guests at a gloomy 'café', however, sent him a different message. A group of young men was sitting at a bar, all dressed in military jackets and boots, all with the same indifferent expressions on their faces covered with days, or weeks, old stubble. They all as one turned their stares away from the new visitors, disappointed perhaps that they weren't someone else, someone who lived a "real life," like themselves. In one of the booths at the far end they spotted a group that used to hang out at the school playground.

"Hey," Dean approached them cheerfully. Some of them muttered a greeting. The blond girl, Dean's default partner at their nocturnal games past summer, attempted to shake off the layer of ash on her burning cigarette and missed the ashtray by a couple of inches. In a slow, labored and uncoordinated motion she repeatedly wiped the spot in her

lap where she thought the ash fell, while the girl next to her gently took the cigarette away from her. The others in the group more or less successfully concealed the true state of their mind, but remained mostly unresponsive to Dean's attempt to reinvigorate their friendly ties. He knew of one certain way to do it and it was about the right time since his lungs, nostrils and the entire body ached for the intoxicating fume, which this group in the booth seemed to have been consuming in abundance. If not the fume, then at least one of those tranquilizers he knew were in circulation; mixed with a shot of vodka in orange juice—that could knock a horse down. Dean glanced at the blonde, the look on his face telling Diana that he so much wanted one of those pills.

After what seemed an eternity to him, one of the men got up and went out with Dean. Diana looked around helplessly and rested her elbows on the back of one of the seats. Every joint in her body ached. She shuddered from a sudden chill, while her face burnt in fever. She regretted following Dean to this place, desperately yearning to plunge her head into the pillow and tangle her body into a warm comforter. I am sick, she admitted to herself, determined to ask Dean to go home as soon as he came back. Dean returning to the booth was not the same Dean leaving it. In an instant Diana recognized his state as not completely coherent, an outcome of an intoxicated system. The mayor's sister, a doctor's brother, a criminal of international caliber as Dean put it, and all the tobacco stench at the house they left moment ago appeared friendly and welcoming at the sight of Dean's bloodshot eyes, this gloomy place and her achy, feverish body.

A mixture of emotions I interchangeably sensed in the past days filtered into a distinct feeling of growing rage at the thought of *Sultan*. An impulse to slap him. . . and keep slapping him, first emerging on a couple of occasions when his face appeared to me as a muzzle of a sly cat—due to various inflictions I thought *Sultan* caused me— kept reoccurring and intensifying in the long, cold days and nights before I could materialize it.

I will not send him any more emails and I will not contact him in any other way, I decided. I wanted to finish whatever real or imaginary relationship I entangled myself into and I wanted to have the last word, or the last move. A dozen of multifarious CDs *Sultan* left at my place were lurking at me from a shelf next to the desk in my office, a small den at the end of the hallway indeed, where I spent hours and hours trying to direct my thoughts, my love and my hopes at one person I thought was worth it. These remnants now, this music as diverse as Johnny Cash and Santana, Vivaldi and Bach, announced its presence every time I turned away from the computer screen. *If only I could listen to the "Four Seasons" and not think of him. . . if only I could see those objects and not think of him...* Then I had a plan: I was going to return them to him as soon as he comes back to his office, I was going to scatter them all over the floor and deliver a long yearned punch in his face, with or without glasses on it.

Meanwhile, painful as it was, I was going to finish my emotional cleansing and free myself from him. He spilled his charm and chivalry and took pride in what he called the "last remains of gentlemanly bearing," often referring to himself as the "last gentleman in the world," but where did his *gentlemanly bearing* leave me or his . . . girlfriend? I gulped a bubble of air at the thought of her as one swallows a partially chewed dumpling and all my ego pep talk went away. She was a middle-aged grandma and yet *Sultan* chose her over me. There wasn't any ego-strengthening exercise I could think of that would erase a sense of failure and disgust at my own actions. This sense of disgust was even stronger at the thought of *Sultan's* actions, but there wasn't a condemnation that would touch him, no punishment that I could contrive that would force him down on his knees, force him to rethink and reshape his character. However, there wasn't a condemnation good enough that would transform him from a "last gentleman in the world" into a real slime ball either. *A new nickname could do perhaps*, I thought. *This slime ball thought that the Vivaldi from a computer speakers and his office chair made him an epitome of charm... Charm he had dispensed in all but gentlemanly way.*

Sally was slightly amused with my plan of ousting *Sultan* out of my system, at least the executive portion of it, a part when I would be slapping, or punching him in the face.

"But where is the love, the exaltation, rejoicing over every line of words he wrote to you?"

"It's still there, as much as the growing impression that he faked everything; faked the passion, the understanding, listening... And, even if it seems to you now that I am taking all this too lightly, just because I have decided to wriggle out of his grip doesn't mean that I am forgetting . . . anything. It's the questions, such as the one you asked that force me not to forget and debate with myself if it's appropriate to forget. To keep forgetting, at least the physical memory? Part of me wants that grip, vividness and passion of the shared past months to never go away for if we keep forgetting, who are we then? Starting anew seems like a punishment and a faded replication. Copy of a copy. How will it be ever possible, I wonder, to experience the same passion, with the same intensity—and with someone else? Even if every single move was a mistake I am still trying to convince myself, and perhaps you," I paused, expecting some body language, a grimace or a reaction of any kind from her, "that I was only following my heart . . . that's what this was all about. I am giving up because I can't compete! How ironic! In the beginning, the more he revealed about her, the more I uncovered about her, the more confident I felt... And losing him for all other reasons, all but her, wouldn't be as much . . . humiliating and . . . disheartening. Where am I now? Who am I now? You are right: the legitimacy of my whole life in the past months depended on the ability to hang onto him, however impossible, however sick any prolonging of such a nightmare might have been."

"Wait, wait, wait..." she interrupted me, in a somewhat softer tone of voice. "I didn't mean to say that your feelings were not legitimate; maybe it is the right way to end it . . . I am not the best person to tell... No one is..."

"All I am trying to figure out is why we have to hang onto pain. And yes, I feel miserable and will feel miserable for a long time, but the way I handled my, how'd you call it, *other womanness,* had nothing to do with the legitimacy of my feelings. And yes, I was in the clouds, didn't listen to your warnings, your down to earth reasoning..."

"Down to earth? I don't know if I can take such a compliment!" Sally burst. "The intensity of your feelings and the uncertainty you faced terrified me on occasion. I admit that. I just thought that there was a way to set things straight. You reminded me of *young Werther*—that I remember from school—with your sublime feelings, the sorrow you turned into sort of a poetry."

"Hm, now you almost turned me away from sharing more of my literary jewels with you. I had this . . . perfect letter I was going to write him, before . . . before he cut me off with cheap politicizing and whatever plan he had to present to the dean... And do I have to tell you that those plans of his are always just that—plans, figments of his imagination?"

"No, I think you don't," she said after a short pause, as if deliberating to come up with a most unbiased answer, as if her "expertise" were deciding in both assessment of mine and of *Sultan's* character and sanity. And in a twisted way I personally carved for her, allowing her to *probe* into my most intimate sphere, her half-scornful, half-derided expertise mattered.

"To admire . . . literature . . . and poetry . . . to have them aid one's everyday life is so much more than just word mastery and adorned phrases ... Grin all you want, but aren't all our struggles generated in an attempt to be, significant or insignificant, contributors to timelessness in our personal quest to defeat forgetfulness and defend *truth*, whatever that might be? And if some of us praise God and *her* word, timelessness and universality of the canon, why can't some others praise more creative expressions with the same ultimate aim? God couldn't possibly describe how I feel, but some other humans could."

"Who? Dr. Phil?"

"Gustave Flaubert! I am not the first *mistress* who resorted to him, seeking expiation, trying to exorcize a *demon* pushing her into a spiritual and emotional desolation, in affiliation with equally spiritually and emotionally desolate companions."

"Madame Bovary sought expiation?"

"No," I insisted, "the ones after her, the ones who recognized the value in her creator's literary work. Flaubert said once that *he* was Madame Bovary. And I am almost Gustave Flaubert, minus his fame, since "There is now such an enormous gap between me and the rest of the world that sometimes I am amazed to hear people say the simplest and most natural things. The most commonplace remark sometimes holds me rapt with admiration,"[12] I grabbed a piece of scratch paper from the bottom shelf of the coffee table and read a quote, dramatizing."

"Why Flaubert? And where did you possibly find that quote?"

"I don't know why Flaubert. Spur of the moment. Here," I invited her into my den at the end of the hallway and opened a bookmarked internet page, "These are all Flaubert's quotes . . . I don't particularly care how the critics interpret them, I just felt a certain . . . connection. Oh, here is the rest of the one I read, "There are gestures and tones of voice which utterly undo me, and stupidities which almost make me dizzy. Have you ever listened attentively to people talking a foreign language which you did not understand?[13]

"Interesting . . . I just never feel like diving through an ocean of someone else's thoughts to justify what I think at a given time."

"I don't see it as justification . . . It's a. . . ." I struggled for words, strong enough to convince and to *convert*, "a narrative," I said, not too happy with the word choice, "testimony of a great human character who cared enough to share it with the world, not only in his but in all future times, and it's a powerful testimony, telling us, if one'd like to tune in, that past was not much different than the present, despite all the deceptions of today..."

Something in my and Sally's relationship was lost with my interactions with *Sultan* losing their intensity and, what we both may have thought of as, spectacular aura. It was as if Sally knew me only through a prism of my disconcerting turmoil with him and she wanted to prolong it to continue my wistful performance of which she was an eager spectator and a judge. The last spectacle I was going to stage for all of us was going to be my last visit with *Sultan* when he comes back to his ten by ten feet office. After our *never-ending conversation*, and strangely I still hoped that it still didn't end, I caught myself in a never-ending analysis of the cause of my infatuation with him. Was it an impending rejection, my fear that he was going to choose someone *who couldn't compete with me*? Someone who was like a well-fed cat in Simone de Beauvoir allegory, over me? But who was I

---

[12] September 1845 (he was 24) Gustave Flaubert
[13] Ibid

237

in his eyes? An unfinished story? A woman with too many plans and too little time? Stationed in life of interchangeable domesticity, school and job insecurity. *Sultan* and his well-fed cat were beyond such volatility: they were both well-fed in their neighborhood on a main street of a small, blue collar town and they were worry-free. Except in unforeseen circumstances of a fugacious love affair for which *she* had a pre-made sentimental speech of *life with him better than life without him* and a generational appeal of a steadfast, reliable, domesticated mistress, all the attributes I was missing.

I was defeated … It only became clearer through the silence that followed his impersonal attempts to communicate with me by means of a political pamphlet. Yes, we lived in economically turbulent times, but we had our ways of addressing it. We had our subtle, seductive way of getting under each other's skin while discussing the most delicate, or the most pressing problems of the world. And every one of my words carried a part of me that I was willingly giving away, thinking that he did the same. After days of silence he responded with a short message that he was working on something for the dean. He welcomed my suggestions if I had any. Suggestions? For "energy efficient transport to and from campus?" I was going to suggest for him to give up on another one of his projects that was never going to materialize, but suspected that wasn't the kind of suggestion he had in mind. Any *suggesting* now would make me more his personal assistant than anything else I aspired to and I convinced myself that I didn't want to be part of an increasingly twisted and infantile game anymore. Or was it him that didn't want it? I have to admit, at the time I didn't possess the clarity of mind to declare who didn't want what. Perhaps I wanted peace of mind . . . or freedom if there is such thing.

My freedom, however, was limited by what was commonly accepted and conventional. I had to come to terms with it long time ago. I have seen my most recently attempted *liberation* in action—with *Sultan*. The liberation of anyone is just a chimera, and I in particular still no less passive than medieval bachelorettes waiting for my knight in shining armor, or at least dreaming about him. It was an expectation, or hope, so powerful that no *Sultan* or his ensuing false alarm could extinguish. I'd like to think that I was not waiting, that I was too busy to live like anyone else, to be normal to be precise, or was even *normal* just an illusion? I was not the only one to try to make sense out of life and I was wrong to disdain others for stereotyping and replicating the reality and life itself. Was I fiddling with the case of hubris when declaring not so long ago that *I won't be forgiven for never reaching a climax in life after which only aging and stagnation followed*? On the other hand, I knew how persistently and sometimes in futility I tried to make meaning out of everything and that once I used to live a life devoid of stereotypes. It terrified me to think that the time finally came when I would be nurturing that wild and uncultivated side of me only in my thoughts and memories, barricaded in constraints of a new reality and helplessness. A culmination of life after which aging and stagnation followed?

I have lived through days and months of contrasts. The greatest tragedies, in life and art, always begin in a way that the protagonists experience an idyll, live through a stretch of time filled with harmony and happiness. It's the contrasts (but not extremes) that create perfection in art, literature and life. But maybe not; interplay of colors and words is constantly misappropriated and imitated in interplays of real life protagonists' intentions. I was trying to immerse myself in one of the Hallmark's Hall of Fame movies, in which the main character learns she has leukemia. Her personal drama culminates in interchanging scenes of family happiness and neighborly love in a small town on the one, and her current pain and suffering on the other hand. Now isolated in her private world, world into which she voluntarily exiled herself, she keeps the secret to herself, secret that can only bring life or death. The other world, from which she departed, and its simple pleasures are becoming increasingly remote, strange and unimportant. That was life sometimes, at the edges of its own existence and so close to its own annihilation, so that even its everyday flow appears unreal and deceptive. Sally said that for her, and she suspected me as well, a possibility of ruin and death was for a long time closer than life itself, for much longer than one might find tolerable, and it took her a long time to accept life and its simple pleasures later. She seldom talked about movies, but in one of the better ones she watched, I think she said it was called "The Big Fish," a man is struggling through the woods, while the trees suddenly come to life and twist their branches, like tentacles, around his body. Terrified at first, he then livens up and exclaims, "Wait a minute, this isn't how I die." The branches immediately release their grip, unwrap and everything goes back to normal.

Buried under the comforter on my sofa, watching a Hallmark's Hall of Fame classic, I was trying to tell myself *Wait a minute, there must be something else, something better. Why don't you live in that instead of this illusion you created?* At that moment I wasn't sure if the *better* was in the past or in the future—and that was the problem I realized. It is true that we like to idealize past, but it is also true that we like to invoke the old demons from the past that take us to dangerous and unknown places. Those demons are especially strong if one believes that nothing new can be created if the old and well known past cannot be recovered, past resurfacing in fragments, more or less powerful. After reliving one of those moments, the past and everyone I knew in that past would perish for a moment and leave me alone in my new reality. Comical, hopeless, kind and atrocious faces would fade away. As in a perfect cycle, I would then start idealizing my new reality where I had, I admit, some beginner's luck, same luck Paolo Coelho talks about in *Alchemist*. He says that, if you stay on your life's path, all the forces in this world coalesce to help you persevere and succeed. I wanted to be strong, to save the world filled with people, images of people at least passing in front of my eyes, subjected to life under a millstone, but all I was trying to do now was to save my own life. One time I remembered I wished to alleviate the suffering of a refugee family portrayed in some international news I was watching, faces without a smile, with clenched fists in powerless rage, by chanting every time those images would come to mind, *may hope and happiness return to you even if some of my own had to be taken away.* I couldn't offer more.

Alexandra leaned over me, over my shapeless body under the comforter and said that she had an idea for a New Year's celebration, "Why don't we go shopping in Chicago?" she suggested. "I could take two of my friends too and we could also visit some other places. . . Shed Aquarium, museums, spend some time at Navy Pier. . . ." *Shopping. That's all I need.*

"Oh," I said, "that sounds. . . ." I looked at the streaks of hair curling around her still baby cheeks, her still innocent baby cheeks, and locked my gaze with her curious, deep blue eyes, and was suddenly overwhelmed by guilt. "That sounds great!" I exclaimed, rising up and pushing the comforter away at the same time. I continued listening to her, indeed listening, for the first time after days of delirium. I knew then as I knew before that I would give up *all* my happiness for hers, if it were possible, I would assuage her crises and her frustrations with all my love, I would hold her hand for as long as necessary—until she is able to fence off all the horrors of the real world, with its traps and pseudo-freedoms, until she is able to master such world's discrepancies and navigate its contradictions.

My years of *free-thinking* were not mine anymore, it was just a meaningless prelude to an inevitable time when I would have to settle my dues and show the way to someone for whom I had elaborated a different life philosophy: path of least resistance. Will she want me as a cushion? Walking the path of least resistance and happiness I want for her might be another one of my self-deceptions and those children, including Alexandra, whether we wanted it or not, will have to fight their own battles and raise their own revolts. Few of them will fit the mold of their parents, but havens, I did not want her to fit mine! I wanted her to know that she can trust me and count on me, even if it only entailed the least desirable trip to Chicago and freezing on its streets for a day. I would do whatever it takes, for I had only one motive: to spare her. To be there for her with all my heart and soul meant that I'd have to give up other pursuits, especially the one of fugacious happiness with *Sultan.* He did, however, catalyze a *self-discovery* that my heretofore more or less compact personality was splitting in two: one of them alert and constantly watching over Alexandra and the other one wild and non-subdued, pledging to freedom and unrestraint. Were all of my struggles just the birth pangs of a new multifaceted identity? *"The issue of identity is a thorny one," Sultan* wrote to me, knowing perhaps how multifaceted, salient and dynamic this identity thing was. My new identity, if that was the case, mustn't betray her, or even me.

Someone, a philosopher I was sure, called it once the path less traveled and there I was, looking at her deep blue eyes, realizing that our love for each other was not so simple anymore. Times of unconditional love, giving and endless loyalty were giving way to the new, unexplored potentials our mutual love carried. While my love might have remained unconditional, hers might have been evolving. I forgot about a leukemia patient and the parallel worlds she lived in when Alexandra snuggled next to me and wrapped her hand around my shoulder, "We'll have the best New Year ever!" Meanwhile, I decided to keep nurturing my secret file, to continue my never-ending story, even if it ends up as *Sultan's messages in the bottle* rants he wrote to me not so long ago.

> *Diana's illness turned out to be a strap throat, an extremely painful one with swollen, inflamed tonsils. Throughout the night after they came back from an obscure café, after she dragged herself to the house and bed, the fever overtook her body. Dean must have alerted his mother that she was sick since she came to the room the following morning and shortly examined her. Touching the glands on her neck and asking if she had difficulty swallowing, his mother expertly decided that it was "just a strap throat," but "it had to be treated." She promised to come back from work at a local clinic with penicillin injections. Meanwhile, she sawed through the throat of a miniature bottle with an instrument that appeared as a miniature replica of a real saw and popped open its tip.*
>
> *"This is usually administered intravenously, but you can just take it orally too. It's called Demerol."*
>
> *Diana poured the thick, colorless liquid into her mouth and at first its viscose texture clung to the roof of her mouth and a long minute passed until its slow flow reached her throat and she was able to painfully swallow. Its bitter, sticky aftertaste roused an asphyxiation-like sensation, her esophagus contracted and she covered her mouth thinking that such a childish gesture could stop whatever was happening in her stomach. Dean's mother told her to take a deep breath and that Demerol was not known for inducing vomiting.*
>
> *"It tastes horrible, I know, but you don't want that to stick to your veins. This is better. Here are two more if you*

need it later." Then she explained how to saw off the tip of the small bottle,

"Do you think you'll know how to do it?"

"Yes, I think so."

The next pill she gave her temporarily stabilized her body temperature, sopping her clothes with sweat. She felt relief for an hour or so and, in a slow motion, peeled off her wet clothes. Dean was downstairs watching TV. Body-aches, fever and a sharp pain in her throat only intensified after the medication wore off and she grabbed one of the two Demerol bottles Dean's mother left. The tip of this little bottle appeared more stubborn than when she was just watching his mother snap it open. The bottle, made out of thin, fragile glass, broke into shards when she squeezed it to detach its tip. Thick liquid oozed out, coating the palm of her hand with a honey-like, slow stream.

"Damn it," she swore and laboriously got out of bed to clean up. She could ask Dean to help her open the last one, but if he destroys it the way she did, she'd have to wait for his mother's return in excruciating pain. Now careful, she told herself, tilting the bottle and positioning the mini-saw so that it worked most efficiently and through the narrowest part of the bottle throat. This time it seemed to be cutting straight through the glass and after a while she grasped its tip with the thumb and the forefinger and gently twisted and pulled. The glass breaking clanged more pleasantly this time, producing a desirable pop and she swallowed another gulp of bitter-sweet, sticky, bile-like medication.

The taste of Demerol faded in comparison with the pain of penicillin injections later in the day. The muscle spasm paralyzed her entire leg, sending shooting pain as the antibiotic spread through her body. After the first injection she lay motionless for the most of the evening and long after the usual visitors gathered in the living room downstairs. Dean briefly announced that he was going out. *Good, at least I have an excuse to stay here by myself,* she thought. On *occasion, a muffled sound of loud laughing would reach up to her, strangely comforting and brightening her mood, as an unsaid whisper that she didn't have anything to worry about. She discerned the voice of Dean's uncle, slow, powerful and jovial as usual and the sense of protectiveness quickly supplanted the anxiety. Those voices eventually became soporific and seemed as if singing a lullaby to her exhausted mind and body, rocking her into restless sleep.*

Whichever pleasant murmur lulled her into sleep, a thunder of Dean's rage woke her up.

"Who does she think she is, that little piece of nothing?!"

Diana awoke in an instant, as if she never closed her eyes and then heard his mother's concerned and still sleepy voice, "What is going on? Why are you so mad?"

"Ask her why I am so mad!" he rumbled, "that ungrateful tramp!"

Diana put on a sweater and decided to go downstairs. She took small, laborious steps across the room and down the stairs until Dean got in her way. Without warning he slapped her across the face, but Diana caught a glimpse of his mother covering her face in shock. She tried to pull him away, while his fingers entangled in her hair, strengthening his grip and pulling it with all force. Diana's face was suffused with tears, but all she did was covering her face in a mute and helpless protest. His mother hysterically pleaded with him to stop.

"What business does she have with that whore? To embarrass me like that! To embarrass our whole family! That stupid hoochie slept with the entire garrison, sometimes two at a time! How is she any diff . . . " and he pointed at Diana, "how are you any different than her?! Huh?"

Diana's head was threatening to explode and she had to hold the railing to keep the balance, but she braced herself, determined for the first time to stand up for Dana, to defend her against those gruesome lies, "She's not who you think she is."

"What?!" his burst again, "How dare you!?"

As he made another motion to hit her, his mother grabbed his hand, saying, "Stop, can't you see that she's going to collapse?"

"I don't care!" he retorted.

"Well, I do. Come on, let's have a seat. There is no reason for you to be so upset."

"No reason?!" he was on the verge of another outburst.

"You cannot be hitting her and calling her names like that," she reasoned.

"I can do whatever I want!" He turned then to Diana and announced, "I don't want you in my house!"

"The house is mine," his mother intercepted, "and yes, you can stay here," she turned to Diana. "What has gotten into you?" she addressed him one last time.

"Look at you—sometimes I wonder which side you're on…" He slammed the door on the way out.

Diana could stay in the house, but not in Dean's room, at least not when he was there.

"You can sleep here," his mother said. "Do you still have the fever? Let me see. . . ."

Her hand on Diana's forehead felt as a balm and her feverish, tense body slowly relaxed.

There must be an end to this, she thought later in the shadowy darkness of the room, wet towel on her face heaving the fervent heat and slowly soaking up with tears.

Even if I have to end it by ending my own life.

XXII

The symbolic resemblance between the transition from the old into the New Year and my transition from one rather worn out and undesirable state of mind into what I'd like to imagine as a fresh start, deepened my appreciation for this somewhat neglected holiday in small towns and my need to celebrate it. The neglect largely emerged as a consequence of a mass hysteria during Christmas time and, though acknowledged and celebrated, the New Year (at least in the time and place where I was) did not have a significance of the holiday preceding it. I have lived to experience the opposite scenario at a different place, sometimes nostalgic for that time, idealizing the time in which everyone would be equally looking forward to such an inclusive, though conventional, celebration. Days and even weeks of playbacks of the past would impeccably start for me during a new year or an old year's season. I created it, not because of the resistance to the populist, overly consumerist and distorted Christmas season, but because it better suited my desire to reflect on the past few hundred days, to cherish the good ones among them and to try to dispose of the weight of those dreadful and dragging ones.

The pressing weight of the old year, along with its baggage of missed and discarded opportunities, could be especially lasting and unrelenting. Hence I had no special desire to *celebrate* the old year, but to wait for a new one with calm anticipation and greet it—quiet and hopeful. Why celebrate the New Year, I heard often, when it only reminds us of the clock ticking and an increased incertitude about the future? In response, I came to realize that it should not be about the celebration—it is a kind of recycling of the past resulting in receiving a renewed opportunity to carry on, evolve, become wiser. It is an opportunity to discard the old one as a used and threadbare toy. In this vein, making a new year's resolution does afford some flavor and festivity to it, far from the glory of Christmas, but somewhat significant.

The morning of January first this year broke somehow cleaner, innocent and newer (although a contradiction for time does not reset at the beginning of a new year and a cleansing of our souls does not transpire only because of the construct we call a *new year*). Looking at Alexandra's and the thrilled faces of her two friends all lined on the king-size bed of a hotel room, I decided that my feelings had something to do with these young girls that were entrusted me for the day. The previous evening, the last day in December, I spent chasing after them from one store to the next and they kept marching up and down the hotel long after I passed out on the sofa-bed in our room. Bitter coldness and wind outside touched upon my total experience of the last day of the year as a clement nuisance in comparison with excess stimuli of flickering lights on the trees and on strings suspended across the street lights on lavishly decorated Magnificent Mile. It made perfect sense not to enhance the magnificent experience and celebrate the first minutes of a new year with noise and distorted perception. If, in a personified sense, the New Year "arrives," then such arrival (quiet and inconspicuous by virtue of any product of imagination) is waylaid by the racket and fireworks. I greeted its first minutes peacefully—in the same rhythm they arrived. I greeted the following morning peacefully, smiling at the three sets of baby cheeks lined on the bed and deep in sleep. The racket, the noise of celebration and fireworks are a human expression of fear, a way to dispel the "evil spirits," erroneously appropriated in celebrating a most peaceful day of the year. I was imbued by its rhythm and steadiness while running after the girls on our final sight-seeing tour, while circling around the block to find a parking space near a vintage book store, while reading a map to get to an obscure boutique they found on the Internet and, finally, on the way home to a life I temporarily placed on hold and was going to resume—inspired, or *recreated*.

Diana saw Dana one last time, as she snuck back into the apartment in the city. She decided to wait for as long as necessary until she'd show up. And she did. Their last encounter seemed casual, almost cold, even though they knew that what they experienced together created a bond, however reluctant, that neither one of them would forego. "Come inside," Dana invited her, as if she knew that standing by the door as she appeared was not exactly a coincidence. Diana wanted to hear if she was safe, if anyone threatened her life, if the police visited, however unlikely the latter possibility seemed. For a few minutes, Dana was rambling about different conspiracy theories, war lords' rivalry, and none of it made any logical sense in Diana's ears, by which a person lives a life by following certain rules and regulations and, in turn, faces the consequences for failure to do so. The reality she was observing seemed as if belonging to a different dimension, a realm of phantasy. She was happy that Dana somehow managed to stay alive and wiggle her way out of trouble and danger, but didn't they all do the same? I don't think she'll want to see me anymore, Diana thought, without sadness or any other feeling. The difference between them was in the intensity with which they clung onto what they knew and experienced as "normal." Dana was living the other alternative for some time now, and Diana kept trying to recreate a normalcy she imagined once existed, but each attempt would throw her into the fangs of yet another abnormal monstrosity. Long after this last encounter the night at the murder scene became a vague memory, but Dana's last confession to her lingered in her thoughts like a ghost:

"Nobody has ever authentically shown a sense of shame and embarrassment of being confined, no, not confined, detained at a place where you used to walk freely. In the movies those are the solemn victims of an aggressor, sacred and avenged in most cases, but in circumstances when the victim and the aggressor are conjoined in Kafkaesque way the victims have to deal with the additional burden of shame, or what they are forced to perceive as shame. Because they are left behind enemy lines, because they are accused of crimes they didn't commit and because they are so obviously not important to anyone to fight for them. "Something has to

be sacrificed," I heard once. For what? I, for example," and she rose and started orating in a pompous, deep voice, "was and am sacrificing my dignity. I was first begging the sick enemy bastards, yesterday's friends, to spare me because I was a human being, somehow distinct from all other human beings on the slow-death row, and therefore worth living. I was and am flirting with the death if you'd like me to speak as a poet." She dropped back on the sofa, silent for a moment:

"I never wanted to know how close I was to the death, even when it was as close as you sitting next to me because in the moments of gravest danger and exposure to it life would always triumph and the cycle was repeated over and over again. The summer was followed by fall, the fall by winter. I thought the winter had no end..."

"We can flirt with the death, but we can't flirt with the nature," Diana attempted a joke. "I remember it. I left my home—what I was calling home until then—in the winter time. I felt an almost physical clasp between me and that place, no wonder we talk about our "roots" when we talk about our place of origin. Uprooting, the separation from home, in those circumstances should have felt as liberation, cutting a cancerous tissue, but it didn't, it was still painful."

"Painful because of the most terrifying experience that you don't belong anymore. I didn't realize it when I was exiled, but long before . . . People are sheep, easy to allure and quick to stray. My terrible isolation didn't start behind enemy lines, but when I refused to believe that the decisions made for me were the right ones. In a movie, I would probably receive some kind of an award for my voice of reason, an award matching the recognition those lone and brave fighters for justice against all odds receive, but in reality I received a simple isolation and invisibility by everyone around me."

"I know, Dana," I interrupted, "something like an unasked question, an unasked accusation, 'who are you to judge everyone else?' and 'what did you do for others? You don't even have others' respect' and so on. With me, it wasn't

*even generational, it was universal. I watched my coevals'
disapproving of me the same way an old grandma did; no,
I can't say I lost my ground with the ad hoc confinement,
portrayed as a proof of "coexistence." The world didn't have
to know that such coexistence meant a certain vegetative
state for some . . . those held hostages, right? So that they can
receive punches of reprisal and vengeance. But still, I lost my
ground much earlier, when the monsters instead of heroes
began populating our myths and memories. And it seems like
there are monsters wherever we go."*

"Listen," and Dana's voice sounded comforting, "I am
beyond fear and you should be too. Do you really think you
have to lose much more than I do? Free yourself from fear of
losing something and you'll realize that you are closer to a
miracle of survival than to a certainty of death." The sudden
glow in Dana's eyes testified, more than her words, that she
truly believed in her repeated resurrection from a certain
death or, as it appeared to her less enlightened friend, she
simply didn't care anymore.

"I'll tell you about another miracle," Dana continued,
"the one you might not even think of as a miracle, but I do.
Remember that there was some kind of a numerical code on
our identification cards that had to be issued to everyone at
eighteen years of age?"

"Yes, what about them?"

"Well, the first four digits stand for a month and a day
of your birthday," she stood up and strode to her purse on the
kitchen table. "I still have the old document somewhere…
You never know when you might need it. Here." She opened
a small, two-by-three inch brownish booklet, and showed
Diana a set of numbers right underneath the photo. "See, one
of the digits on this identification card number represents the
ethnicity. I am not sure which one exactly and am not sure
which number stands for which ethnicity, but mine should
have been "undecided" because that is what I chose."

"Why?" Diana asked, lightly amused.

"*Because I was simply undecided about it when I turned eighteen. Contrary to everyone else at the time. They were declaring it so proudly, as if bragging about the greatest accomplishments. Do you wanna hear how "undecided" saved my life?*"

"*Yes.*"

"*OK. It was a freezing cold day in January when a group of war profiteers took my mother's money, a really small stack she saved for the days of greatest hardship, and promised to take us through the barricades, to "our" side. I said to you earlier that we left in a trunk of a car, but that was a slight aberration,*" she smiled. "*My mother and my siblings were lying under the awning of a pickup truck, covered with auto-parts from a junkyard, and I was sitting on the passenger seat along with the driver's companion. In case they get pulled over, they'd simply say they were going to a nearby town to deliver those auto-parts and that I was a hitchhiker visiting relatives, hoping to be able to buy some scarce provisions, abundant where they were headed to. It was one of those oases, strategic points for all involved in the conflict, far away from the trenches, something like this town where we are now, a town spared bombing and other horrors and where people and goods circulated relatively freely. Made you wonder if it was some kind of a sick agreement among the warring parties, an advanced plan in favor of all participating in their war games.*

Anyways, those two were pulled over at the first barricade and the uniforms asked to see the identifications. I handed my document to one of the soldiers and he looked at the picture, then looked at me and then at every letter and number from the first two pages of a small booklet. Every second seemed as long as an hour. When he slowly handed me my identification document back I almost shrieked, but my face turned into a petrified mask the longer he stared at me. "What do you have in the back?" the uniform finally asked the driver and this one replied in a rehearsed speech and with a deferential grin, purporting daily struggles of a man trying to get by. Both of the uniforms at the check point went around the truck and lifted the awning. I saw it in the rear mirror, still motionless on the one end of the passenger seat. In the corner of my eye I noticed the annoyance on their faces and they let the awning down in a manner one covers a carcass. The driver, slightly bowed, genially extended his hand for a handshake, which those two accepted in a half-hearted motion and it all seemed as if heavenly forces of good conspired again to perform another miracle. If they were not so tepid and took just a little bit closer look . . . Do you understand? Even if I die after all, it'll happen in a way I wanted to die. But my family and I were given another chance to continue this miraculous life."

Diana lowered her eyes, not sure if Dana really praised life or resorted to sarcasm again, "I do not have your grit and I am not ready for anything life throws at me. I mean, am I supposed to be ready? For this?"

"You don't know where your strength is, that's all. Don't despair, don't give up! Own up to your actions; don't let a group of villagers decide who you are. If we survive, this all will be just a faded memory."

"You don't have any idea what odds I am fighting here. You . . . too," Diana stuttered, apologetic.

"I do," Dana protested. Why can't you see it? The moment you realize you're fighting the odds, you're the winner."

"Oh, it didn't occur to me."

"Our escape was an adventure; they drove across the hills and through the woods to a town that was only twenty miles away. And I don't remember other details of the journey, the questions my companions asked and am sure they did, I just remember the checkpoint, those faces, the cold of the kind that penetrated bones and a town somewhat different than the ghost dwellings I was seeing in the past months. It seemed secluded in the twilight shades and I couldn't see the names of the streets from a greater distance. And however apocalyptic the whole journey appeared at first, we were *saved, at least from the dangers of imminent persecutions and possibly execution. At the time, the town in-between two enemy lines that thrived on war profiteering, human trade and other black markets, was our refuge, a starting point for rebuilding our shattered lives. Do you understand it now? From the bottom you can only go up, not down."*

My inexplicable need for theatrics, a fuel I was feeding my starved soul with for months, took me to a yet another dimension of entanglement or disentanglement with *Sultan,* and at first I wasn't sure which it was. The thought of existing in the first few weeks of January was painful, but only in a *grand-narrative* sense, as I realized later. I was uncertain about what to do with my secret, *never-ending conversation* with *Sultan* in a secret folder of my obsolete computer. *What do I do with Diana,* I obsessed. Mine and *Sultan's* union lasted at the most a hundred days, hardly acknowledged by a single human being, and far from the glory of one thousand and one nights of Scheherazade. He didn't think it was possible to go on and our correspondence extinguished. *Do I want Diana alive or dead,* I continued on my metaphorical journey to decide the faith of a spasmodic grip I called a life line. However, and this was also true, we don't decide a comfort level of the life support we need. This time around, mine was exactly like that—spasmodic. I decided to put Diana on hold, finding her now somewhat irrelevant and anachronistic. Then I remembered another one of *Sultan's* lines, the one about reverberations of the conversations even after one dies, so I decided to keep that—the reverberations. I was also hoping to keep the sound reverberations of a slap on the face, once I get a chance to do it.

An unusual peace overcame me in the first few weeks of the new year. At times, staring at a gray landscape of the driveway in front of my deck, interspersed with slushy dirty-brownish trails of snow carved by car tires and blending into dirty-whitish cover occasionally replenished by new layers of dusty snow, I expected stormy, heavy waves of remorse and *If-I-Could-Turn-Back-Time* sentiments to overwhelm my unsettled mind. Instead, I received peace, a hopeful, uplifting peace. *Sultan* and I, however reluctantly, rode on our linguistic waves, while all the while I was steering those waves in a more visceral and palpable direction. That was my idea of our *connection,* subsequently often doubted and questioned as if unreal. But, even if there is a *real* connection between two people, beyond *let's-procreate, provide-and-be-provided-for* connection, is it not marred, desecrated somehow the moment it enters the world perceived by our five senses? Such *connection,* often expressed in most mundane of places, places where structures of corporatized, "real" life rule, might appear as inane as a stroke of one's palm, longer-than-usual gaze, and as fragile and indefensible as a whim. Most often, it is all of it because our senses are purged of a most important and pure of all senses: sense of beauty and ability to create it. Our senses are obtuse and dull to a call of nature beyond brick and mortar confines and manmade laws. Perhaps that is why *Sultan* was only able to produce delayed and convoluted reactions, and that is why I burned through our encounters like a wild fire, annoyed at times with his passionless "glacial modes." Now I caught myself riding on waves of vindictiveness. *"Yes, I can be vindictive,"* I thought I told him once. But what is the point, when the other party does not play along.

A month without a sunshine, that was the January following *Sultan's* departure. A few weeks later, as planned, I packed the concoction of CDs he gave me and headed toward his office. That old, maroon-brownish Chevy was sitting in the parking lot. It looked as if this winter took more bites off its rusty fenders than all the previous ones. Entering the space that I once cherished almost felt like trespassing. *This IS trespassing,* I chuckled silently. Considering my intentions... I glanced at him standing in his office, statue-like, fixated on the empty boxes on the floor. As I pulled the door wide open, he was caught off-guard and yelled "What are you doing here?!"

As rehearsed in my thoughts over and over again, I ordered him to sit down. He obeyed, like a remorseful child caught in mischief. I took the CDs out of my bag and let them fall out of my hand. Some of the frames opened upon hitting the ground. Resisting the temptation to stomp all over the pile at my feet, I looked at him from above and said, "I don't think there will be a single day that you won't be thinking of me." I stepped back and he slowly got up, giving me a good angle for a nice swing. Another step back and a glance at the door signaled him that our encounter was over but then, before he was able to conceive of and process an alternative, I slapped him as forcefully as I could. His small, untidy office might have dampened the sound of a fleshy slam, but his thundering "Damn it!" might have raised a few eyebrows in the neighboring offices. I think his glasses were still on, so my earlier hesitations to slap a person wearing glasses proved to be unfounded. *So this is how this ends…* I believe that something died in both of us that day, even if only temporarily. However, it was a good death, a due death so to speak. We set each other free, for this was a different kind of freedom, the one not bound by "nothing left to lose," but by the impossibility to feed a *never-ending conversation.* Some conversations must end, in order for others to be born.

Printed in the United States
By Bookmasters